58 Bed Stories Stressed Out Adults

The Proven Guide To Sleep Like A Baby.

Relaxing Tales To Overcome Persistent Insomnia & Powerful Guided Meditations To Defeat Anxiety And Daily Stress

Violet Deep

© Copyright 2021 - All rights reserved – Violet Deep

The content contained within this book may not be reproduced, duplicated or transmitted without direct written permission from the author or the publisher.

Under no circumstances will any blame or legal responsibility be held against the publisher, or author, for any damages, reparation, or monetary loss due to the information contained within this book, either directly or indirectly.

Legal Notice:

This book is copyright protected. It is only for personal use. You cannot amend, distribute, sell, use, quote or paraphrase any part, or the content within this book, without the consent of the author or publisher.

Disclaimer Notice:

Please note the information contained within this document is for educational and entertainment purposes only. All effort has been executed to present accurate, up to date, reliable, complete information. No warranties of any kind are declared or implied. Readers acknowledge that the author is not engaging in the rendering of legal, financial, medical or professional advice. The content within this book has been derived from various sources. Please consult a licensed professional before attempting any techniques outlined in this book.

By reading this document, the reader agrees that under no circumstances is the author responsible for any losses, direct or indirect, that are incurred as a result of the use of information contained within this document, including, but not limited to, errors, omissions, or inaccuracies.

Table of Contents

INTRODUCTION.. 1

BEDTIME STORIES FOR ADULTS.. 5

The Trip after the Wedding.. 7

Inspiration in the Unknown... 11

Solar System... 15

Infant Soul... 21

The Bridge of Life... 27

A Kind Stranger.. 31

Love at a Glance... 35

The Rain... 39

Because I Love You... 43

Fulfilling a Dream... 47

Two Inspiring Places of Peace... 53

Clara's Inner Awakening... 59

The Pleasure of Friendship.. 63

A Trip to Emerald Island.. 67

Henry and the Mountain Gods... 73

Trip to the National Park... 79

The King and the Charity Works.. 85

An Extraordinary Heritage... 91

Back Home.. 95

Snow Day... 99

Sisters.. 103

The Proposal... 107

My First Friend.. 113

A Beautiful Flower 119

The Road to Happiness 125

The Park 129

Happiness above All...133

The Roller Coaster...137

Life in the Countryside..143

Family Vacation 147

Autumn and Cinnamon 151

The Teaching Keychain...157

The New Awakening of a Young Man 163

From Accountant to Drummer 169

Holidays in Lake Auyahú 175

Back to the Region 181

The Day I Met You 187

A Journey through the Mind..191

The Art of Being Persistent 195

The Dragon and the Hunter 201

The Power of the Mind...207

Between Love, Chocolate and Madness 213

The Wonderful Power of Self-control 219

Jade's Interesting Experience 225

The Sweet Chains of Love 231

A Special House by the Sea 237

Travel to a Distant Past..243

Field Trip with Students 249

The Color of Amethyst..255

Joseph and the Fascinating Orchids 261

Good Actions...267

After the Storm 273

FOREST FAIRIES 279

SAM'S DREAM 285

TIME AND ITS WHIMS.. 291

THE TRIP 297

THE BUSIEST CITY 303

ANDREW'S SUDDEN PEACE 309

RELAXING MEDITATIONS AND POSITIVE AFFIRMATIONS FOR ADULTS 315

A WONDERFUL BLUE.. 317

A WALK THROUGH THE HEIGHTS 323

AN ADVENTURE THROUGH NATURE... 329

AN ENCHANTED PATH 335

THE INNER LIGHT 341

FLOATING WITH THE WIND 347

A MAGICAL PLACE 353

EXPLORING THE SEA 359

EAGLE EYES 365

A TRIP TO PLUTO 371

ATTACHED TO NATURE 377

THE ROAD AND THE TRAILS 383

THE RUINS OF A LIVING CITY 389

A PINK DOLPHIN IN MY LIFE 395

FLASHES OF PEACE 401

LET GO 407

THE PERFECT COMBINATION 413

THE ART OF PAINTING IN YOUR HEALTH.. 419

THOSE WHO DO NOT LIVE TO SERVE, DO NOT SERVE TO LIVE 425

RECEIVE AND GIVE LOVE 431

HYPNOSIS FOR A SOUND SLEEP 437

MEDITATION TO SLEEP AND RELAX DEEPLY 443

MEDITATION TO END YOUR DAY 447

A UNIQUE TREE 453

RELAXATION BEFORE SLEEP..459

A HOLIDAY DAY 463

ONE DAY AT ROSE'S CABIN..469

A SEASON OF HIBERNATION 475

CONCLUSION 481

Introduction

We all know how exhausting it is to get through a night without a good rest. Sleep, like eating and breathing, is necessary to survive. Attaining deep quality sleep allows the whole body to rest and prepare for the day ahead.

When you sleep well, you can improve memory and problem-solving skills; you are motivated, alert, and participatory, and you improve your mood and help prevent depression. A quality night's rest helps keep the immune system strong, repair important cells and tissues, and maintain a healthy heart. People who do not sleep well at night often feel tired.

Their performance suffers, and their ability to think clearly, react quickly, and form memories. They are more prone to accidents because they place themselves in risky situations, making bad decisions.

Most who have trouble falling asleep at night suffer from anxiety and depression, chronic diseases that cause pain or shortness of breath, such as fibromyalgia, asthma, cardiovascular problems, reflux, sleep apnea, among others.

This work was born from the need to create a storybook especially for stressed adults, to serve as an instrument of help for those who need to disconnect from their day-to-day and achieve a state of relaxation, allowing them to fall into a deep sleep. To achieve this, simple stories were written, the objective of which would be to capture the reader's attention and set their imagination free as they read or listen to the stories, achieving relaxation that allows them to sleep.

Many methods are used to help people sleep, but nothing is better than reading a good book before going to bed. It is a book that transports us with its narration, no matter if fiction, adventure, love, or funny stories. Tales aimed to create good habits in the reader before going to sleep, teaching them various simple methods to relax, meditate, and show them the steps to follow before going to sleep.

Reading is one of the most widely used methods for managing a good night's sleep. Through it, the reader focuses their attention on the story heavily. Your mind visualizes characters, landscapes, tastes, smells, scenes. Reading makes the reader feel like it is inside the story, either as a simple spectator or a participant.

Using the concepts, the body and mind relax, the heartbeat slows down, blood pressure normalizes; the person forgets all the problems they have, the mind calms down, and without realizing it, the desire to sleep returns, achieving deep and uninterrupted rest.

As a result, the next day, the person feels refreshed, active, and full of energy. It's almost as if they had charged their batteries overnight. They see the glass as half full, have a better disposition to face the situations that may arise, see the problems from another viewpoint, make decisions, and be in better spirits.

Contemporary adults will find respite among the pages, offering unconditional support for those who cannot fall asleep after a long day.

The process offers two stages. You will find funny, romantic, fictional, fantasy, adventure, personal growth, and reflection stories in the first. The reader will have a different story at their disposal each night, help them to distract themselves and thus achieve a night of deep and restful sleep. The second part of the book consists of stories aimed at helping the reader relax and meditate, learn new habits before going to sleep, replace old beliefs and bad habits that contribute to sleep disorders and replace them with positive thoughts that naturally lead to sleep.

Bedtime Stories for Stressed-Out Adults is a tool for those people unable to sleep soundly at night. The goal is reducing stress and anxiety levels by bringing readers into the story, where their imagination begins to fly. Similar to children, they begin to visualize the characters and the scenario where the story takes place. Without realizing, readers begin to detach themselves from everything that stresses them out, and gradually, their mind relaxes, heartbeat and blood pressure slow, and they calm down until they fall asleep.

For this and so much more that we invite you to read this work, through the pages of which you will find a healthy, natural, fun, and educational tool to help you fight insomnia through stories to make your imagination fly, and that will induce you to achieve a night of deep sleep.

Bedtime Stories
for Adults

The Trip after the \

In the world of union, what everyone longs ,
what the world shares, whenever possible, bo
together and provide tenderness, no compassion, ι
love. The wedding took place with a few details, but ι
that couldn't be fixed. The united family was one oι
designs of life between the bride, who appeared to be one ,
the most beautiful women ever described, and the groom, who
was always aware of the wedding. The families met, and under
the veil of happiness, everyone remembered his rusty smile.

After the wedding, the party was the ribbon that ended up
tying those who love could not find. The joy overflowed when
unknown people met at a party that was for the union of two
people. The couple received the blessing of each person who
attended the big gathering. Words of romance were said, a
sign of little strength among those present, who applauded the
enthusiasm shown by all.

When the wedding came to an end, no one was crestfallen.
Everyone had their own to woo those who were due. They felt
new ways of loving, not only strangers uniting with them. They
had enriched that essence of love within the family, especially
when they felt the family grew as the years allowed
congratulating the newlyweds. It was the beginning for a new
couple, who was looking for nothing but happiness, and who

l find it every morning when they saw the smile of the
,on they loved on the side of their bed.

ιe honeymoon was the right foot in the history of the couple,
,here they decided to travel with the money they had saved.
They said that it was a better decision and that it would serve
to get to know the world while getting to know better the
people with whom they decided to marry. She always said that
one does not finish knowing each other unless they began to
live under the same roof and began to do it once they were
married.

He always had the brief desire to get to know Corsica. He liked
the areas where they couldn't find him, and even more so with
what he claimed to be the love of his life. In addition, he
wanted to know the history that encompassed that small
island next to France. So it was the two of them with the
money saved to satisfy the desire of one of them, while the
other party was pleased to find her husband's happiness.

They came by renting a house in the best part of the town on
the island. It was a very old town. Since colonial times, the
façade of the houses had not changed, but they were seen a bit
retouched by an artist. His house was the one that everyone
admired when they crossed that street. The island was
inhabited by people of the third age who inherited the crops
and traditions of that town.

The couple liked the house, but they visited and learned, as they did with each other, a new way of life they would not think of on an island. It was all new to them to see so many elderly people walking without distractions and living while their sighs were exhausted. It was a new world they tasted from the first day they arrived. They always wondered what made the elderly enjoy the silence and the tranquility.

Newcomers ran like people who come to a new place just to know; as tourists, they got to know the mythical homes of ancient Corsica. They told them stories of pirates who smuggled the coasts of all Europe. They said that treasures were kept underground on nearby islands at the time when ships were the most massive investment method. Gold and jewels asked to be found; all the money in the world was hidden from greed.

Similar stories were heard from the villages. Walking the colorful streets with pure emotion, they went to the beach at night, as they said it was the perfect time to get lost in the waters and the darkness. On one of those nights, they preferred not to go into the water and enjoy the view. The environment was dark, comfortable, and sensational.

The cold was obstructed by their bodies together, listening to the waves that washed up on the shore of the beach. They talked about his decision to have gone away, leaving all the people who told them that it was better to save as much money as possible for the expense of the child they did not want to have. They laughed at them because they always told them what to do, what was right, and what they believed they should follow the example of their brothers.

They always disagreed with others because, and it was true, they liked to have their own opinions. For them, life was about listening to silence, and if they could not hear it, it was not tried; rest would come when he wanted, and it was not a priority to push what cannot be moved. They only needed each other, and that was the law of life that had moved them to meet and keep together. Love was the most they could feel, and although it might hurt them too, they never felt the stab of separation. They showed eternal dedication.

When they decided to have each other, without more than that, that was when the smile was drawn, and they knew they needed to do the bonding ritual. They had never been patient. It was a ball of desires together that haunted them in their youth, and they did not know how to deal with it. But if the same person cannot deal with ghosts, it was necessary to have someone to support them. They understood it the way they knew that their parents had advised them. They were always moved by their mutual love; no one bothered them afterward.

Inspiration in the Unknown

John had sat on his balcony. He liked his house; it was spacious and had details that gave him comfort. One of the details that most caught his attention was the exaggerated lighting due to the number of windows. He believed that all those windows increased the lighting, and it was no wonder; his house was placed on the top of a hill. It could see the entire city, and it did when it was in good weather. That was rare; for him, the best situation to appreciate was under the good presentation of the tropical temperate.

When he was ready to feel the breeze, it was when it was shy and light that it did not suffocate him like the wind in Antarctica on his vacation. Not only because of the strong breeze that brought but the force with which it was approaching. Also, in his free time, when twilight came, the sun meditating to hide and rise on the contrary when the Earth was ready to take a turn in itself, John would take a book and with a freshly brewed cup of coffee, he decided to take his free time as what it was made for, to have fun and entertain himself.

He took that sheaf of white sheets as a whole center for the improvement of many of his factors, but, above all, he was amused by the stories that in life could be treated, or at least taken as true. All this under the calm of the weather and the sunset that fascinated him since he was a child.

That afternoon he went out without a book. The weather was perfect to just admire, from the top of the hill with the help of that balcony, everything that surrounded. He liked that dividing line that was taken as the horizon. It was the division of heaven, divine creation, with urbanization, totally terrestrial creation. Each had its own perfections. One maintained unique cleanliness that human beings would never think of being able to replicate. What was edible in books escaped from their hands. The other maintained an order established by the perfect regiments of common sense.

He liked to admire the authors' works. No matter what the authors wanted to say with their projects, only the beautiful mattered. The sun began its reverie, which, drunk with sleep, forced him to leave the day as finished and resolve, like all living beings that he could see from an extreme height, to sleep. But the ants were incredibly intelligent. Although the sun was a source of vision and that it was not always present because everything needed a change, they created small suns that allowed them to have the same vision as before the star disappeared.

He had never thought about it. Therefore, he never tried. But at that moment he felt an opening between his emotions that shook him on how many veins he had. It was a moment that was never specified. His conscientious smile, which only took its own will, followed the imaginations that crossed in the voluptuousness of the right hemisphere of his brain. John vibrated at what his imagination was playing, and he did not want to interfere. He did not agree to take control of the emotion that made the images pass naturally in his consciousness.

He recognized that he was having a process of creation. That is why he did not want to interrupt the process that arrived alone, and alone leaves, but leaves its mark in the sinister depths of the supreme art. After so many stories told and received by unknown authors, he had his opportunity and did not miss it.

That same afternoon he took his computer and began to write after months of dedication with his eyes glued to the computer. He knew that this work was his greatest and that everyone would want to read it; even if those same people did not have the habit of reading, it was not necessary to take the boldness against cheap entertainment, to take a time of silence and concentration to be reading in the most comfortable place they have.

He put himself in each letter, and each sentence stood out like the books of the Bible, with so much power in their enunciations that a synonym of surprise emerged on his face. He did not know he could write so easily. But it was his style, and since he liked it, surely many others would be excited to read it. Sure enough, he put out his book for sale and it flew off the bookstore shelves. He made brief comments on his work and rose to stardom in literature very quickly. It was a total success. His fame did not disturb his life or his vision of it, which was extremely centered with small traits of the delicate ethics of the great artists. It was not false humility; it was that, like every artist who knew how to relate as in Victorian times, he knew how to behave at such a height.

John's life passed between novels that commemorated historical events with the rich lexicon he recognized in high places. Each time his fame grew, but his ambition succumbed with the years that were beating his physique.

But, while in his life, the silhouette of his fame changed and transformed more to the same brilliance of the diamond. He always liked to go to the balcony, where he had such a wonderful idea. The sun and the city were the same, but he wasn't, and that didn't bother him. His ritual continued without alterations: Afternoons of coffee and books. Still, this time he added the fiery imagination that became normal for him to feel whenever he arrived as a domesticated animal.

He resolved not to change his view. He was in the best point of the city, and close to divinity, so close to heaven that the priests came to visit him very often. John loved his ideas like anyone loved their loved ones, afraid of losing them.

Solar System

Once upon a time, there was a large meteorite that circulated through the surrounding areas of the solar system inhabited by terrestrials. It was a meteorite that always passed the solar systems, and he said he had never witnessed such a beautiful sun.

The sunlight attracted him, causing him to slow down at the extraordinary speed he was carrying, a speed common among meteorites. He looked around him, seeing that other large stones, which the terrestrials took for space junk, were gathered next to him to admire the light that the sun lavished. They all agreed. They remembered, in their estranged journeys, having observed millions of suns, many more than God himself, and they assured, in unison, that this sun was not the one that shone the brightest in space, but it was the one that best intoned its strength. That light was a provider of life, which he gave to the earthlings.

That life, which they knew resided on Earth, also disturbed them in many ways. Meteorites knew there was more life besides terrestrial ones, but surely none had created objects that could navigate the depths of the dark waters. But they knew that humans supported each other, and although they were small dust in the desert, it was the dust that dominated physics and threatens to be the first race to colonize a planet foreign to theirs.

All the gathered meteorites, seeing that solar system, agreed to become one of them. That little group of five asteroids set off. From Earth, some children played at night in the large yard of their house, enjoying the freedom that it resembled. Tired from running and screaming, they lay down on the green grass that, thanks to the moonlight, was able to help them to be aware of their happiness. When speaking of the constellations, they saw a shower of stars, which were the five meteorites that put the plan they had stipulated in motion. Excited, the children yearned for the truth and serenity that this rain professed for them, desires whose property was in the hands of humility. Children's wishes are usually the most real.

The five meteorites traveled great distances, where human capacity could not understand—everything to find a good area to settle. But, what they did not concern, was where they were going to create a sun, or at least, as they had seen when they traveled great leagues, that some suns were alone in the space. But they were not going to go back to occupy one of those suns, they went forward, and they found one of them. In front of the sun, they got ready to talk to him, proposing to be planets that will go with him. The sun, undecided about such an unsuspecting offer, was indifferent the first seconds, but then, it needed company, and its existence needed it.

16

The five meteorites searched for places where they felt comfortable, but this time following ovoid routes, they formed triangular circuits. They didn't care about physics, they created it. The meteorite that was the first to admire the terrestrial solar system, chose the place farthest from the sun. He felt comfortable having the best view of all. He was able to procure from his thoughts and feelings that he would be satisfied with what others left them, even if they thought he was lonely, he liked having a family.

He saw the sun when his fellow men ceased to obstruct the path of his sight. He would never imagine that scene that called him to be calm with all the space he had traveled, the work he did, and the wishes that he always listened to when he crossed the darkness and the inhabited planets. He did not know why all kinds of good fortune were being asked of him in lives he did not know. He could not help them, the only one who could deliver what they asked for, was the almighty. But, despite those superstitions that did not bother him because of the confusion, it was good that they could believe; it was established in his memory that it was better to believe than not.

He was with his family and he didn't need more. He boasted of his new state, although back he had the darkness that he traveled for millennia, now he had the constant light direct to his face. He knew he couldn't be in a better place. Although unexpected was the solution, he was happy to be with them. For years they supported each other and remained faithful.

Over the years, what were colorless asteroids became planets fit for life. Each of them had a life of its own like the Earthlings they had seen in previous years. The solar system where asteroids were, and planets became, was made in a very short time, one of the most fortunate solar systems. They don't need the help of the almighty to create life in them, and they rejoiced in that because each one helped the other. It was a happy family, nobody could be separated, and the rocks that passed greeted them. When they passed, they felt shaken by the noise that was in them, they knew that it was the millions who remained faithful to the desire they professed to the asteroids. The planets laughed at that event since they suffered the trembling of all their guests screaming at the rocks.

Life became comforting, as millions of asteroids were looking for a place in a solar system, and that, as they were daring, had achieved it. In the same way, stars were born and meteorites grew. The cycle of life held them all to be in it, to keep smiling, they wanted to be calm with themselves. During their travels, they learned different secrets about the planets, and they applied it so that the future of their solar system would emit peace and modernizations, which they so badly needed.

Dreams come true, and theirs was real. They could touch them, each one of them. They were happy.

Infant Soul

Maya was a 31-year-old young woman whose attitude was gradually becoming a little darker than it used to be, she was losing her sympathy and her soul as a child. Her friends already noticed something strange when she no longer went out to any of the meetings they organized. She only dedicated herself to working without rest, completely isolating herself from the world.

However, this was not always the case, she used to be a very cheerful and quite lively girl. As a child, she loved visiting the forest near her home. Her mother insisted that she not go too far into that place, but she never paid attention; there was something in the forest that called her joyful girlish heart. More than anything, it was someone.

Maya used to have a best friend who lived inside the forest; his name was Rock, and he was a magical elf. The truth is that he was not very similar to the goblins of the cartoons; he was someone quite short in stature. He was barely 1.40 meters tall, had reddish hair, clothes made from tree leaves, and always carried a bottle with him containing a highly concentrated fruit juice, which could be smelled from several meters away. He was a little curmudgeon, but also very nice once you met him.

He and Maya used to play every day in the forest, in search of magical adventures. Often, Maya would come home from the forest and tell her mother about all the exciting and unreal adventures she had with Rock. On one occasion, they found a deer a bit sick, so they prepared some medicine for him together to make him feel better. The result was a healthy and grateful deer with both friends.

Of course, Maya's mother didn't take any of this seriously and only sensed that Rock was an imaginary friend, a product of her daughter's highly creative mind. However, that did not matter much. The really important thing is that Maya did know of Rock's existence and trusted their friendship was something real and lasting. Unfortunately, we all have to grow up at some point.

As the years went by, Maya no longer went to the woods as often to play with Rock. At first, she went a few times a week, which then turned into visits once a week, then a few times a month, until she finally lost interest and never visited the forest or her friend again. Inside Maya's mind, all she lived through as a child was not real, and as her mother said, it was only the product of her creative imagination.

Now, as an adult, she felt that something important was missing in her life to be happy, but she did not know what it was. She sought comfort in obtaining new titles and promotions at his job, but nothing was enough to fill the void within her. She needed her inner child again; she just didn't know.

One day, Maya left her work early in the morning and set out to go to the coffee shop in an attempt to lift her spirits. Upon arrival, there was a very long line. It was somewhat annoying to have to wait so long, but it was not like she cared much about that. Something caught Maya's attention: the person in front of her must be the smallest man she had ever seen in her life. The man was wearing a coat and hat; his face wasn't very distinguishable, but he still looked very familiar for Maya.

Suddenly, the little man opened a bottle that he brought with him, and from it, a very strong smell of fruits came off, which everyone in the coffee shop could easily notice. As soon as she smelled that concoction, all the memories returned to Maya's mind; she already knew who that small man was. "It's been a while, Maya. I see you've become a whole woman; that makes me very happy," said the little man, who was none other than Rock the goblin.

Maya just couldn't believe it, "Rock? Is it really you? I, I thought you weren't real. That all that stuff in the woods was just a figment of my imagination," said Maya, to which Rock replied, "I'm very real, honey. And what it is also very real, it is that I notice you are sad, and without the same spirits that the nice girl I knew used to have." "Yes, well. We all have to grow up sometime," added Maya.

The goblin extended his hand to Maya and said, "You don't need to grow up so fast. Come on, come with me." Maya decided to listen to her heart for the first time in a long time and left the coffee shop together with Rock. The two walked through much of the city, finally reaching the huge forest where they used to play together every day. Maya's eyes were brimming with the greatest of joys, it was like being a child again.

All that day, the two friends were playing like old times. They gathered fruit, cooked some of Rock's famous forest stew, made clothes out of leaves, and even got to visit the deer they had helped many years ago. He even already had his own sons, with whom the friends played for several hours. There was a lot of fun, but the night was getting closer and Maya should already be coming home. Not before, of course, give the strongest of hugs to his best friend Rock, and thank him warmly for having returned the happiness for life.

As a final message to his best friend, Rock said, "Remember, Maya. No matter how old you are, there will always be a little girl inside your heart, waiting to come out to play now and then. Oh, and by the way! Come visit me more often!" Maya replied with a big smile on her face, "Thank you for reminding me of all these things, Rock, I really needed them. And don't worry, I'll be back tomorrow to visit you!" Maya learned the importance of always taking care of her little inner child, and from that day on, her life regained the shine it had lacked for so long.

The Bridge of Life

Chris and Darcy were a pair of 17-year-old twin brothers who were about to once again visit one of the most magical places in the world for the two of them, their beloved grandfather's old beach house. Many years ago, the two brothers used to go to that place very often, it was like their predetermined family outing plan. However, they moved from the city where the house was, and they went to visit it once a year alone.

The reason why this place was so special to them was that this was not an ordinary beach, it gave off an unimaginable good vibe and positive energy. Not for nothing did the brothers nickname that place as the sea of miracles. Very special and magical things always happened when they crossed those crystalline waters.

Many years ago, on the twins' last visit to the place, incredible events happened to them during their stay. First of all, little Chris enjoyed swimming at full power in the immense sea in front of him. He was truly a great swimmer, later he would take it as the flagship sport in his life. After getting out of the water, the little one noticed something shiny on the floor and like every little child, he was curious to take it. He couldn't believe it, it was a real gold coin, right there in front of him.

Immediately, he ran to his grandfather's house to confirm its authenticity. "Grandpa, Grandpa, look what I found on the beach. It's a real gold coin!" said the excited little boy. The old man used his knowledge and experience to check if it was real gold, "Wow, wow, little Chris. Looks like you just found a gold coin, and very old from what I see. It must be worth a lot of money," said the grandfather, there were no more doubts.

Chris said, "That's great! In that case, I'll make a lot of money if I sell it well," the old man interrupted him and said," Don't even think about selling this jewel, you little rascal. This is a gift that the sea gave you. It has been granted, and the gifts that the sea gives us must be treasured for the rest of our lives."

The man took the coin and a string, and with it, he made a beautiful necklace for his beloved grandson. "Keep it, son, it will bring you good luck," said the old man. The little Chris replied, "Thank you so much, grandpa! I swear I will treasure this necklace for the rest of my life," sweet words, which ended in a very loving hug between grandfather and grandson.

Meanwhile, the then little Darcy was searching for treasures on the shore of the beach, without much success. He noticed that something was moving very close to a palm tree in his search, so he went to investigate a bit. His face went from intrigue to one of emotion and tenderness when he discovered that what was moving was nothing more than a small puppy rolling in the sand.

Immediately, Darcy went to his grandfather to introduce him. "Grandpa, grandpa, look what I found on the beach. He's the most beautiful puppy in the whole world!" said the excited young girl. His grandfather was always a big fan of animals, and dogs especially. So, he took the little puppy and took it home, where it received all the food it needed.

The kind man said, "You know, little Darcy. This puppy is still very young and will need a mother to take care of him, and give him a lot of affection. Why don't you keep him?" Hearing such a thing, Darcy's eyes began to glow with excitement and happiness, "Can I really keep him, Grandpa?" asked the girl; and the old man answered, "Of course you can, my little one! I don't think your parents care. Also, if there is a girl with a heart of gold which is capable of caring for this cute animal, that is you, Darcy." Moved by the words of her sweet grandfather, little Darcy gave him a very big hug, and her new pet, which she decided to name Dustin.

At nightfall, in the far reaches of the starry sky, a kind of natural bridge was observed, made up of millions of stars. The little grandchildren had never seen something so beautiful in their lives. Their grandfather explained to them, "What you children see there, they are not ordinary stars. That luminous path is known as the bridge of life," said the old man. "And what is that, grandfather?" both grandchildren asked.

"Well, in simple words, my little ones. It is that path that unites us all, and the one that promises we will always be connected. No matter the distance and no matter what happens, we will always see each other again," replied the grandfather—a wise teaching, full of much love.

Now in the present, it was Grandpa who was beyond excited to see his little grandchildren again. When they both finally came to visit him, he could see that they were no longer little ones. Chris was a very strong and athletic boy and quite a man; Darcy was a beautiful young woman, much like her beautiful mother; even Dustin had gone from being that adorable puppy to being a giant guard dog. The grandfather felt somewhat nostalgic; he was still almost the same, and his grandchildren had changed, however, not as much as he thought. During his visit, everything happened as if time had not passed. They played the same games, listened and laughed at the same stories, and even got to spend the afternoon swimming until exhaustion in the beautiful sea in front of them.

Finally, everyone ate a delicious special meal made at home, while in the sky, that endless path of stars was once again glimpsed that united the souls of the people they loved—the bridge of life.

A Kind Stranger

Carly was a beautiful 19-year-old girl who was going through a very common situation in a young adult's life, a very chaotic day. While it is true that everyone has bad days at some point in life, Carly's started as disastrous as possible. She set up her phone alarm at exactly 7 am to wake up and go to work, but this time, the alarm didn't go off for some strange reason. The young woman woke up on her own, and noticed that it was already 8 am. "It can't be; I'll be late for work," the young woman said to herself in her thoughts.

At full speed, Carly made her breakfast and dressed as quickly as possible; she didn't even have time to take a shower. When she went to turn off her television to leave home, she noticed something strange. In the newscast that was broadcasting live, it was 7 am, "But what the heck? That can't be possible. It should be 9 am by now," said to herself. By checking her phone, Carly confirmed her suspicion, the time on the device had been misconfigured, and so there was no reason for such a rush. Something very ironic and funny at the same time, although not for Carly.

The young woman left her apartment somewhat angry after the show that had happened to her, and it was no wonder. When she got to the bus station, it was closed due to a city holiday, so she had no choice but to walk to work—the second misfortune of the day. After walking for about half an hour in some uncomfortable shoes, she finally arrived at her work office, only to discover that they were also closed that day. "But why is this closed? It doesn't make the slightest sense," Carly said to herself, although afterward, she began to remember a couple of things, which she had not realized throughout the day.

In the newscast where she realized that the time on his phone was wrong, they were announcing something about a holiday, and also, the bus station was closed due to a holiday. There was no doubt, Carly went to work in vain since she would not work that day. Carly was exhausted from her bad luck that day, so she decided to take a break and go to her favorite coffee shop to release some stress. When the young woman got ready to buy a coffee and something to eat in the cafeteria, she was very surprised, that she did not have her wallet with her. "I don't know why I didn't see it coming," she said.

Defeated and penniless, Carly sat on one of the coffee shop furniture, to rest a bit, and ponder why the hell she forgot her wallet. At that, a young man her age sat in front of her and was carrying in his hands the order that Carly tried to buy. The boy said, "Hi, how's everything? Hey, I could tell that you couldn't buy what you wanted, and by the way, you looked pretty sad sitting here. So, I decided to buy it for you. If you don't mind, of course." Carly felt very flattered by the boy's gesture, she didn't even know what to say. "Oh my God, thank you very much! You don't know how happy you just made this bad day, friend," she said, mercilessly devouring that bag of sweets, which scared the boy a bit, but nothing out of the other world.

The girl said, "Hey, my name is Carly. Do you have a name? I would like to know the name of the person who saved my life," to which the boy replied with a smile, "Sure, my name is Matt. A pleasure to meet you, Carly." "The pleasure is all mine, Matt," she replied. After that, they chatted for a long time while eating sweets and coffee, they got along quite well.

Leaving the coffee shop, Carly mentioned she would now have to walk home, as there were no buses that day, and it was at least a half-hour walk. Matt, as kind as ever, offered to drive her in his car. Carly seemed a little indecisive, it was not normal to trust strangers who just invited you a coffee, but she could not perceive any bad intention coming from Matt, so she gladly accept the offer.

As they drove home, they listened to loud music. It turned out that they both shared the same musical tastes, it was as if they were connected. While they were on the road, they were stuck in traffic for at least an hour, but that didn't matter, they were having a great time with each other. At that moment, while they were both still in traffic, fireworks began to appear in the sky out of nowhere. Probably due to the holiday that was being celebrated. Carly and Matt watched them in amazement from the comfort and coolness of the car. Carly took a little moment to appreciate all of that and realized that this hadn't been such a bad day after all.

After much waiting, they finally made it to Carly's building. She got out of the vehicle, but curiosity suddenly invaded her, and she couldn't help but ask, "Hey Matt, I appreciate everything you did for me today. I had a great time with you, but why did you do it? We don't know each other, for you I'm a complete stranger." The young man smiled and replied, "Why did I do it, you say? Is that important? Well, it's not like I think too much about why I do things. I only saw one girl who seemed a bit dejected, and I decided I would try to cheer her up. I think there is nothing else besides that!" It was a very simple answer, but it really managed to touch Carly's feelings. "Well, I'm glad you did. And for the record, you did it. You made my day so much better!" said Carly. They both said goodbye, and Carly would never forget those funny moments she shared that day with that kind stranger.

Love at a Glance

It was a calm summer night; the weather was cool, more than normal. It was not too late and despite being Saturday, the streets of the city were clear. For Marco, who lived with a very marked routine, this was indifferent to him, since the night outs were something null in their lifestyle. He was a young man, barely 24 years old, but he lived each day with the parsimony of a man of 80. He avoided stressful situations, commitments, and all kinds of responsibilities to maintain that tranquility that characterized him so much, that Saturday was a little different because, for the first time in his life, Marco felt bored and tired of his monotony.

He had almost no friends, just a few, and surely that day they were all busy with their partners, however, that was no excuse for not calling them and trying to put together a plan that would shake up the night. He picked up the phone and called the first one. There were no positive results, and he insisted once more, but only got answers from silence. He repeated the same plan relentlessly, and with the same result as the first attempt. After dire insistence, Gerald one of his best friends called him back.

Gerald said, "Hey, is everything in order?" to which Marco replied, "Hey buddy, I'm just bored and I've been calling everyone, and you were the only one to call back. Do you have any plans for today?" "More than a week ago we tried to call you to invite you to a trip we took to the valley, but you were unable to answer us, no one is in the city. We all are here," said his friend, to which Marco replied, "Yes, I remember the calls; hey, I'm very sorry. Take care and hope to see you soon."

Seeing his options reduced to zero, with all his friends having a great time in a place far away from the city, Marco wondered more than once about what to do. The plan should be consolidated; he had to leave home. The problem was where, with whom, and to do what. He called a couple more acquaintances without any success. Tired of the repetitive failures, he made the decision to go out alone, go for a walk, get away from his bland reality a bit and maybe find a little fun.

He took the house keys and thought more than once whether to take the car or not. The decision remained firm, that walk would be on foot. He took his first tours outside his house. The wind was blowing; the strong breeze touching his skin not in a tender way, perhaps with a destructive intention, or perhaps it was a warning. He ignored the details of the unleashed wind and continued without major problem. He walked the first 2 hours without a fixed course, taking some photos with his phone of places where he passed during the day, but that got a different vibe with the low light of the nights. In a short time, he reached the boulevard where life rumbled like a drum, people walked around smiling, happy, immersed in that beautiful moment with their families. Nobody was aware of that presence that was looking for some company, although he denied it.

That night, there were some attractions installed around that space, carousels and even small roller coasters. A small mime circus was also in the area. The colors of the fair splendidly decorated the night; the music of the carousels transmitted a unique peace through those light piano notes that made him feel as if instead of being mounted on a rigid horse, he was flying on a cloud.

At the cotton candy stall, it was where their eyes met, where the magic happened, where Marco recovered in a certain way the hope in something he thought he had lost a long time ago. He did not stop seeing her; he blushed just by seeing the yellow light reflected by her square glasses. In that row, there were all kinds of people, some in love, others lonely, and some who, despite being alone, enjoyed their own company.

Marco was never good at initiating the interaction; he was panicky even at the idea of facing such a situation. On the other hand, she was looking at him, and she had seen something that probably no one had ever seen in him before. Both, in the end, managed to buy what they wanted and while they wandered through different places, both ran the strange feeling that the more they claimed, the closer they were to

37

each other and that's how it was. Marco who was about to be eaten by his nerves, took an unprepared step that would unknowingly change his life forever. "OUCH! That hurts," said the girl, and Marco said, "God, I'm sorry, I didn't mean to."

"Don't worry, don't worry, that happens to me for spying on you," added the girl. Marco, who didn't need to be more nervous, almost choked on his breath when he heard her speak; he managed to ask, "Spy on me? Why would you do that?" to which the girl replied, "Hey, I just repeated what you did, then I wanted to know why you were looking at me so much and you didn't come to say hello." "We don't know each other," said Marco; and the girl added, "We are all strangers until one approaches to speak. Nice to meet you; my name is Gina."

After that, what had started as a boring and lonely night was the beginning of a beautiful and new friendship. They both made their attractions, breathing the same air and for one night sharing the same dreams. Their mutual company invited them to believe that everything was possible. Without realizing it, in less than a day they created a bond that takes a lifetime to put together. It was daylight and they exchanged numbers and said goodbye with a kiss, which gave them something very valuable to understand: that love is hidden in plain sight.

The Rain

The rain fell slowly and very closely. He could not touch the drops because Julian wanted to avoid a cold, but the smell of freshwater with divine spring brought back memories of the most fantastic moments of his life. During that spring, little rain had been forecast. It had been a warmer season than usual, sometimes giving the notion that it was already summer. Julian had been at his sister's house for a few years now. After ending a marriage that didn't go well, she lived alone, so she didn't mind sharing the roof with her brother. They had not lived together for more than six years; however, being together again was the same as when they were children.

Rebecca said to his brother, "It's time to eat. Are you coming or not?" to which he replied, "Sure, even if your food is terrible." "I've been calling you for hours, and you looked like a fool watching the drops fall. It made me remember how when we were kids and I caught you in the bathroom with dad's magazines," sharply said Rebecca. Julian just said, "I don't know what you're talking about, I never dug into Daddy's stuff." "Don't play dumb; I'll never forget your face when you saw me. They could even use it for a horror movie," added her sister.

The rain did not stop and consolidated in time, making them lose the notion of the hours and space. While they ate, Julian kept his gaze fixed on the window that was in front of the kitchen. The sound of the water hitting the ceiling, the grass, and the walls, became something hypnotic, causing Julian to gradually lose himself in that one-rhythm orchestra. The dinner, his sister, and all his surroundings little by little seemed to be more distant. Meanwhile, he, or perhaps his mind was swimming in the rain that Sunday afternoon.

The mind tends to be a mysterious place, and as deep as the ocean itself, full of unpublished rooms, where memories of past lives are hidden, of what we were and what we could be, but, giving some clues to what that we can become. Julian woke up in a well-known place with homey smells, freshly toasted bread, freshly squeezed oranges, honey, and butter, all beautifully followed by laughter he hadn't heard in years. The grass was green, and the sun was shining uniquely. It was then when he saw the place where he was and could not believe it until his heart gave him the certainty that he was not hallucinating.

It was the country house, where he grew up with Rebeca and her parents, the same place where he learned to put on his boots, where he rode for the first time on horseback, where for the first time he kissed, and where they also broke his heart. The place was intact, clean, magnificent, the grass freshly cut and most importantly, there were people, it was inhabited.

In the distance he heard voices discussing whether to use ham or pastrami, whether to bring cola or orange juice. They could not see him; and confused he tried to find the purpose of why the rain had brought him there. Everything was still confusing and although he clearly remembered that day, there were some forgotten details. Fear seized him. He was afraid to continue; he didn't want to cry; getting tears out was a waste of time. He looked for ways to get out, hit himself, pinched himself, even washed his face with the water from a pond, but nothing worked. Julian was slow to realize that if he wanted to return, the only thing in his power was to continue the journey of that family.

Since the divorce everything had turned a little gray. Julian had lost his hopes, his motivations, despite being still a young man, with a career and life ahead of him. That event had marked him. He was nowhere to be found; he went through hundreds of changes; he did everything to try to recover what he lost. However, he did not realize that the more he tried, the more he lost within himself. That's when the idea of going with Rebecca seemed good. Being close to a loved one made him regain a lot of confidence. But Julian had to learn an important lesson from someone he could only find in his memories.

The family was going to an old castle located in the surrounding areas of their house in the countryside. It was an old medieval fortress, which, despite the corrosion provided by time, maintained a comfortable aesthetic. The plan was to spend the day there, have a picnic, get to know the place and learn about its history, and the truth was that it was fully accomplished.

A sunset in motion gave a different contrast to the valley with its light, filling it with satin colors, which made him drunk with excitement just by looking at them. Suddenly a boy ran and fell into a well. His sister was the first to realize it and looked for the father with fear for his brother's life. Julian never left the boy behind. He saw in his eyes the fear, the hopelessness that he felt, the feeling that everything was lost. They both cried and then, their salvation was presented. The father, with a rope, lowered himself as he could to the well and with a smile he took his son, looked at him and told him, "How great you are, champion, these things happen to you, and they will continue to happen to you. Falling is very important, in this or whatever it is during life because it is the only way to learn to get up. Come home, son, let's go back."

Rebecca brought him back, saying, "It's time to eat. Are you coming or not?" to which Julian replied, "Sure, I wouldn't miss it for the world." "Are you feeling okay? You hate my food, are you okay?" She asked, and his brother answered, "Wonderful, but we better eat, and then I'll tell you why."

Because I Love You

The waves of the sea were still that morning; he could barely see them reaching the shore. The parsimony of the water generated an unprecedented peace, so much that it could be felt even in the bones. It was already the end of the summer and Luke did not want to leave that bay where during the last months he felt very happy. It was ten years ago since that last day at the beach; from that moment, life has given various changes for Luke, who no longer was a teenager, but a man with work and responsibilities, a wife, a six-year-old daughter, and one more to come. Although many years had passed since he got on a surfboard, he maintained the indomitable spirit of that young that he was.

Luke prepared for a busy morning. Although always with his head up to face whatever lies ahead. He had already a career as an insurance salesman for a few years. In college he had studied to be a teacher, but he found his passion was always being a salesman; he was great at it, to be honest. With already five years of experience in the field, he lived daily with a somewhat hostile environment, among very competitive colleagues, very demanding bosses, and tiresome clients, of those who mentally thought about how to eradicate. However, his brilliant attitude was unable to cover himself with such bad energies, and he always ended up moving away with the rhythm of good music.

His boss came to him and spoke. "LUKE! Where is my superstar?" to which he replied, "Here, Mr. Fox, what do you need?" "Well, son, and I don't say that because my daughter is your wife; you are like the boy I never had, I couldn't take my daughters to poker." An uncomfortable laugh came from Luke's mouth. It was not easy to have your father-in-law as your boss, and although Mr. Fox was not the president of that firm, he was de facto the one who gave the orders. He was a kind and kind-hearted man. Yes, he was very demanding, especially with his son-in-law.

"I know that you recently left a job that took you a long time to solve. You made an effort as few do and you deserve a good rest. However, something came out and therefore we must suspend your vacation; well, more or less," said Mr. Fox. A little indignant but still not fully understanding what Mr. Fox was saying, Luke was trying to answer all the doubts that began to come to his head after that moment. To then inquire, "What do you want to tell me? Will I have a vacation?" to which Mr. Fox replied, "How funny you are, son; nor that I was an exploiter, of course, you will have your vacations, but so that you do not miss the office so much, you will take a little of it for your rest." "And how am I supposed to rest if I have to work?" asked Luke. "Good question, boy. I bet you will find a solution. I have already bought tickets for you and the girls. They will go to a beautiful port in the bay. Our client will also be there; he is a very big fish and that is why I have chosen my best fisherman. Go, bring him to put him in Wall," answered Mr. Fox.

A little defeated, but determined to carry out what was entrusted to him, Luke left his boss's office, with the devotion of going home to tell his wife about the new plan for the summer. At home, Luke arrives at the best place in the world for him: the arms of his wife and daughter, ready to talk about everything that had happened to him. Iris had been his girlfriend since adolescence, his best friend and confidant. They had a relationship as solid and firm as a mountain, capable of coping with everything. In recent years, Iris had been very concerned about her husband, who, despite being an excellent father and partner, had lost a lot of himself to give his family everything they needed. The fact that he no longer went to the beach for so many years is a living example of that.

Luke had arrived stressed, he was trying to hide it, but there was nothing he could hide for Iris. He trusted his wife, "Your father hates me, dear. Now we must go to a place that he chose for the holidays: I thought about staying here at home. I wanted to take that time to finish the baby's room and paint your study." Iris replied, "Luke you do so much for us; I never imagined this possible. He doesn't hate you, maybe he just trusts you too much." Luke did not suspect what his wife was up to. In reality, there would be no fat customers to visit, even the tickets were rigged. They would go to the other side of the coast, at the beach house where Luke grew up. The fix was thanks to certain influences from Mr. Fox, who always kept those kinds of tools for situations like these.

The days passed without major inconveniences; they already had everything prepared and ready to leave home and take the so-called business vacation, as Luke baptized them. On the other hand, Iris had already spoken with her daughter so as not to reveal anything to her father. At the same time, she had also communicated with old friends and acquaintances of Luke, in addition to doing the same with her relatives, who had not been able to do so for a while. Now, with each subject discussed, they began their journey. They slept the entire flight.

It was then that the surprises did not stop arriving. When he left the building, all those faces from his youth were waiting for him, hugging him and welcoming him, "Welcome home and to your vacations," they said, Luke asked, "Did you know anything about this dear?" to which Iris said, "Sure, silly; I planned everything. There are no clients; there is no work, just us and everyone who loves you." "And why did you do it?" he asked, to which his wife added, "Because I love you."

Fulfilling a Dream

It was getting dark in London, it was the first week of winter and the streets gradually began to stain a thick aged orange, leaves everywhere, on the road, and along the sidewalks. The trees left an interesting well-defined mosaic along the streets of the Gaelic capital. Walking in a carefree way, humming the notes of an old song, was Jason, a young redhead, inveterate lover of life and his island. For being so young, it was impressive for some that he knew with such precision the culture and customs of his land and, if you ask another boy his age, they would even lack the imagination to invent an answer.

Jason was walking with little direction. He loved taking that kind of walk after finishing his job as a postman, an ironic situation since the young man's job consisted of taking long and long walks to deliver packages, letters, and other parcels. He liked to walk; apart from music, walking through the streets of his city generated immense and insatiable pleasure.

Upon arriving at the pub, he met Jack and Wayne, his best friends. The pub on O'Higgins Street was one of the oldest in the whole city, preserving different things and souvenirs from all its long history. There were photographs of the Prime Minister, some dukes, famous rock bands all over the island. The essence of that bar was unique in the world; it was surely one of the places that every Englishman should visit at least once in his life.

"I would not change this place for anything boys. It is a fantastic feeling, the people, the music, and the girls; here come the most beautiful of the whole island, and do not doubt my words: The best of England is here," said Jack, to which Wayne replied, "Of course the best is here because we are." The laughter at that moment did not stop, followed by some sincere looks, the kind that you receive not only from your friends but from a brother.

They had known each other for years and had a relationship like few there are now. They shared some dreams, among them: to know South America, go to Siberia, and navigate the narrowest stretches of the world, but all these goals were not compared to their greatest desire. What Jason, Wayne, and Jack most wanted was to form their band.

They had tried before. Jack played guitar and bass; Wayne was terrific on drums; none of the three was a splendid singer, but Jason was the one who had the most appropriate voice for the sound they had and he was also a good guitarist and songwriter. From a very young age, Jason had started a taste for reading great authors from his land and from all over. He had even learned Spanish and French just to be able to read the greatest exponents of writing in these languages in their original versions. Since then, the lyrics did not leave his mind.

In good and bad moments, Jason's muse was present in his mind. Songs, poems and all kinds of stories were part of the entire repertoire of our protagonist.

"Guys, to tell the truth I would not change these moments for anything, we should toast, to be grateful for being alive, and together. There are few people who dare to do this, and I assure you that we are fools, but not cowards and less ungrateful," said Wayne. They shouted and cheered with extreme emotion; the jars made a roar. Thank heaven they only splashed drops of beer and not broken glass. The hours passed, the music improved, the night somehow was telling them that the best thing was to continue with those smiles and that perhaps in that same evening, the opportunity they wanted so much could present itself.

Jason stopped for a moment and said, "You know what would be great? That we could sing tonight. I know the next band has a member with diarrhea and there is no other alternative besides us, which would be great." "It definitely would be, besides who better than us for this?" replied Wayne. The night continued as if nothing had happened. The last band was about to appear, they were some Scots who came directly from Edinburgh; they were widely listened in Scotland and had sown certain fame. The promotion to that first concert in London had been one of the most brutal and colorful. Everyone knew about that presentation. Even people from the corners of the island and beyond came to O'Higgins Street to attend.

The pub was on the edge. The bar staff was not enough, with so many people invading their spaces, demanding from minute one the start of the long-awaited presentation. However, due to fate or some divine effect, three of the group members had a fever and powerful indigestion. That was all; there would be no concert. Dylan, the pub manager, did not know very well how to talk to all those people who had his establishment packed. The disappointment was going to be great, and he knew that, although telling the truth, he could lose many customers that night. It was then that Jason noticed the strange situation and confronting Dylan, they came up with what could be an intrepid solution.

Jason: "Hey guys, I hope you can understand this; we'll play right now. The Scots have diarrhea. We'll do it instead," said Jason. Jack and Wayne could not believe what they were hearing. The opportunity they had been waiting for so long had presented itself; they said yes and they got ready to get on stage. In their whole life, they had only practiced a couple of times. They knew only five songs, and although the public's reaction at first was not expected, his charisma and talent were the only elements necessary to get the crowd in their pocket. At the end of the night, Jason and his friends realized that to fulfill their dreams, it is only necessary to start with the first one.

Two Inspiring Places of Peace

Once upon a time, an elderly man named Luke lived in a beautiful country house located on the outskirts of the city. He was fascinated by gardens, so he had built one himself with numerous beautiful plants with lush flowers in his home. In addition to the garden, Luke's house was surrounded by a majestic forest full of leafy trees, shrubs, ferns, and other types of plants that gave the place extraordinary beauty. One day when Luke was out for a walk in this forest, the old man suddenly saw, at a distance and hidden among the foliage of some bushes, a small being about two feet tall that seemed to be very busy with something.

When he approached to see it, Luke discovered that the strange creature had a youthful appearance and was dressed in extravagant outfits, bright and brighter colors. "Who are you? What's your name?" asked the old man. "My name is Nemur, and I am a gnome, a spirit of nature," replied the little man. "Wow! I had heard of your existence, but I never believed it to be true," Luke commented, surprised.

"We are not used to being seen by humans," replied the gnome. "And what are you doing here?" asked Luke. "I'm working. The gnomes are the guardian spirits of the earth. We take care to protect it, keep it free from all impurity and protect it from all disturbances. In addition, we prepare the ground so that Mother Earth shelters in her entrails the seeds that, when they germinate and bear fruit, will serve as food for the human race", explained Nemur.

Luke didn't know what to say. He had been dumbfounded by the shock. Then, the gnome took him by the hand and said, "Come, I will take you to see my village." The creature made a movement with its right hand, like one who opens a window, and soon a kind of colony made up of hundreds of small colorful houses appeared before them, inhabited by gnomes of different factions and clothes, all fascinating.

The panorama was amazing, thousands of bushes with beautiful flowers in bright colors adorned the houses, and beautiful waterfalls with crystalline waters culminated in rivers or splendid ponds. "Looks like I'm in heaven," Luke thought, dumbfounded. And Nemur said to him in a funny tone, "It is not paradise, but it must be very similar to it." "How did you guess what I was thinking?" asked the surprised man. And the gnome replied, "We gnomes can communicate telepathically with each other or with others." "I would like to stay here a while longer," Luke said to his companion, but the gnome announced that it was time to return to the real world. Making another movement with his right hand, now like someone closing a window, He made the forest where they had long met appear before them.

"I didn't want to go back so soon," Luke confessed, a bit sad. "Don't worry, one day we'll meet again," Nemur replied. And when Luke turned to say goodbye to his friend, he had disappeared. The old man returned home excited by all that he had seen and heard, but soon had to return to his daily occupations, so he forgot about his encounter with the gnome.

Several months passed, autumn was about to end. Luke was visited by his daughter Laura and some of his grandchildren. These restless and playful children, out oversight of the adults, went to play in their grandfather's garden, leaving everything trampled and battered. "Oh, my garden!" The old man yelled with his hands on his head. But there was nothing to do. The man was filled with resignation and continued to attend to his visits as best he could. When his family left, Luke began to work intensively on the recovery of his garden. In the days that followed, the old man tried to sow plants and germinate some seeds, but all to no avail. The arrival of winter was already imminent, so the water in the ground was already beginning to freeze and made it impossible for the growth of the seeds to grow plants.

Winter has arrived. The snow-covered everything, and its flakes fell like soft cotton on the skin. Desperate, Luke couldn't see the day when spring would come so he could dedicate himself to his gardening work.

When spring finally arrived, Luke got up one morning excited to go to work. He was aware that arduous restoration work awaited him, but he was not daunted by this fact. The old man had not woken up well even when he saw how his garden had been restored and improved with surprise. Not only had they planted in it all kinds of herbs and bushes full of the most varied and fragrant flowers, but they had also provided it with practical paths upholstered with colored flagstones and luminous white benches that invited you to sit on them. Furthermore, a charming fairy-shaped fountain with a pitcher was placed in its center.

"How beautiful is this all!" Luke exclaimed ecstatically, feeling a soft touch on his back; it was Nemur's hand, who suddenly appeared at his side. "Friend, how long no see!" exclaimed the excited man. "Yes, I told you that one day we would meet again," replied the gnome. "So this is all your doing?" asked Luke, touched. "I had many collaborators, including some gnomes, undines, and fairies," Nemur replied proudly. "Oh, Nemur, forgive me for not having gone to the forest to visit you again," the old man said a little sadly.

"Don't worry, remember that we gnomes are capable of stealthily observing human behavior, and we saw in you an enormous love and concern for nature, so we decided to do this for you," said the gnome. "Well, they did a great job," Luke replied, with tears of gratitude and happiness in his eyes.

Then, the two friends sat on a bench in the renovated garden to tell each other everything that had not been said in months.

Clara's Inner Awakening

Once upon a time, a very educated and professional lady named Clara had spent a large part of her life dedicated exclusively to work and the financial support of herself, her children, mother, and siblings.

As Clara was divorced and her children had gone to live outside the city, one day it occurred to her to take a tour of the most beautiful places in the world. The lady quickly consulted a travel agency, where they recommended visiting monumental and amazing places such as the Egyptian pyramids, the Milan Cathedral, the Parthenon in Athens, the Great Wall of China, and many other places of extraordinary beauty.

Clara gladly accepted the agency's suggestions, joining the lists of several tours in Europe and Asia to visit the recommended places. However, after touring those beautiful and spectacular places in the world, Clara still felt as if something was missing in her life. Then, one day, a friend named Olga invited Clara to spend a week at her beach house. Clara gladly accepted, so the two women soon found themselves in a simple and humbly decorated dwelling. The house had a wide corridor that faced the seashore, a beautiful garden, and huge windows that let light in.

"Your house is very cozy," Clara said to her friend as she entered the house. "Yes, it is an inheritance from my father," Olga replied. "What do we do now?" asked Clara, smiling. "We are going to put your things in the guest room and then we will prepare a delicious dinner with what we brought," Olga replied. The two women began to cook, and to cheer up more, they opened a bottle of wine that Olga had kept in her refrigerator. "With this delicious wine, we are going to toast for our health and friendship," said Olga enthusiastically. "Cheers!" Clara exclaimed, clinking her glass against Olga's.

Later in the afternoon, Olga took her friend to walk barefoot along the seashore. "Oh, what a wonderful feeling!" Clara expressed this when she felt the softness of the warm sand under her feet, the warmth of the seawater, and the spectacular view of the sun setting. "Yes, walking barefoot on the beach is always very relaxing," said Olga. "Hey, how about tomorrow we go fishing?" Olga asked her friend. "I would love to, although I have never caught anything in my life, except several colds," Clara replied in a good mood.

Clara and Olga went to sleep so that they could get up very early next day. The next morning, both women had their fishing rods, hooks of different sizes, and tasty baits ready. Then Olga opened the house's garage doors where a boat with four oars had long been stored, two on each side. "Come help me get it out!" Olga said to her self-absorbed friend. Clara and

Olga took out the dusty boat, and after taking it to shore, Clara got on it while Olga pushed it into the sea.

"Take the oars tightly and do this undulating movement from front to back," Olga explained to her friend while rhythmically moving her arms, clinging to her pair of oars. "Like this?" Clara asked. "Exactly, you learn quickly," said Olga. The two women paddled slowly out to the shore, and then Olga said, "This is a good place to bait our hooks." That morning the sea was very calm and the sun was not so strong, so the fishing became very pleasant and entertaining.

"You know, friend? I didn't think fishing would make me feel so serene," Clara said in a soft voice. "I'm glad you enjoyed the experience," Olga replied. Clara and Olga did not fish much that day, but they did fish enough to prepare a delicious meal. Then they sat on the seashore, in two very comfortable plastic chairs whose front legs almost touched the water.

After telling Olga about her travels abroad, Clara added, "I have visited beautiful places, but in none of them did I feel as calm as I do now." "That's because ..." Clara had not finished completing her sentence when suddenly a neighbor knocked desperately on her door, "Neighbor, my wife is giving birth and I don't know what to do!" Olga replied calmly, "Don't worry, let's see how the labor is going,"

Olga was a doctor, so that afternoon she had to attend the emergency delivery of her neighbor. Clara, with great dedication and integrity, helped her in the process. And when Olga handed the newborn baby to her to clean, Clara's heart was flooded with indescribable tenderness and emotion. Two tears rolled down her cheeks, but they were from the joy of witnessing the miracle of life. When they finished attending this unexpected delivery, the two friends returned to the beach house, tired but happy.

Again they sat down in their plastic chairs on the seashore, where Olga told her friend, "That great feeling of tranquility that you were talking about a while ago is nothing more than inner peace, something that just it is achieved by experiencing a deep feeling of acceptance or reconciliation with oneself, with others and with the daily events of the world." "Right, friend," Clara replied. "And it is that inner peace that allows us to appreciate every beautiful moment that life offers us, no matter how simple and insignificant it may seem," added Olga. "That's right, friend, fishing with you today, our quiet and pleasant conversations, the light that enters through the windows every day, the flowers in your garden and the fragile and decent appearance of that child that I held today in my arms, made me feel like the happiest person in the world," said Clara, who never felt empty again.

The Pleasure of Friendship

Rose and Jane were two friends who had met while studying in the city's capital. Both came from distant cities in the interior of the country, where they worked as professors at very prestigious universities. When Rose finished her studies, a year before her friend, she had to return to her university to work, leaving Jane devastated. But the distance was not a problem for them at that time, because the daring Jane every so often took her vehicle and traveled for seven continuous hours to the city where Rose lived.

Then it was Jane's turn to finish her high degree studies in the capital, so she also had to return to her job in a city far away from Rose's. The two friends could no longer meet for a long time, limiting themselves to communicating only by phone or e-mail.

Years passed, Jane had married and had a five-year-old son, while Rose had divorced and now had a new life partner. "We have to find a way to meet again, friend," Jane said to Rose as they spoke on the phone. "Yes, I have many things to tell you," Rose replied.

After a few days, Jane called Rose to say, "Friend, I already found a way for us to meet. In a month, we will both be on vacation, a time that we should take advantage of to share it in a place close to the two cities where we live." "What a great idea! What do you think if we meet in Puerto Santo? It is a beautiful coastal city where we could have a great time," proposed Rose. "Excellent, I will find out the hotels that this city has, I will search where we can stay, and then I will call you to make our reservations," replied Jane.

After all the arrangements, the two friends finally met in Puerto Santo, at the doors of the Blue Bay hotel. Rose arrived alone, while Jane arrived with Gabriel, her little son. Upon seeing each other, the two friends hugged deeply emotionally and soon began to chat about everything that had happened in their lives during the six years they were apart. "Come on, let's go get settled in our rooms, and tomorrow we'll start our planned tour," Rose suggested. Jane followed her with the child in her arms.

Next morning, the girlfriends and the boy headed to a nearby beach to spend the day. This beach was famous in Puerto Santo not only for the quality of its waters but for the restaurants near it. In this place, Jane, Rose, and Gabriel had a great day. The boy had fun playing in the sand with other children and making sandcastles with his mother and Rose, while the two friends sat and chatted placidly in comfortable folding chairs placed under the shade of a huge umbrella.

In addition, they took the opportunity to enjoy the food offered by one of the most popular and distinguished restaurants in the area, one where customers took their orders and served dishes wherever they preferred, either sitting on the sand, in chairs, or even plastic benches in the water. From her folding chair, Jane ordered the waiter, "I want some overflowing shrimp with a salad of lettuce, tomatoes and olives, and some steamed potatoes." "Excellent choice, ma'am," said the waiter. And then, turning to Rose, he asked, "And what would you like to order, distinguished lady?" Rose, smiling, replied, "I want the same as hers, but add two very cold fruit cocktails."

While they waited for their food, Jane commented, "Hey Rose, do you see that island in the distance? It's called Snail Island and they say it's very interesting. Do you think we could visit it tomorrow?" "Of course, we just have to find out where the boats that lead to her are," Rose replied. After a while, the waiters approached with the two ladies' food orders. And right away, Jane called her son to share her plate with him.

Next day, the trio of vacationers was already very early at the dock to embark for Snail Island. While they were on the boat with fifteen other tourists, the two friends and the boy listened attentively to the story the tour guide was telling. "This island we are headed for was once much higher above the surface, but then mysteriously sank under the sea, taking with it an entire city whose ruins can still be seen clearly through the water." "Oh, that's amazing!" exclaimed Jane excitedly. "Yes, it is also said that some beautiful fairies have been seen in this area guarding the ruins," added the guide. "How interesting!" Rose exclaimed.

The other tourists were also listening carefully to the guide's narration and when the ship finally docked on the island, all the passengers ran off to explore the place. Indeed, through the crystal clear waters that surrounded some areas of the island, some roofs, streets, and walls of the ancient submerged city could be seen.

When the walkthrough of this interesting area ended, the guide led the visitors to a nearby beach where they could bathe and enjoy the sun. It happened that at a time when the guide was carrying a tray with sandwiches for the group, he tripped over some rocks and injured his right hand. Then Gabriel immediately took out a precious blue stone from his backpack, placed it in the guide's hand, and it was quickly healed. Everyone was stunned. "Where did you get that stone from?" They asked. And the boy replied, "It was given to me by a beautiful and resplendent young woman whom I ran into a while ago in the ruins of the submerged city." And so ends this story about two inseparable and adventurous friends who always fought to be together and enjoy life.

66

A Trip to Emerald Island

Jonathan's dream had always been to sail his own boat. So one day, barely reaching the time required to retire, this professor requested his retirement without hesitation, and with the money he received for all his years of service, he immediately bought a boat. It was not a very sophisticated boat, but it was very beautiful and comfortable. It had two floors, a lower one where the kitchen was located, a small living room and two cabins provided with bunks to sleep, and an upper floor where the control cabin was located. "I finally have my own ship, and I can be its captain!" Jonathan exclaimed as he stood in front of his valuable acquisition.

Since Jonathan was not an expert navigator, and as he was a little afraid to travel alone, he invited some of his colleagues, also biologists, to go with him on his adventure. The men accepted immediately because they would take advantage of it to make scientific observations and study nature closely. Among them were Peter, a zoologist specializing in sea turtles; Joseph, a botanist, and Gerald, an ornithologist. In addition, they would be followed by Alonso, a young sailor who would be the captain's assistant.

When everything was ready, Jonathan and his companions set sail for the Emerald Island. The journey was somewhat long, about seven hours, but between the great blue of the sea and the sky, the pleasant sea breeze, and the dolphins that every few hours curiously approached the boat, the way to the island seemed shorter.

Suddenly, the sailor exclaimed, "Land at sight," and all excitedly ran to the side rails of the ship to look out and scan the horizon. There was Emerald Island, a small flat oval, surrounded by stunning white sand that sparkled in the sun. As the boat approached the shore, the sailors were able to appreciate the greenish reflection and the crystalline nature of its waters. "Look at this, no wonder they call her Emerald," Peter said ecstatically.

One or another fishing village could be seen from the Victoria. That's what the boat was called. And to everyone's surprise, there was a helipad where the newcomers could see how a helicopter landed and dropped off some tourists. Among the few tourist boats that could be seen, there was a very striking one with its hole at the bottom and some narrow sailboats that seemed to glow in the evening light. This whole image was beautiful and peaceful. Jonathan and his companions were ecstatic and happy at the beauty in their eyes. "Look at that clean white sand," Peter said raptly. And Joseph replied, "Yes, it looks like a dream."

As it was getting dark, Jonathan ordered the anchor to be lowered and invited those present to enjoy a simple and exquisite dinner. Then they all went to sleep in their cabins.

The next morning, Victoria's passengers were ready to begin their exploration tour of the island. All on their bathing suits, their respective light clothing, and the necessary material and equipment, including notebooks, food, water, GPS unit, and cameras. Since Jonathan was also a biologist and nature lover, he couldn't help but go along with his colleagues on this exploratory journey.

"Get the support boat ready, you leave us on the shore and then you go back to the Victoria," Jonathan ordered Alonso. "At your command, my captain," replied the sailor. Jonathan, Peter, Joseph, and Gerald sat carefully in the support boat while Alonso started the motor to take them to shore. "How will Alonso know when to come back for us?" asked Peter, curious. "Don't worry, that's why we have our communication radios," replied Jonathan, showing a small device that he took from his backpack.

Once on the shore of the island, the scientists quickly changed their clothes. It was so sunny that it was necessary to wear long pants, long-sleeved flannels, boots, and a hat. As they toured the island, the explorers noticed how it was covered by countless limestone rocks that gleamed in the sun. Abundant cacti poked their heads between the furrows of bare soil, and some scattered bushes could be seen across the surface of the land.

For these botanists and zoologists who loved their work and nature, they were in a paradise. "Look at those white lizards!" Exclaimed Joseph, surprised. "Yes, they are as white as the rocks that cover this island, a camouflage that has surely served them for years to survive in this environment," Peter explained. Soon the song of the birds began to be heard and Gerald, excited, began to observe and photograph how many birds crossed his path.

Suddenly, the travelers' stomachs began to rustle with hunger, so they all agreed to find a suitable place to eat. They sat under the shade of a tree and there, at the moment when Joseph opened a bottle of water to drink, a small lizard approached them without any fear as if waiting to be invited. "Look how daring this animal is!" Exclaimed Peter smiling. And they all smiled too. At the end of lunch, the captain ordered, "Let's take one last look at the island and go back to the ship."

They did so, and then they returned to shore to wait for Alonso, who soon arrived with a cellar full of cold drinks that he distributed to each one. Later, the travelers could not hold out on the boat and jumped into the water to swim and splash like children. "This is life," they all said while enjoying the wonderful transparency and excellent temperature of the water where they bathed. "And did you see that view?" Asked Joseph, smiling, as he watched a beautiful tourist strapping her bikini on an adjoining sailboat. "Yes, that is also part of the wonders of nature," replied the rogue Gerald. And so the four friends, biologists, and fellow travelers continued to enjoy their fortunate and pleasant journey.

Henry and the Mountain Gods

Henry was a man who had a modest life, his house was comfortable and spacious, where he lived with his beautiful family; He had a vehicle and a good job, but that was not enough, he always wanted more. This man went with his family to spend a season in their country house, which was in a mountainous area. This place was beautiful and full of peace, and there they could enjoy the rich aroma of flowers, the sweet song of birds, and the gentle fall of the waters.

There her family had a great time and her children loved the place. "Look, dad how cute and colorful that bird is!" Said his daughter Carol. "Yes, it is really beautiful," Henry replied. "Come on Toby, let's play on the grass," his youngest son Edmund told his beloved dog. "Take care, children! I am going to prepare the food," said his wife, Catherine. "I'll join you, sweetheart," Henry said lovingly, and they went to the kitchen.

One day Henry decided to go alone to walk the mountain at the back of his house. Everything was green and flowery, with many streams, ravines, huge trees, and many animals. He walked for a long time and entered the mountain. He came to a rather steep area, where there was a cave with many mosses and ferns at the entrance, which looked like the entrance to a beautiful dwelling; strangely, from inside you could see bright and colorful rays like a rainbow.

These charming images prompted Henry's curiosity to venture inside. Internally, everything was magical. There was a lot of brightness on the cave walls like precious stones were upholstering the multiple corridors that were formed. There were also beautiful flowers adorning the place, and springs that flowed with golden and blue colors. Henry was perplexed by such beauty. As he entered and observed everything, he heard a melodious voice that asked, "Who dares to disturb the peace of this place?" "Excuse me, I didn't want to bother," Henry replied, startled. "Don't be scared; we just have to take care of this place," said the voice.

At once, several majestic figures appeared that seemed to flower and settled in front of him. They had very white skin and golden hair and beautiful clothes with colors similar to nature, of different shades of green. "We are the gods of the mountains, and with our powers, we try to keep these places healthy and beautiful for everyone," said one of them. "Yes, the wonders you see in these mountains and everything fantastic about this place is our work, we can do these and many more things," added another. "Very few have found this place, and we never allow it, but today we were all gathered in a room in this place, discussing some matters about nature, and we neglected the entrance," said the first. "When we are accidentally discovered by some human, we must grant them a wish, so you can ask for anything for your life," said another.

Henry thought for a while that it would be more convenient to ask, "A vehicle, a house, a job, the love of my family, I have all that," he told himself. But after meditating a while more, his ambition overcame him and he wanted to have much more material things. "If you allow me to choose, oh exalted gods, make everything that I touch with this finger (pointing to the right index finger), become money."

The mountain gods agreed, regretting that he did not make a more sensible request. Satisfied with the random gift, he thanked and said goodbye to hurriedly return home. On the way he wanted to make sure of the truth of what happened and of his gift, so he touched with his finger some leaves, which instantly changed their greenness to take on the color and shape of money. "How wonderful!" Henry yelled euphorically.

He touched a stone on the ground and immediately began his transformation into precious money. The herbs, the fruits, everything he touched underwent that change. Out of joy, he ran home, and when he turned the knob, the door opened, but it was also made banknotes. The very playful dog ran to the entrance to meet him and jumped on him. At the moment in which Henry reached his hands to catch him, unconsciously, he also turned him into a bag of money. At that moment, Henry realized how risky the gift he had asked for, because at any moment, accidentally, he could irreparably harm his family and everyone he touched. He hurried back to the mountain to see if he could reverse his terrible gift, before his children noticed the absence of his precious dog, and before anything else happened.

He ascended as fast as he could up the mountain until he reached the cave he had previously visited; this time some gods were waiting at the entrance and allowed him to pass. There were several of the gods, who seemed to be waiting for him. "Go ahead, tell us what you want," they said. "Oh, I have realized my terrible mistake, in requesting that they grant me such a gift! I don't want to lose what I love most, my family and all the people around me because of my excessive ambition; I prefer to continue having everything I already have, which now I see is more than enough, especially the love and happiness of my whole family. Please can you undo this spell?" said Henry, very remorseful.

"We knew it was a foolish wish you requested, but it was our obligation to grant it to you; Even so, we perceive that you are a good man and that you were only confused and a little ambitious, so we can reverse the spell. As a gift for having reconsidered in time, you will preserve throughout your life the happiness that you already have with your beloved family and with your environment", said one of the Gods. "You must put your hand in that light source and everything will return to normal," said another.

Indeed, everything returned to normal, including the bag of bills returned to return to the form of Toby, who returned, received him wagging his tail and jumping on him, as always. He tenderly embraced his family, and since then he has been very happy, grateful, and successful in his life.

Trip to the National Park

A group of friends who lived in a coastal city decided to take a leisure trip to the National Park, located in a mountainous area. Although in their city there were beautiful beaches and other spaces for recreation and fun, they wanted to know new places with other colder environments. Someone had told them about this park, located approximately four hours away by road, so they made telephone reservations for a recommended inn. They did some shopping, packed their things for the trip, and left in the morning.

As they left their city, it was possible to perceive that even when it was not noon, the sun was already strong enough and the heat was beginning to increase in the environment. They traveled a stretch of highway where they could see, on the small sidehills, the typical vegetation of that city: many cactus, prickly pears, and thorny bushes. The soil was quite dry, since the dry season had begun, and which would last about six months.

They moved away until they took a road that led to a more wooded municipality with a little more altitude. There the vegetation changed, it stopped being xerophilous to have taller plants, with fewer thorns, many trees, and herbs. At some points, they could see a majestic river snaking along the road; between it and the highway, several villages appeared at every certain distance, with somewhat rudimentary houses, made of wood and roofs of zinc or asbestos, but very beautiful. The locals walked along the side of the road or rode bicycles.

After an hour, the friends began to see many sugar cane crops on both sides of the road until they reached the capital, which was a small and picturesque city, located in a valley, surrounded by large mountains. Upon entering, one of them said, "I'm a little hungry," while funnily touching his abdomen. "You are always hungry Adam, you are very gluttonous," Barbara replied, and they all laughed. "Let's ask where we can eat, Adam infected me with his hunger," said Edward who was behind the wheel. "Now it turns out that hunger is a contagious disease!" Camilla exclaimed, and everyone laughed again.

A passerby indicated a place, which was inside the market, where he could eat. They went in and tasted a delicious meal with pork. They then toured the place for a while, where they bought some cookies and drinks to go. They left the market and walked through some of the few streets in the small town. "Look! There you can see the factory where they process all that cane that I saw when entering the city," said Stephen. "Yes, a lot of the sugar they produce here is what we use in our city to sweeten our lives," Adam said.

They moved to the central square, where there was an old church, its façade faded and stained by mold and rain. Still,

80

the structure was beautiful, and internally it was even prettier. They made a few more turns and continued on their way, leaving behind many more cane fields at the exit of that quiet city. They continued on the road, always on the rise, while listening to music and singing. After about two hours had passed, they began to notice the weather was changing again, it was getting colder and there was mist in the environment. They observed the entrance to a military training camp and later found another village.

"There is a pleasant cold in this place," Barbara said, crossing her arms. "Good thing we brought our coats!" Camilla added. "These areas are much colder than our city, as we were told," Edward indicated. "Look, you can see several pine plants already," Adam pointed out. Then the route went downhill, the cold was less, but there were still many hills, in which numerous plants were appreciated, among them pine trees. Also, there were various crops on both sides of the road. Later, they came across a dam, built to direct the watercourse for irrigation of crops.

About forty minutes later, they reached the border of the National Park, which had an area of 627 km, there they began to climb again, but this time much higher, to visit a cave where numerous colonies of nocturnal birds, typical of that place, lived. The place was beautiful, with abundant trees, very tall, on which grew mosses, ferns, and orchids with flowers of extraordinary beauty and exquisite smells that permeated the whole place, in addition to bromeliads that hung like curtains with a grayish-green. The weather was much colder but pleasant.

"Let's take the tour inside the cave," suggested Barbara. "Sounds like a good idea, let's go check on the recommendations to enter," Edward said, and they went to the facilities located in front of the cave. "You only have to collaborate with an entrance fee, and you will be provided with plastic boots since inside the cave there is humidity from the springs that come from the depths," explained the manager. They made the tour and were fascinated by the figures that were formed thanks to the sediments of the waters that flowed and originated these stalactites and stalagmites in different ways. In addition, the sound of the birds in their nests was heard. After leaving the cave, they visited an impressive waterfall, located a few meters from there.

They then went to the inn they had reserved, which was located half an hour from there. They settled in, ate, and then went out at night to see the town. "There, it says they sell strawberries with cream, let's go try them," invited Camilla, and everyone agreed. "How delicious this dessert is!" Said Barbara, very pleased. "We also have a hot chocolate that is very tasty and helps calm the cold," suggested the owner of the place. They accepted the suggestion and then Adam said,

"This chocolate is delicious."

Then they returned to the inn to rest peacefully in their rooms, sheltered to mitigate the pleasant chill of the environment. They had had a very pleasant and fascinating day, and they already planned to continue their tour the next day.

The King and the Charity Works

There was a king who was very kind and concerned for the welfare of his vassals, in addition to ensuring they were compassionate and virtuous with others. For he considered this to be part of his mission. Yet as he traveled the various regions of his reign over and over again, he found that many of his vassals lacked altruism. His advisers had already mentioned it to him, "Your Majesty, we have observed the unkind and ungenerous behavior that has grown in the population." "We must think of something that allows good feelings to emerge in my beloved people," said the king.

At the beginning of the New Year, he met with his advisers to entrust them to spread to all the peoples of the kingdom, his willingness to give an award to the person who had done the greatest work of charity during the past year. He was convinced that with gestures like these, he would encourage the altruism of the settlers.

His advisers left to carry out the delegated order, sent emissaries to disseminate the information. They went from town to town, through all the streets, houses, crops, and other places to participate all population, in addition, they placed written announcements everywhere.

After a week, everyone went to the castle, as that day had been set for the awards. Many people had attended, from all parts of the reign, some because they considered having done the greatest work of charity, and others as mere spectators. "Before you, His Majesty the King," one of the heralds announced, and immediately everyone bowed. The king greeted them warmly and personally confirmed what the award consisted of. Then, they went one by one to expose what they considered their best charity work, for their king to decide.

One came up and said, "Your Majesty, I built a beautiful teaching center for orphaned children in my village." The king's heart was filled with joy when he heard his words and he asked, "But is it fully built and working already?" "Not yet, because it only needs to place a statue of me with an inscription in gold, which reflects by whom and on what date it was built, so they will never forget me." The king thanked the man and passed to another, which said, "Kind sovereign, I have paid from my own wealth, a monastery for several religious men who are in my town." The monarch rejoiced at his action and also asked him the same question as to the previous one, to which he replied, "I just need to finish a beautiful room for me because I plan to retire to that place when I am older, to practice religion."

The king thanked him, as the next participant passed by. He said, "I have also used my fortune to build a new cemetery in my region since the one that was there was very small and with defective pantheons, and I would not like anyone in my family to have their eternal rest in that place." "Yes, it is indeed a necessary work," said the sovereign, "I suppose it is already completed and at the service of all the inhabitants of that region?" he added. "Soon it will be completely ready, I am only polishing the magnificent pantheon that I am building downtown for myself and my whole family." "I understand, thank you, let's hear someone else tell his work," said the king kindly.

In this case, a royal guard spoke, "Your exalted majesty, I have traveled long roads and steep mountains for many months for the sake of your excellence, just with the idea of getting this beautiful plant as a gift to your beloved daughter." "I appreciate your care and dedication, but I don't see where the charity is in that work," said the king, a little surprised. "Don't you see it, Your Majesty? It is said that this plant is miraculous and can lengthen people's lives, and I want her to remain for a long time next to her future husband, who, with all due respect, I hope to be me."

The king, who was a gentle and peaceful man, smiled at the boy's audacity and turned to the next one. This time it was a lady, who expressed the following, "Dear sovereign, I believe that I am the one who deserves this award because my charity work has been more vital since I have picked up an orphan girl

who was dying of hunger and I have fed her like a daughter."
"Sounds good work to me, is she still with you?" asked the
king. "Yes sir, I was never separated from her, because she is
so diligent that she has transformed my house into a very
clean and beautiful place, she also attends me with love and
dedication; how good I found someone like that!" the king
kindly asked them to sit down, asking if there was anyone else
who wanted to intervene.

It seemed that there would no longer be more people who
would exhibit about their works, when suddenly a commotion
was heard within the crowd, which made way for a pretty girl,
who was holding the hand of a very poor old woman, with her
patched clothes and a walking stick. The old woman was
reluctant to go to such a congested place. The king lovingly
asked the girl what she wanted, and she replied, "With your
permission, sir I consider that this pretty old woman is the one
who deserves the award for the greatest work of charity."
"Ignore her, sir, I have not done any work to deserve such an
award, I am just a poor old woman who lives on what little she
gets," said the old woman. The girl replied, "However, she
gave me a piece of bread." To which the old woman added,
trying to avoid the subject, "You see, so much fuss over a
breadcrumb." "Yes, but she gave it to me when I was very far
away from home, alone and hungry, she was also in the same
situation, and even so, she gave me the only piece she had,"
replied the grateful girl.

The king, shocked by such good feelings of altruism, did not hesitate to consign the award to the pretty old woman, in addition to inviting both of them to taste delicious delicacies. From that moment, all the settlers learned the importance of doing charity works, without expecting anything in return, while the king continued to lovingly watch over them.

An Extraordinary Heritage

Robert was a young and single man who worked in the city. As a manager, he lived submerged among papers, calculators, and all kinds of receipts for purchases and payments. Robert liked his job very much, but sometimes he felt lonely, bored, and tired of handling many accounts. One day, while he was in his apartment, someone rang his doorbell. "Good morning," said a man to Robert when he opened the door for him. "Yes, tell me," Robert replied. "Are you Mr. Robert Norton?" asked the visitor. "Yes, it's me," Robert replied, intrigued. "This is for you," the man announced to Robert, handing him a large envelope that appeared to contain many documents. "Thank you," said Robert. When the postman left, the young manager immediately set about uncovering the delivery.

Among the documents he had just received, Robert found a letter from his uncle Henry, who had died a few days ago, informing him that he had inherited a valuable property near Lake Blake, in the vicinity of the city of King. The surprised Robert did not know what to think or what to do. The property he had just inherited was a long way from where he lived, a few hours' drive overland, so moving there would mean driving a long time to get to work every day. Then, the insecure boy decided to request a two-week permit at the agency where he worked, carry out the necessary procedures of his new acquisition, and visit and inspect it in detail.

When everything was ready, Robert took his bags to the city of King. When stopping his vehicle in front of his new property, the man was impressed by the house's beauty and by the large expanse of land where it was located. Between curious and excited, Robert got out of the car and hurried to open the front door. An inspection of the property revealed that it not only consisted of a spacious and beautiful home furnished and decorated in great style, but included a huge land full of leafy trees, shrubs, and a great variety of plants that gave the place an impressive beauty. In addition, a charming lake with warm and crystalline waters was part of the boundaries of this place.

With the passing of the days, the young heir was feeling more and more comfortable and attracted by this environment. Every afternoon he would sit on a bench that he had placed near the lake, and there, permeated by the calm that the place inspired him, he would dedicate himself to reading a book, solving a crossword puzzle, or simply contemplating the immensity and splendid beauty of the lake and its surroundings.

And it happened that one afternoon, when Robert was standing in front of the lake, thinking about how to get a fishing rod to use in these waters, a spectacular multi-colored fish poked its head above the surface and swam in such a strange and special way, that the young man soon gave up the idea of fishing. Robert had been so impressed by this fish beauty and strange swimming path that every day he returned to the lake to see it. His curiosity and attraction to the animal were so great that one day this man decided to use an old rowboat that was stored in a warehouse in his house to peacefully navigate in it and take a closer look at his admired fish.

The two weeks of leave requested by Robert from his agency had passed, so the boy had no choice but to return to his apartment. When he told some co-workers about his inheritance, they got so excited that they immediately set about organizing a visit to Robert's new property. After several days, Robert and a large group of colleagues arrived at the farm near Lake Blake. Everyone was amazed by the construction and the surrounding nature.

In the afternoon, Robert and his guests began to cook an outdoor barbecue. And in oversight of the owner, Brandon, one of them, headed to the lake. After a while, Brandon appeared smiling with a container in his hands. "Look what I brought to complete our lunch," he said. When Robert got closer to look inside the bowl, he was stunned to discover that his beloved multi-colored fish was among the captured fish, splashing through the scant water spilled into the bowl.

Desperate, Robert took the container and quickly carried it to the lake, where he immediately submerged it and prayed for the fish's sake.

Meanwhile, Robert's guests waited in confusion. "I think I was wrong to catch a fish without the owner's permission," Brandon said shyly. At the lake, Robert's soul had returned to his body when he saw his favorite fish revive and swim nimbly. When Robert returned to his guests, he explained that he had promised never to fish in that lake for a personal reason. Everyone understood and soon forgot about the incident.

As they all left, Robert went once more to the lake. He sat placidly on his bench until nightfall, and then, under the reflection of the bright moon, a nymph of extraordinary beauty emerged from the waters. She wore an almost transparent bluish dress, like chiffon, and her hair was multicolored, identical to that of the body of the fish that Robert admired so much.

Before the young man spoke a word, the nymph approached him and said tenderly, "I am a special kind of elemental of the waters, and I have come to thank you for saving me today." After this meeting, Robert decided to move permanently to his house on the lake.

Back Home

Monica was a 26-year-old young woman who came from a small village called, The Village of Petals. This was a picturesque village, where a great number of honest, hard-working, and simple people lived. For the most part, they were farmers. In this place, Monica lived most of her childhood with her loving family. She lived with her parents and her younger brother, Tommy. Together they divided up the housework and worked every day to earn money on the farm. It was a somewhat hard life but at the same time very happy the one they lived.

As time went by, Monica was presented with the opportunity to leave the village to study abroad; she was already 18 years old, and she could take care of herself. She was very insecure about this decision. She did not want to leave her family alone, but her mother insisted, "You do not have to worry about us, my little one. We will be very good here," to which her father added, "An opportunity like this one doesn't show up every day, Monica. You are a smart young woman, you deserve more than this humble life as a farmer." Her little brother Tommy finally said, "Don't worry about a thing, sister! I can easily take care of all the work here on the farm, trust me!"

Seeing the unconditional support she received from her family, the young woman hugged them all with happiness and promised to take her feelings with her on her journey. "Thank you very much, everyone. I promise to always carry you in my heart." And just like that, she left her village, in search of a new life.

Many years passed since then, Monica met a kind and gentle boy named Frank, and they both fell in love and began to live together. She managed to finish her studies and graduated with a literature degree. Reading was something that made her very happy, it was her passion without a doubt. Day by day, Monica wrote letters to her family to tell them how her life as a couple was going and to ask how they were in the small village. Everything was wonderful for both parties at that time. One day, Monica wrote a letter to her family, informing them that she was going to visit the village with Frank and that she also had a little surprise for them.

Meanwhile, in The Village of Petals, Monica's parents were eager to see their little girl once again and to meet their new son-in-law of course. "I'm so glad that our little girl is finally coming home! But it bothers me that she brings a boy with her," Monica's father said, somehow angry. His wife replied, "Frank, don't even think about being rude to Monica's boyfriend. Besides, she is already 26 years old, she's at the age to hang out with whoever she wants," "Yes, I suppose you're right, Muriel. Although I still don't like the idea," he said. Mr.

Frank was an old curmudgeon, especially when it came to his little girl.

To celebrate the return of the eldest daughter, Tommy, who was now about 17 years old, went to the lake to catch his sister's favorite fish. Monica's father was in charge of collecting the most delicious vegetables from his garden for the occasion. Monica's mother used all the ingredients gathered to prepare a delicious banquet in honor of the return of her beloved daughter, who would not take long to arrive according to her letter.

The family was waiting impatiently outside their home, but Monica or her boyfriend was no sign. At that, Tommy saw something that surprised him, "Hey, guys, who's that little girl?" he said, pointing to a little girl who was sprinting towards her home. When Muriel detailed it well, she couldn't believe her eyes. That girl was Monica, at the tender age of 5, or at least she looked exactly like her. The little girl came to the home of the confused family and jumped directly into Muriel's arms as if she had known her forever.

Muriel was waiting for the girl to call her Mom, just like Monica used to do when she was little. But instead, the little girl said, "Grandma!" which left everyone in the place freezing. "Did you just call me, granny?" asked Muriel, "Well, yes, I have only seen you in photos, but you are my grandmother, Muriel!" Nobody could believe what they heard. Behind the little girl, a young couple in very formal clothes was approaching. The little girl ran up to them and said, "Mommy, daddy, I just met my granny!" with that there was no doubt that beautiful and well-dressed young woman was Monica. Her mother and father ran to hug her when they saw how beautiful she had become and they were super happy with the news that they were now grandparents.

At home, they all caught up. Monica told them that that little girl was her daughter Sasha. It was the fruit of the love between Monica and Frank. Seeing that she was so happy with Frank, Monica's father relaxed a little and decided to give the boy a chance. Tommy showed his sister what a great job he had done on the old farm and she couldn't believe that he was now such a strong and vigorous young man, very different from the little boy she lived with many years ago. Without a doubt, it was a good decision to have left her family in his hands.

The whole family gathered. They spent the night eating from the delicious feast they had prepared while telling funny stories about their day to day on the farm and in the big city. Tommy played with his little niece; father and boyfriend had many things in common to talk about, and Monica and her mother were planning a future wedding in the small village. Without a doubt, a very moving reunion for everyone.

Snow Day

Samantha was a young and cheerful 17-year-old girl who was about to turn 18 and had only one wish, something she wanted for that day more than anything in the world, to be able to see the snow once more. The city where she lived with her parents had a very hot and tropical climate most of the year; it never snowed in that place. However, Samantha had already known snow for many years. When she was just nine years old, she traveled with her parents to visit their small native town to celebrate their anniversary. Upon arrival, little Samantha watched in amazement how small ice crystals fell from the sky and piled up on all sides, forming a layer of very cold white sand that covered the entire place. All of this was new to her.

"Mommy, what is this white thing that falls from the sky? It is very cold, but it is very pretty," asked little Samantha. Her mother carried her in her arms and replied, "This is snow, my love. In this little town it snows most of the year; your father and I fell in love walking through this sky full of snowflakes. It is beautiful, don't you think so?" Samantha found it extremely beautiful, the most beautiful thing she had ever seen in her life. Little Samantha started playing snowball wars with the other children in town. Although she had never done something like that before, the truth was that she was very good at the game, everyone else wanted her on their team, and she had a lot of strength in her arms for her young age.

While playing games, Samantha accidentally hit a boy who was sitting on a bench drinking hot chocolate. The sad girl ran straight to see how he was, "Are you okay, friend? I'm very sorry I hit you! It's just that I got distracted all of a sudden," the boy smiled and replied, "Don't worry, nothing happened to me, that's very normal here. The good thing is that I did not spill my hot chocolate! That would be sad," it was a very nice boy.

Samantha detailed the boy and saw that, on his cheek, he had a scar, right where she had hit him. The boy quickly realized what Samantha was thinking and clarified, "It's not what you think! I have this scar from when I fell while riding a sled, you had nothing to do with it." Hearing such a thing, Samantha relaxed a lot and said, "What a relief. I did not know that you could go sledding in this place," "Yes, it is something very fun! If you want I can teach you. My name is Claus, by the way," said the boy, to which the girl replied, "My name is Samantha, but you can call me Sammy. And yes, I would love to go sledding with you, Claus!" And so, a new friendship had been born under the snow.

Samantha and Claus became a pair of totally inseparable friends, they always played together throwing snowballs or building funny snowmen; it was a very pure and innocent friendship. However, after a month had passed, Samantha and her family had to return home, saying goodbye to the great friend she had made under the snow.

Now 17 years old, Samantha had the desire to see the snow again one day, which was her greatest wish. While she was sleeping, her parents entered her room and woke her up, with a big birthday cake in their hands, "Happy birthday, dear! Make a wish," her parents told her and she already knew exactly what she was going to ask for. As she blew out her birthday candles, the young woman wished, "I wish to see the snow once again," a request made to fate, from the bottom of her heart.

The next morning, Samantha felt a little chilly, which was strange since she had left her air conditioner off all night. The now eighteen-year-old girl finally got up from her bed and got ready to go brush her teeth to start her day. When Samantha stepped in front of her bathroom window, she couldn't believe what she saw through it, "Snow, real snow!" she said. It was something unreal, a storm of white and cold snow was falling in her city. Samantha immediately went to her parents to ask how that was possible, but they had no idea what was happening. It was the strangest case of climate change ever seen in years.

Samantha didn't much care why, she only knew one thing for sure, that she would make the most of that day. The cheerful young woman wrapped herself in her best sweater and went to explore the lively and cold city. In it, hundreds of children were playing snowball wars and Samantha ended up joining them, she had the heart of a whole little girl. While throwing frozen balls left and right, she accidentally hit a boy his age who was sitting on a park bench with one of them. The grieving young woman approached the boy and said, "Are you okay? My dear, I'm so sorry! I guess I got carried away with emotion," the boy laughed a little and said, "Don't worry, don't worry. Well, I didn't spill my hot chocolate! That would have been sad enough." This whole scene was very familiar to Samantha.

The girl saw that the boy had a scar on his cheek. Curiosity washed over her and she couldn't help asking, "Hey, how did you get that scar?" to which the boy replied, "Oh, this ugly thing? I get it riding a sled in my hometown, it was many years ago." There was no doubt, they had met again after so many years. "Claus, it's you, right? Do you remember me?" Detailing the girl's face well, Claus couldn't believe who it was. "Sammy, is it really you?" he asked to which the girl replied, "Yes, it's me. I'm also very surprised by this." "Well, you're not the only one. Do you want to chat for a while? I have hot chocolate," asked the boy. "Of course! I would love to," answered the girl, and the two good friends sat together to enjoy their sudden reunion on that wonderful and unique snowy day.

Sisters

Karla and Mika were a couple of beautiful and very loving sisters, who enjoyed spending quality time with each other and always looking for new adventures around their little town. Karla was the older sister, she was an 18-year-old, beautiful, and quite a kind girl. For her part, Mika was an 8-year-old girl, very cute, but somewhat hyperactive at times. They both lived together with their mother and were humble farmers.

The name of his native town was Camino, a quite beautiful place to live, surrounded by abundant nature and a summer climate most of the year. It was never too hot, not too cold, it was a perfect balance of both. Despite being nothing more than simple farmers, the truth was, that Mika and Karla were quite popular in the town. Mika was a happy girl, but at the same time somewhat unruly, she was full of energy and often got into a lot of trouble. On one occasion, a folk dance contest took place in Camino, which was subsidized by the mayor's office. The winner would take an incredible amount of money with him.

During those times, the girls' farm had not been able to produce much due to bad weather, so they were somewhat short of money. Little Mika, seeing that there was a possibility of winning that great cash prize, did not think about it for a second and took the dance stage, even though he hadn't even signed up. She came up with an old dress belonging to her mother and performed a strange dance she created with her imagination. "All of you admire me! This is the dance that will take home the award!" little Mika said to her beloved audience, which brought a big smile to everyone present.

Karla ended up taking her little sister off the stage and apologized to the organizer of the event. "I'm very sorry, I promise that something like this will not happen again!" said the embarrassed older sister, to which the organizer replied, "There is nothing to apologize for, dear. On the contrary, it was the most special dance I've ever seen in my life!" After saying this, all the audience present began to applaud the interpretation of little Mika. It was without a doubt the cutest thing they had seen in years. In the end, Mika did her job and won the dance contest with a majority of votes. Thanks to her, the family now had enough money to live well for a whole season. Although Mika was a rambunctious child, everyone on Camino adored and cared for her as if she were their little sister. But, if there was anyone who truly loved Mika madly, it was his older sister, Karla.

Karla, unlike Mika, was a sweet and quite calm young woman. Not to mention, she was someone extremely beautiful, who attracted the gaze of everyone on Camino. It was the beauty of the town. On one occasion, Ryan, a young chef from Camino, tried to ask Karla to go on a date with him, bringing her the largest bouquet of roses she had ever seen in her life. "Karla, would you agree to go on a date with this poor cook?" Ryan said on his knees before his beloved. The boy had already taken several attempts to ask Karla out on a date, but there was always an eventuality in the process.

Karla didn't even know what to think, she was literally in shock. Ryan was cute, but she never thought the two of them would ever go on a date. Seeing everything from a distance, was little Mika, beckoning her sister to accept the invitation. That made her somewhat uncomfortable, but no more than Ryan, who had already been kneeling for about a minute waiting for an answer. Finally, Karla took the beautiful bouquet and said, "Ryan, it will be a pleasure for me to go on a date with you," to which the very excited boy replied, "Thank you so much, Karla! You're not going to regret it! Do you think tonight, here in the restaurant?" "I'll be there," replied the girl, to which the boy added, "Perfect, I'll prepare a banquet worthy of your beauty!" and the appointment was made.

After that, both sisters headed home. The older sister said, "Mika, why did you insist so much that I go on a date with Ryan? Don't tell me you want us to be boyfriends to eat for free at his restaurant." The energetic little girl laughed and replied: "None of that, sister. I just think you both look great together! Besides, I've always seen him trying to push himself to ask you out on a date, it just didn't come off very well." Now it was the older sister who was laughing. "Very good, little cupid. Since I accepted thanks to your suggestion, you will have to help me choose a good dress for the occasion. Got it?" said the older sister. "Of course I do! You know that I love to help you choose new clothes," said the little one, and they did it like that.

The sisters spent an entire afternoon trying on a wide variety of dresses for the occasion. For her part, Mika liked them all, but Karla didn't think they were cute. The nerves of the date were already affecting the young woman. In the end, both sisters decided on a beautiful navy blue dress and Karla now felt much more confident for her date. The older sister said, "Wish me luck, little one," to which her little sister replied, "You don't need luck, just being you is more than enough!"

Karla and Ryan had a great evening that night. While Mika waited patiently at home for both of them to arrive and give them a little surprise. When the young man happened to drop off Karla at her house, Mika was waiting, smiling at the door, and gave both of them a pair of small bracelets made with small flowers; they were simply beautiful. Moved by the little girl's gesture, the beautiful new couple took her in their arms and the three of them decided to take a relaxing walk through the town together, under the moonlight.

The Proposal

Richard was a very kind and friendly boy of about 23 years of age, who was planning very carefully the most important words he would ever say in his entire life. Those words were, "Do you want to be my wife, Amelia?" For six years now, Richard had been in a dating relationship with his beautiful beloved, the charming Amelia. She was a somewhat rude girl with the rest of the people, except with Richard. The story of how they met, dates back to their high school years.

Richard had always been the typical boy who bullies teased at breaks, a sucker for most. Almost no one talked to him or wanted to be his friend, because no one wanted to get in trouble with the abusers at school. One day, Amelia came to the school as a new student, and she was in the same class as Richard. "Hello, my name is Amelia. What is yours?" she asked very kindly. Richard was a shy boy around this time, especially when it came to pretty girls like her.

"My name is Richard. It is also a pleasure for me to meet you," he finally said, after gathering a lot of courage, Amelia found her shyness adorable. "Nice to meet you too, Richard! Hey, since I'm new, and I still don't have anyone to show me what school is like. Would you mind showing me around after school?" she asked, to which the boy replied, "Sure, no problem." They both began to walk through the corridors of the school, while Richard taught Amelia everything important. He was still very nervous about being around such a pretty girl, but he was reassured that she was so kind to him.

At that, the two of them ran into the group of bullies who always annoyed Richard, and they took the opportunity to start insulting him in front of Amelia, which made him feel even more ashamed. Amelia was so furious at how her new friend was being treated, that she stood in front of those bullies and said, "If you continue to bother him, you will deal with me. Is that clear?" His voice and his gaze were so cold at that moment, that the bullies left the place terrified of the girl. Even Richard was a little scared by her tone of voice. Amelia smiled again and extended her hand to Richard and said, "You see? You just have to know how to put them in their place. Come on, let's get on with the tour!" to which Richard replied, "Sure, let's get on together!" taking Amelia's hand and promising not to let go of her again for the rest of his life.

Over time, their friendship escalated to something much deeper than just that. At 17 years old, they officially became a couple, sharing many unforgettable moments. They even supported each other in their studies to get into college. They were a very close couple. Now both twenty-three years old, they had moved together into a small apartment paid for by their jobs. Richard worked making deliveries for a pizza place, and Amelia worked full time at her parents' flower shop. For

108

Richard, seeing her surrounded by flowers was the best sight on the planet.

Richard had been saving for several months for a beautiful wedding ring with his salary as a delivery man. The efforts had been worth it; it was a very beautiful gem, worthy of his true love. Now there was only one detail in his plan, and that was, how on earth would he make his proposal to Amelia.

"Come on, Richard, think. There must be a great way you can ask her. Playing her a song? No, I sing terribly. Taking her to dinner at a restaurant maybe? Neither, that's very typical; with a bouquet? Oh, but of course not, she works in a flower shop for heaven's sake! Think, Richard, think!" The frustrated young man said to himself. After so much thinking, Richard came up with a great idea, "I'm a genius, and this can't go wrong!" said the excited boy, while jumping for joy throughout his apartment.

The next day, Richard texted Amelia to meet at a specific location. This was the park where they had had their first kiss. "Hey Richard, why did you want to see me here specifically?" asked the confused young woman, to which her boyfriend replied, "Oh, for nothing in particular. I just wanted to visit this old place. Do you remember, right?" "Well obviously! This was where we both had our first kiss. I remember your face from that day, you were so nervous you looked like a scared puppy!" she said. A memory, which got a lot of laughs out of both of them.

Richard's plan was simple but powerful, take Amelia to all the places where they spent their most beautiful moments, and then finally make his proposal. The park was only the first stop. Then they went to the movies where they had their first date, to the mall where they held hands for the first time, and they even went by the fountain where Richard asked Amelia to be his girlfriend. All of this, while bringing back all those beautiful memories of moments past.

Finally, Richard took Amelia to the place that he considered most important to both of them, the high school where they met. "Almost nothing has changed, don't you think?" Richard asked, and Amelia replied, "No, not really. Although, we have not changed that much since those years. You are still that cute boy that I fell in love with many years ago." Richard took his girlfriend's hand and said, "Amelia, I never told you this, but. Many years ago, when you defended me from those bullies and extended your hand to me for the first time, I could only think, that I never, ever wanted to let go of your hand again. And today I plan to fulfill that promise." Richard's words touched Amelia's heart, so much so that she didn't even notice when he put the ring on her finger. He said, "Amelia, do you want to be ..." "Yes, I do! Of course, I do, Richard!" Amelia said and lunged to hug Richard, and they both fell to the floor hugging and laughing very happily like little children.

A successful proposal, full of tenderness and a lot of love.

My First Friend

Annie was a cute, but somewhat bitter girl, who was going through a somewhat difficult time trying to adjust to her new lifestyle in the big city. For a few months now, Annie had moved from her small town, to start a new life a little more independent. The main reason for this is that she could no longer endure life at home. She lived in a small country house with her parents and with her four brothers. Being the oldest, she also had to be the most responsible. So, day by day, she took care of her household chores and taking care of her little brothers. The truth was that it was a fairly peaceful life, but she wanted something more.

Ever since she could remember, Annie was always a great artist, she had the talent of a professional painter. She applied for a job at an art company, and she ended up getting the job because of her talent. It certainly hurt Annie to leave her family behind, but it was a small price to pay for meeting her goal, and she still went to visit them from time to time.

Once in town, it didn't take long for her to adjust to the new life. She got a small but elegant apartment in the central part of the city, with a beautiful view of the greenest parks in the area. It was something very warm and comforting. As for the work, everyone recognized the great artist that she was and often congratulated her for her great effort, everything seemed to be going wonderfully. There was only one small problem with this fabulous new life, and that problem was that Annie had no friends.

It was not something to be missed in her. Even in her hometown, she was not very sociable. Normally she had a somewhat dull and simple character, which did not allow her to socialize much, even with her brothers it was difficult at times. She insisted that having friends wasn't something that mattered much to her, but deep down, that was a very strong desire she had. One day, Annie was walking home after getting off work. However, she realized that the route she always took was closed due to repairs. Seeing this, she had no choice but to take another way home.

There was only one small problem with this and that was that Annie had never taken another route since she was new to town, so she had to ask strangers for directions to get back home. In the end, she ended up getting lost in a park. She was already somewhat frustrated and checking her cell phone for online maps to get home, but there was no signal at the time. Already fed up with everything, the young woman began to walk angrily everywhere and unintentionally bumped into a boy in the middle of the park. They both fell to the ground. "Hey, watch where you're going!" said an angry Annie. The boy got up and said, "I'm so sorry! I must be more careful next time. Come, I'll help you," and extended his hand to the angry young woman, who accepted reluctantly, although also a little sorry for the situation.

The boy smiled at her and then started looking for something in his pockets and the rest of his body, "Hey, haven't you seen my glasses? They must have fallen off when we collided," said the young man. When Annie looked down at the floor, she realized that the boy's glasses were smashed on the floor. She had landed on them. Annie took them and very embarrassed said, "I'm so sorry! I swear I didn't mean for this to happen." The boy smiled again and replied, "Hey, don't worry! You'd be surprised how many times these glasses have been broken. It's not something new anymore." Hearing such a thing, Annie was able to calm down and smile a little after so much stress. It was as if that boy had infected her with some joy.

"Hey, if you like I could repair your glasses. I'm very good at that," said the girl, to which the boy asked, "Can you really do that?" "Sure, no problem. I used to repair my little brothers' glasses." The boy smiled more than ever and accepted the offer of that stranger he met in the park. "Thank you very much! My name is Leo, by the way. What is yours?" he asked, "My name is Annie, it is my pleasure," she said.

Annie explained to Leo that she was new in town and was having trouble finding her apartment. With the boy's help, they both made it to Annie's home and she began to repair the kind young man's glasses. "Here you go, Leo. I hope they serve you," said Annie, handing him his now repaired glasses. Leo's face of shock and euphoria said it all, "Annie, they are like new, you are incredible! Thank you very much," said the energetic young man. It was something strange, Annie normally did not feel comfortable with most people, but with Leo something was different, he inspired confidence.

Leo was surprised by the huge number of paintings and pictures in Annie's apartment, so he said, "Hey Annie, you never told me you were an artist." "Oh, yeah. I've been drawing since I was a little girl, and I work in an art company here in town," said the girl, to which Leo added, "That's great! I'm something of an artist myself." Leo took a small notebook from the desk in the room and began to draw something on it. When he finished, he revealed an ugly, poorly drawn doodle, which made Annie laugh a lot. She had never felt so comfortable with someone in her life.

The two of them continued chatting for a long time, but it was already late and it was time for Leo to go home. That made Annie a little sad. Before saying goodbye, young Leo said, "Hey Annie, you told me you haven't made any new friends since you got here, right?" "Well, I'm not proud to say it that way, but yes," replied the girl. Leo gave a very warm smile and said, "Well, perfect then. I'll be your first friend! What do you think?" Hearing such a thing, Annie could not help but feel a warmth inside, what she had just heard made her very happy,

"Yes, I would like that very much, Leo," said the young woman, with a tender and shy smile on her face. The two exchanged phone numbers and finally said goodbye. A chance meeting, which ended up being the beginning of a new and beautiful friendship.

A Beautiful Flower

Carmen and Francis were a pair of 16-year-old twin sisters, who came from a distant kingdom very popular with tourists, the glorious kingdom of Dancroft. The reason this kingdom was so special was because of the beautiful flowers that grew in it. Year after year, the most beautiful flowers ever seen by the human eye sprung up in the huge gardens of all its inhabitants, there were very rare species of all kinds. Giant roses, lilies with the color of the very rainbow, and even sunflowers that were capable of reflecting sunlight as if they were lanterns. These beautiful and special flowers could only be obtained in the kingdom of Dancroft, nobody knew how or why. Their lands had special properties that no other possessed and, in addition, the climate was suitable for these plants to grow as beautiful and healthy.

Many other kingdoms tried to grow their plants using the seeds extracted from this kingdom, but these simply died instantly, the conditions were not ideal. Thanks to that, Dancroft earned the famous nickname of, The Kingdom of Flowers. In this place, Carmen and Francis had a small flower shop, which they attended with their mother. Running the family business was not an easy thing, basically because everyone in the place had their own flower shop. It was not surprising, the flowers were what gave the kingdom its name, which was the disadvantage of living in Dancroft. However, the twins' business was not like other businesses, they not only sold flowers, they also made crafts with these flowers. They made everything from simple but beautiful hats adorned with rainbow lilies, to dresses made entirely of bright, never-fade flowers. Imagination was what kept the business going.

One day, a somewhat older lady went to the twins' flower stand, Francis was serving customers that day. "Good morning, my lady. How can I help you today? Would you be interested in buying a bouquet, or perhaps you have a craving for some handicraft made with rainbow petals?" said the kind and energetic young woman. The lady took a small hat out of her bag and said, "I want a handicraft, young lady. Nothing complicated really, I just want you to add a flower to this little hat." "That will be a piece of cake, my lady! And tell me what kind of flowers would you want?" asked the girl, to which the lady replied, "A sunrise rose, please."

Upon hearing the lady's request, Francis was very confused, she had never heard the name of that flower before in his life. Not knowing what to do, the young woman asked the lady to please wait a moment while she went to consult her request with her sister. Francis told Carmen about the lady's request, upon hearing it, the young woman looked quite intrigued and said, "Are you sure she told you she wanted a sunrise rose? Francis, the sunrise rose, is a very rare flower, almost nobody

120

has seen it, and it is like a legend. It is said that it shines as much as the sun itself and that its pollen brings with it healing properties." Francis was very impressed with what she just heard, so much so that she said, "If so, we must get it, I bet it must be worth a lot of money!" to which her sister added, "And how do you think to find such a rare flower that hardly anyone has ever seen, genius?" "Well, with a lot of effort, of course!" answered Francis. It is said that in each pair of twins, there is the smart one and the clumsy one.

Carmen spoke with the lady who made the order and clarified that they did not have such a rare flower. "I see. Well, you see, my little ones. I am only interested in that very special flower. So much so that I am willing to pay a huge amount of money to anyone who helps me find it. What do you tell me? Do you accept?" said the lady, as she put a huge amount of cash in front of the twins' noses. Both were shocked, they had never seen such an amount of money in their lives, it was enough to buy ten flower shops twice the size of theirs. Without a bit of hesitation, both twins replied, "We accept, we will gladly find that flower for you!" initiating the search for that flower of legends.

Carmen, Francis, and the mysterious lady entered the enormous forest of Dancroft in search of that beautiful rose. The forest was the natural habitat of countless species of flowers and special plants, some of which were even worth a

121

great deal of money. The group spent hours searching the vast forest, but there was no sign of the sunrise rose. A frustrated Francis said, "Sister, is there no special method to find that silly flower? There must be something," Carmen stopped to think for a moment and remembered something, "Well, it is said that the flower is so rare that it only comes to people who have a pure heart and who love nature with all their being. But I don't know how that could help us," she said.

Hearing that, Francis immediately had a great idea. She always carried with her a small tulip seed that her mother gave her many years ago; it was her most precious treasure. The young woman planted the seed with all the love in the world in the immense forest. "Francis, are you sure about this? That is your most valuable possession," asked Carmen to which Francis responded with a big smile on her face, "Mother said that one day it would bring me a lot of luck. Today is without a doubt that day, sister!"

After finishing planting his beloved seed, the soil of the place began to behave very strangely, and roots suddenly coming out of it. And so, before the three adventurers, was the very rare, sunrise rose. With a brightness comparable to that of the sun itself. The lady couldn't help but contain her excitement and hugged the twins. "Girls, for many years, my only goal has been to find this beautiful flower. It was the thing I wanted most in the world and now, my dream has finally come true.

122

Thank you, thank you very much!" she said. The lady hugged them, and they were very happy to have fulfilled someone's golden dream that day.

In the end, the lady was very happy with her now super shiny and beautiful new hat and the twins surprised their mother with the absurd amount of money they had made that day. With that amount, they did several major remodels to the shop, and it became one of the most popular in all of Dancroft. A dream come true and another that was just beginning.

The Road to Happiness

Some years ago, a woman named Stella, met a little boy who helped her find the path from which she was lost. She was a lady who lived only for her family, and this caused her indescribable stress because all the responsibilities of her closest circle fell on his shoulders. One day, while cleaning the living room of her house, she decided to take a walk in the park. Everything that had happened in the week had overwhelmed her and she needed to relax, "What a long week, I have many days without sleeping well, I feel that my eyes will fall at any moment," exclaimed the exhausted Stella, who decided to sit on a bench to sunbathe while enjoying the nature that surrounded her.

The day was wonderful, at times she felt how life passed in front of her eyes. She began to see her past, beautiful memories that had made her very happy a while ago, life tried to give her a new perspective. Suddenly, a small and damaged ball hit her heels; this made her come out of her state of meditation and reflection. She noticed a boy with considerably old clothes was approaching her at the same time that he said, "Excuse me, ma'am. Could you return my ball?" Stella took it very gently and replied, "Sure, honey, here you go," and gave it to the boy. He took it in his hands and proceeded to run in the opposite direction from her, leaving her with a series of doubts that would not let her enjoy her day; so she began to follow the little one to see where he was going.

After a long journey, the little boy stopped in an alley and she said to herself, "How strange, it must be that the ball went to that place," said the curious woman. But she was not prepared for what she would see. The boy sat on a small sheet that was on the ground; this made her understand that this was the place where he lived. Stella's heart broke into a thousand pieces: she could not hold back her tears. She approached the sweet child and said, "Hello, sweetheart, are you okay?" The little young man was moved to see that someone had taken an interest in him, for which he replied, "Great! Today I met some children in the park, I made new friends." Immediately the woman decided to ask, "Why do you live here? Where are your parents?" "I do not have, I never met them, but that does not matter, I am very happy because I have my ball," said that boy, those words surprised the lady a lot. She had never seen so much energy in a single body; the little one was someone happy no matter the difficulties that life gave him.

"What is your name?" she dared to ask. "My name is Fred and I am twelve years old," replied the infant. She could not allow himself to get to her comfortable home knowing that adorable child was in those cold streets. Fred accepted with great emotion; it was the first time that someone cared for him. The walk was long, so they took the opportunity to talk about many things. "My dream is to have a family with whom I can share everything," said the little boy. "Don't worry, from now on you will live with me, we will be a very close family; you will love to the rest of the members and they will love you," said the woman. That news was impressive for the child; it was the best day of his life; so he stopped to give a huge hug to his new mother.

Upon arrival, Stella introduced Fred to his family, explained the situation to them, and asked for their support so that the little one felt comfortable. Life had been very rough with him and he deserved a new beginning. After the basic introductory conversations, Fred went to play with his new siblings, while Stella stayed in the kitchen talking to her mother; his innocent attitude had opened her eyes. "Fred taught me many things in a few seconds. He is someone who has never had good times. Life has hurt him a lot, but he never lost his faith and the desire to be happy," said Stella. His mother, who was a very wise woman replied, "I hope that will serve as an example for you, my little one. Not only can we learn things from older people, we can also learn from younger people; Fred is an example of improvement for all; he is someone worthy of to admire." Stella nodded her head and said, "I know that life can be very difficult, but the only way to get ahead is by being happy. Everything is temporary and nothing that happens to us has to affect us, we are the masters of our destiny."

For his part, Fred spent the entire afternoon playing like never before. He was happy, his brothers were the best and he had a new ball to play with as many times as he wanted. At the end of the afternoon, Stella called the boys to go to sleep. After that, they went to bathe and each one went to their room to wait for their mother to kiss them good night. The woman went one by one, leaving Fred last, whom she had prepared a few words to thank for everything. "You have no idea of everything you taught me today. I have always been a very stressed woman, someone who he lets himself be consumed by pressure and difficulties, but when I met you I noticed how beautiful life can be if we learn to enjoy moments of happiness. I promise you that from now on you will lack nothing," she said to him. So, Stella, Fred, and their family continued with a life full of peace; the one that Stella had lost for a moment, but with the help of Fred, she took back.

The Park

Derek was a man who lived very stressed, his work was his entire life, but he was also responsible for each of the gray hairs that he had in his head, he never married and did not have children because he only dedicated himself to work. He thought that money would give him a lot of happiness but it wasn't like that. He had few friends since he said he didn't have time to see them because his work kept him very busy.

One hot morning, Derek woke up very early to go to work; he dressed while he had breakfast so as not to waste time. When he was ready he went out the door, stopped for a moment to pick up the newspaper, and continued on his way. He got in his car and drove to the company where he worked. During the ride, the busy man watched through his window as people casually walked along the sidewalk, mothers took their children to school, some young people walked their dogs and others simply enjoyed the surroundings. This caused Derek to slow down while saying to himself, "Maybe those people don't have a job as stressful as mine. I would love to have time to do the things I like." The man's thoughts were interrupted by a car horn. He decided to continue on his way to work.

At the end of the day, the exhausted man left his office and went to his car. When he got into it, he released all the air he contained in his lungs, looked at the lights that were around him and again said to himself: "I should relax a little, all my life I have worked hard, I deserve a break." Having said this, he started the vehicle and finally got ready to go home. When he arrived, he opened the door and realized how lonely he was. This made the man reflect. He told himself that it was time for a change. Although he was afraid to get out of the routine he had, he knew he had to do it. He walked to his room, put on his pajamas, and was finally able to sleep peacefully.

The next morning, the loud alarm clock on his nightstand interrupted his sleep. He remembered that he had a lot to do that day, and jumped out of bed to put on his usual clothes. While having his coffee, he got into his car and took the familiar route that led him to work. When he was almost arriving, he noticed there was a beautiful park near the company; it caught his attention and the man decided to go to that place. He parked his car and walked to the magnificent place. The little birds recited beautiful melodies that made the stressed man completely forget all his worries. Sitting on a sidewalk near some bushes, he prepared to observe everything around him.

The gentle breeze that brushed his face made him relax little by little; he lost track of time and forgot that he had to go to work. That place had completely trapped him. His mind thanked him for taking a break. "It is time to relax; it is time for me to do the things that make me very happy. I was a slave to my work; I cannot continue to allow my life to pass in front of my eyes. I have to enjoy the following years. It is time to start living," he said to himself. Derek took his cell phone to make an important call, dialed the familiar number, and after several seconds, his secretary replied. "Anne, I want you to notify the boss that I am resigning. From now on I will dedicate myself to being happy; I will seek my happiness. I hope you have a good day," he said.

He hung up the call and began to walk around the place, he was fascinated with all the small animals that ran freely through the green grass. He felt that he was as free as they were; now he could do whatever he wanted. He decided he would look for a job that did not completely consume his time. He wanted to fulfill all his goals but felt that he could not do it with the loneliness that followed him. After walking around the place for a while, he decided to rest his legs for a few moments, he sat on a bench that was right in front of the park and took a happy breath, closed his eyes, and seconds later he felt someone sit next to him. When he opened his eyes he realized that it was a beautiful woman. She managed to capture all his attention making Derek be delighted with her.

The woman felt that someone was watching her and turned her head to the left, the man came out of his little trance and scratched the back of his neck as a sign of nervousness. "Hello, do I know you?" asked the blonde with great curiosity. Derek simply answered, "Hi, we don't know each other, sorry if I make you felt uncomfortable." The woman smiled tenderly and said, "Don't worry, my name is Tina, I've never seen you around here." And that was how Derek, the man who lived stressed by his work, met the love of his life and completely detached himself from all his responsibilities. That place had made his mind fly to another dimension in which he learned that money does not give him the happiness he had expected for many years.

He moved to another city and got the job of his dreams. After a long time he felt satisfied with everything he had achieved. He finally had a beautiful family that loved him and loneliness did not accompany him on his way; he was someone very happy and he was very grateful for everything he had experienced. He felt very proud for having removed the chains that bound him to unhappiness. He finally felt complete and that mattered more than all the money in the world.

Happiness above All

This is the story of Flic, a young med student who wanted to learn from the best doctors. He was always looking for ways to improve in his field and invented many elaborate excuses for his parents to let him go to the conferences of the best doctors in his city. His life had entered a vicious circle where everything that happened around him was related to his studies. One day, while preparing for his final biology exam, he began to remember all those good times he lived in the past with his good friend Ben, who had moved away from his life since Flic's time was only dedicated to studying.

Flic had good intentions. He wanted to take his family name to the top so that he could pay the debts that his parents had accumulated over the years, but little by little he began to feel an emptiness inside him. He knew that something was lacking, the desire to excel had reached a very sick level that caused him to distance himself from all his friends. "This can't go on like this, I'm one of the best students in the entire history of the university, and I let happiness drift away from my life just to fulfill my goal. I haven't talked to Ben for months, I'll go visit him," the young man said to himself very concernedly.

Flic put his belongings in his backpack and went to his best friend's house. All the way he thought about the words he would say to him and how he could take his unexpected visit.

"I hope he doesn't take it the wrong way; I'll explain everything to him when I see him. I know he will understand me; he always does," he said in his mind. The road was made a bit long by all the thoughts that flew through the mind of the overwhelmed boy, but after several minutes he finally found himself in front of his friend's house, filled his lungs with air, went to the door, and rang the doorbell.

An eternal silence took hold of the moment as Flic waited for an answer through the intercom. The wait seemed endless but after a while, someone answered, "Hello, who's there?" said a familiar voice through the device, and the young boy was frozen, he didn't know what to say because he had not visited him for many months. After several seconds he took a breath again and said, "I am Flic, do you remember me? I would like to talk to you." A short silence took hold of the moment. Several seconds later Ben replied, "Good to hear from you, friend. I would love to take a walk, wait for me," those words calmed the dismayed young man, so he decided to wait for him on a sidewalk that was near him.

After a couple of minutes, his friend made an appearance in front of the future doctor and said, "I have not heard from you in a long time, what has happened?" and received a sincere apology in response, "I'm sorry. I put aside all my happiness; I believed that I could complete my life if I graduated." Flic looked down at the ground as a sign of regret and added: "I am someone unhappy because of the attitude I took, I only think about my studies. I want to change. I need to learn to combine my responsibilities with my hobbies; I want to get my life back."

Ben was very surprised to hear the words of his dear friend. He never would have imagined he would visit him to apologize. His tone of voice showed him he wanted his help; so he approached him and they both melted into a warm hug. He said: "Easy, brother, I will help you; 10 years ago I promised not to leave you alone, and I will not do it now; don't worry." When they separated, Ben invited him into his house, greeted his parents, and began to think the plan that would help Flic to give a great twist to all his reality, "The first thing you should know is that nothing is impossible in this life. You will see it will be very easy to combine your studies with your social life. You just have to find a middle point between those two things so you will not affect either side," said Ben.

Flic pondered his friend's words and asked, "How can I do it?" His friend responded immediately, "It's easier than you think. You have to learn to use your time; you can use a calendar, alarms are also very useful, and they will serve to remind you of all the tasks you have to do during the week." Flic liked that idea a lot. He took his cell phone and made different reminders that would allow him to organize all his homework with a predetermined time. In this way he could have several

135

hours for his enjoyment. "I will try, I had never organized my time. I believed that the only way to pass was to dedicate all my hours to study, which is the reason why I never had time to do other things. Thanks for helping me with this, friend," he said.

In this way, the boy returned home very happy. A world of possibilities was in front of his eyes; the advice that Ben gave him was very helpful. For the first time in a long time he was the owner of his time; he decided how to manage it and how I could enjoy it. The years went by and Flic regained his happiness little by little. He was already able to sleep peacefully without the need for therapies. The high levels of stress that attacked him disappeared completely. He was someone who lived calmer and more relaxed at last: he had freed himself from all his worries.

Ben never left him alone during all that process. He was always present and helped him with whatever he needed no matter what time or time it was. In this way, Flic understood that being happy is very important. The emptiness he felt inside was caused by his desire to want to achieve his goal. During the journey, he lost himself, so he promised that he would never fall into that state of mind again.

The Roller Coaster

Jerry was a very studious young man. He always had the desire to be a great entrepreneur and he knew that to achieve it he had to work hard, so he made sure to get the best grades in college. His life was very monotonous; he only focused on his studies and always said that he could not waste his time going to parties because that would not lead him to the future that he longed for so much. One hot morning, the young student woke up at the same time the bright sun rose. He wanted to study before arriving at the institute because he had a very important test that day, so he took his big book and gave it a few peeks.

The minutes passed and the boy lost track of time. He turned his eyes to the small table clock he had in his room and made a little jump due to the surprise he received: there were only a few minutes left for the exam to start and he had not even brushed his teeth. So he quickly got dressed, took a breath mint, and ran out of his house.

When he got to the university, he breathed a sigh of relief. The teacher was a little late, so he felt very calm. He walked to where his friends were and greeted them with great enthusiasm. "Hi guys! Did you study for today's test?" Rob returned the greeting very animatedly. "Hi, Jerry. Yes! Last night we got to study together, then we watched a few movies and told very interesting stories. The only thing missing was you." The boy was going to reply to his friend, but the professor's deep voice interrupted him.

When the test was finished, Jerry left the classroom and went to the dining room to take breakfast. Throughout the journey he meditated on the words his friend had told him. He had always focused on his future, forgetting his present. He considered the idea that maybe he needed to distract himself a little more and start enjoying his youth. That same day he decided he would change his life completely: he would continue studying as he had always done but now he would go out with his friends; he would sleep like never before, and would just let himself go.

When he got home he remembered he had a few chores pending, but before doing them he realized his new plan, so he just went to sleep for the rest of the day. His body was very tired and he was crying out for him to laidback on his comfortable bed. He walked to his room so he could rest and it didn't take long for him to fall into a deep sleep.

Next day, he was very excited because he knew that in a few hours he would meet his new best friend. It was a very sunny Saturday, so he could take as long as he wanted. He prepared his favorite breakfast and he tasted it very happily while watching a fun series on television. After taking a well-deserved shower, he prepared to leave his home. The sun was brighter than ever; the little birds recited beautiful melodies that slipped through his ear canal. Without a doubt, it was a wonderful day. After two hours he returned home. He was very happy because finally his body was free of worries and he knew that the puppy he was carrying in his arms would give him the company he needed so much.

They both played all afternoon in the little garden. Jerry and his playful dog, Tim were very tired. The young boy decided it was time to eat. They went to the kitchen and while serving the happy animal a sandwich, he remembered he had to make a call. He took his cell phone and called his faithful friend Rob. Jerry told him that his words had motivated him to make a big change in his life and he raised the idea of going to the amusement park. When the call ended, the young boy did some chores. He could not completely forget about them because that way his life would have no direction. When night came, he decided that his cute pet should stay home. It was very cold outside and he didn't want him to get sick. He left food and water for him on his little plate, and he was finally able to go out.

He had already arrived at the meeting place. He had been the first to arrive but he did not last long alone. In the distance, some familiar silhouettes were approaching him, "What's new, Jerry?" They all greeted him very happily; he returned the greeting and they immediately his friends wanted to know everything about his change. They were excited and very happy for him. The cheerful young man explained what had happened.

As they went to the place they wanted to go, Jerry told them about what he had done the last few days. They were all very astonished because they did not believe their friend the scholar had changed overnight. After several minutes of walking, they finally reached the desired place. Everything was lit by the different colored lights. The atmosphere was a bit cold but that would not impede having a good time. They all agreed to go to the big roller coaster, and talked about the different attractions they wanted to visit while they waited for their turn to go up. Rob approached Jerry and made a face at him so that he could move away from the group so they could talk better.

"I notice you differently, you are more relaxed and very happy. This change did you good," said his friend while looking at him happily. Jerry did not take long to answer him. "Yes, my body deserved a break from so many worries. I feel that I am capable of achieving all the things that I propose." His friend smiled as he told him: "I am very proud of you, you finally understood that you have to live life." Jerry saw his friend and happiness invaded his body. They were the next to climb the great attraction. They both looked at each other and fists clashed as a sign of brotherhood. They got into the small cubicle and fastened their seat belts. The adventure was just beginning.

Life in the Countryside

Some time ago, there was a small community of peasants. That place was very far from the city, but there lived an older man who dedicated his life to work. His name was Carl; he and his children did different tasks to have a good life and get out of that place. One sunny morning, Carl woke up very early to start the day's tasks, got out of bed and put on his work boots. Quietly walked up to his son Rick's room to ask for help with some chores, opened the door and with a soft tone of voice said, "Little boy, today I have to open the new bags of feed for the cattle, but I can't do it by myself because they are too heavy for me. I'm already a little old, could you help me?"

After several seconds without an answer, the boy finally replied, "Of course, father, if you want you can go ahead while I change my clothes." Carl nodded and headed towards the barn with a huge smile on his face. He was very grateful to life for having the best children in the world. He was very proud of them; they were excellent boys. During the journey, many thoughts crossed his mind, some good and others not so much. He also thought about how much he loved his life and how excited he was to be able to leave the country and go to the city. He believed they could be happier there because they would work a little harder to improve their lifestyle, and he wanted to achieve that goal.

"I have to talk to Rick again. I know they don't want to leave like I do because they think it's something we don't need, but we must do it to have a better future." The man exclaimed as he walked to the barn. Upon arrival, he got ready to put everything in its place to later count how many sacks of food they would need for that day. After a couple of minutes, Rick arrived with his brother Stu, both young people wanted to help their father so that he would not get so tired.

"Good morning, father, how are you getting up?" Stu asked, "Oh! Good morning, champion, what a surprise to have you here. How good that we are all together! I wanted to talk about something very important with you," said the father. Rick responded, "Sure! You know you can tell us what you want. We are a team and it will always be like that." Carl could not contain his emotion when hearing those words. He knew that his children deserved the best, so he said, "I would like to sell all our lands so we can live in the city. There we will have a better life. It is a good place for you to become completely independent."

Stu heard those words and couldn't believe his beloved father was planning this. He stopped him and exclaimed: "No way, father! These lands are the most precious thing we have, here we are very happy. If we move to the city, nothing and no one will guarantee us that we will be happier. We will have to work twice as hard." Rick supported his brother's idea and added:

"Right, dad the most successful people are not the ones with the most money in their bank account. Money is the reward that life gives you for being happy doing what you love the most. We are very rich, we are healthy and we are all together. There is nothing better than that."

Carl was stunned at the situation he was in. All his life he knew that his children did not agree with that idea, but he never imagined that those were the reasons. After meditating for a few seconds, he approached them and they all melted into a warm hug, "Thank you guys. I just wanted to find a way to give you my best. I know you are grown up but that is the job of a father. I always believed that this was not the life you wanted. I love you, my children," said the man very moved. Rick replied, "We are happy with what we have. Let's go to work."

And so, father and children began to do their work. The boys did the tasks that required physical strength while Carl sat quietly in his chair to organize and coordinate everything that had to be done. At the end of the day, the whole family sat in the dining room to enjoy a well-deserved dinner. When everyone took a seat, Carl was silent for several minutes. He was experiencing an indescribable sense of well-being because, for the first time in a long time, he felt complete. Rick noticed his father was in a self-absorption state, so he patted him on the back as he said, "Are you okay?" Carl came back from his little trance and quickly said, "Better than ever, son.

I owe everything to you, I don't know what I would be without you guys."

They all listened to his father's words and were silent so that he could continue speaking. "That talk we had in the barn made me open my eyes. I was losing my physical and mental health due to a whim that only I had. I believed we would all be better if we got away from this life and our past, but the reality was that everything would be worse. Here we have everything we need to be happy. You showed me that the only thing that matters is family moments. Everything else is secondary because with time all will be lost. So thanks for everything guys."

In this way, Carl and his children continued to live in the countryside since that was the place that kept them together. They took care of all their land and made sure they were always united to be able to enjoy all the family moments.

Family Vacation

Steven was a very busy man, he lived in a huge house with his beautiful family. His first daughter was named Rose. She was the one who took care of his home while he was away, looked after the well-being of his mother, Leah and his younger sister Emilly. The three of them fantasized about the idea of having a vacation on a paradise island, but they knew that it could not be possible. One day, Steven left his house very early because he had received a very important call. They were requesting him at the hospital where he worked to treat a patient. He put on his uniform as quickly as he could, took all his things, and headed for his vehicle completely forgetting little Emilly's sixteenth birthday.

When Steven finished doing his job like a professional, he felt very satisfied with what he had done. He managed to save the life of a patient, so he invited his team work to a dinner at a restaurant near the hospital. "Let's go eat, we did a very good job. We deserve to taste some delicious dishes. I invite you," said the successful doctor. Steven and his colleagues went out to enjoy a beautiful evening together. At the restaurant he said, "Ask for whatever you want, don't worry about the expenses." One of his nurses replied saying, "That is too much money, you should not spend it like this." Steven simply replied very proudly, "I have worked hard throughout my life.

I always work very hard; that discipline that I have had brought me as a reward the economic freedom that I have."

The woman listened carefully and said: "Are you sure you are happy with the way you live? You work all day, surely you must miss your family." Those words made the tired doctor reflect. He thought of his beloved girls and remembered that it was the birthday of his youngest princess." It can't be! I totally forgot. I have to go, guys, don't worry about me, I won't be long," Steven exclaimed as he ran to his car to return home. The man drove at a high speed. He was very sorry for having forgotten his daughter's birthday. He knew that everyone at home would be very upset with him. The journey was a bit long and he was still not fully aware of the mistake he had made. "I missed a very special day because I was working all the time; I didn't buy my little Emilly a gift either," Steven said, very concerned.

When he got home, he tried not to make any noise. He didn't want to be responsible for waking them up if they were already sleeping. When he walked through the front door, he met his beloved wife. She was very angry and needed to talk to him. Steve looked into her eyes and said: "Excuse me, darling, work kept me very busy; it was not my intention to leave you alone," said the repentant man as he sought forgiveness from his beloved wife, but the answer he got from her was, "You have to apologize to our daughter. This was another birthday

148

without her father. If you are very sorry, tell her how sorry you are and that it would not happen again. You are a ghost in this house; you are always working. You are only present three times a year. Will you continue missing all the family moments?" The woman looked him straight in the eye and continued saying, "I love you as I always have, but I don't want my daughters to continue growing up without their father. You only think about your work, realize that you are making a serious mistake. I'll go to sleep, it was a very long day. Good night."

Leah's words left the doctor very thoughtful, he stayed in the kitchen admiring the beautiful house he had thanks to his work. He immediately understood that this obsession made him lose himself of something much more important: his family. "I just focus on work. I can't go on like this. I'm stupid, I have to change my life once and for all," Steven said as he took his computer to look for plane tickets to Cancun. He was determined to get back to his beautiful family.

The next morning, he called the hospital where he worked and told the director that he would resign from his job. "I have enough money for my family and me to live well for the rest of our lives; it is time to enjoy it." Then he hung up the call leaving the woman with the words in her mouth and waited for his family to wake up to tell them the good news. The first to wake up was Rose, her eldest daughter. She had the habit of waking up very early to prepare breakfast for everyone at home. "Father, what are you doing here?" asked the very curious girl. Seconds later she got an unexpected answer, "I have decided that we will go on vacation. I want to make up for the lost time. Wake up the others."

Rose was very surprised, but it did not take her long to run and wake up the rest of the family and tell them the good news. After a while they had already prepared everything. They left their rooms and found a very happy Steven. "I want to apologize to all of you. I just dedicated myself to work and neglected my family. I promise you that this will not happen again. We will go on a trip so that my little Emilly can have a happy birthday." They were all very happy, they could finally enjoy a well-deserved vacation altogether. The plane ride was very long, but the wait was worth it. They would relax in one of the most beautiful places in the world while appreciating family time.

It was the ideal time for Steve to rest after so many years of working very hard. Fate had given him a beautiful lesson. He understood that money did not make him happy and that he had to make the most of his life.

Autumn and Cinnamon

The seasons and how they change the mood of the individual is certainly a topic he enjoyed thinking about, especially when he was in a position where he should and certainly could take advantage of the emotions they generated. Winter was when he stopped to relax the most, he still worked, of course, but he could enjoy doing it from home and wrapped in his blankets; he saw nothing wrong with spring. The birth of flowers was a lovely sight, but certainly not his favorite just because of the inconvenience of pollen and his poor immune system. Summer? A nice trip to the beach solved every problem as long as he didn't forget to pack his sunscreen again; however, whoever questioned the particular impatience he had towards autumn could first call him picky or else put himself in his situation.

It was almost funny how in the autumn customers seemed to organize themselves almost naturally to place a large number of orders individually. This wasn't impossible since they were all strangers, of course. It was all the more hilarious considering how different each one was and that such stories were expected during holiday seasons like December and July. It gave him anecdotes to share with the family over dinner, none particularly unpleasant, but it really wasn't in his plans to receive wave after wave of requests for prints late into the night (He was sure the old security guard already knew his name for the times he had to rescue the poor man locked in the elevator).

That day was no different and when the doors were opened from the outside with difficulty, he could not help but smile at the older man in a silent gesture of shame and apology for interrupting him.

He saw the man shake his head, a clear reproachful gesture twisting his features as he backed away from the door to let him out. "Last warning, boy." Threatened the man shorter than him, raising a finger, "If I see you on camera again at this time and without warning, I'll leave you sleeping in there all night."

"I swear to you this time it was an accident, Mr. Hyung, I thought I had programmed the watch correctly," he replied to calm the man, even trying to complement his explanation by lifting the wristwatch with difficulty while holding the bag with merchandise under his arm, "It will not happen again, it will be the last time."

The guard was slow to answer him after several seconds. He swore that reproachful gesture with resignation and, deep down, just deeper inside, a vote of confidence for his words. "I hope so, Hawthorne. I told you, last warning."

As he said goodbye to the man with a final apology, he heard him mumble something about, "Today's youth," and couldn't help but think how after so many days giving him a hard time he should give him a detail. The train of thought only interrupted by the realization of the initial problem: The time. It was late and surely the last bus he could have caught and taken him straight home had already left, which meant a long walk from work to the station, catching the second transportation option and again a long walk home...again.

Fall meant neutral colors, the perfect temperature between the freezing winter and its allergy season, yet at that point, it again meant a busier working season than usual.

"The positive of all this..." He heard a new train of thought resound in his mind, oblivious to his silent childish complaint about the inconvenience, "...I can take a walk." Which was always welcome considering that easily his job could slip into a sedentary life, and if he wanted to prevent his back from developing a shrimp complex at a young age compared to his sister, then the more improvised walks that resulted were certainly a blessing.

The initial discomfort was slow to fade as he lost count of his steps on the way to the station. The line separating the nighttime traffic from his sole against the pavement blurred to simply white noise in the background worthy of the ambient songs on his playlist waiting for him to get home and finally sit down after a long day with a hot cuppa, probably the cat considering it a good time to honor him with its presence by invading his seat like the good royalty it was; a perfect denouement calling to him like a siren to innocent ships.

He could easily have gotten confused in the middle of his reverie. Too busy within the same fantasy, too attractive at that hour for his exhaustion, which took a couple of minutes to process the coffee shop closest to the station cunningly inviting him even though he knew it was late, that he had to go home and the faster he arrived the sooner he could relax. If he took a seat, he knew well that he would not get up. But how to blame him when they seemed to still be open and the sweets at that moment did not seem like a bad idea? Did the end of the world mean such a little indulgence? He would not get any younger and it was not something he would repeat the next few days.

Unopposed to the idea, it didn't take him long to pick up the pace just a bit. In the process better detailing the coffee shop and what he saw right now as a change recently in the vinyl lining the windows of the themed designs. The colors that certainly ten years ago were not decorating the interior accompanying the more modern furniture than the previous and, he remembered, Madame Marie so treasured. Not recognizing the business in his distraction was to be expected, even if that route he took each day to work was the same one he took for a long time. Perhaps it was that sudden realization that made him mentally slap himself; how long had he been working for others' businesses, watching them rise from scratch and perhaps grow enough, but never bothered to visit them, much less after ten years where the familiar person he accompanied to these was no longer in town?

With a shrug of his shoulders, he peeked out only to find a couple of people inside without counting the employees and who he assumed as the manager. The only person with a familiar face who was not the owner of the place and the probable person responsible for the change of image that it was certainly not designed by him. He could see Henry look up from the other side of the bar and, making eye contact loaded with a glow of recognition, waved him in despite the reproachful gesture.

To say that the excitement of coffee, cinnamon and the warm temperature inside the place greeted him with a greeting more akin to a slap in the face was a kind comparison; the ambiance certainly felt different in a superficial way as soon as he stepped inside. But upon reaching the bar and seeing the pair of framed photos serving as decor and the familiar smell of cinnamon that Madame Marie used to add, and now his friend, it proved a pleasant welcome. "Someone took a while to grace me with his presence." Henry sneered; both arms crossed. "Should I be offended that you came just for the coffee, or thank you for visiting, Jonathan?"

"A little of both, maybe?" He replied after a nervous laugh, especially when he found the manager following the black bag with his eyes before returning to focus his eyes on him, "Yeah huh...it's a long story."

"I can see that..." He murmured perhaps thoughtfully, assumed by the clear elephant in the room: Ten years and lost contact was a long time to just blurt out a couple of inside jokes and hope everything was honey on top of the fact that it was late. Maybe they were about to close, and he came in like it was nothing; just getting off work. Be that as it may, a decade in silence was a long time, and Jonathan was no longer able to recognize if the brief grimace of the manager who was his old friend was the involuntary reaction he used to make when evaluating something, or if it was just an unimportant gesture. But he did know how to recognize something about Henry, and that was the nonchalance about issues that were not a drama in his eyes, and that he saw him interpret with his shrug before pointing out to him. "Ten minutes for ten years, coffee with cinnamon if I'm not mistaken."

"You don't." He conceded on an exhale, the weight on his shoulders finally lifting from being able to take a moment in the middle of that fall night to take a seat. "I have a lot to tell you, all funny stories, take it easy."

The Teaching Keychain

George was the oldest of three brothers. Since he was little, he dreamed of traveling to an island called "Valparaíso," which he had seen in a tourism magazine. His family was not very wealthy. They lived comfortably without many luxuries, but they had what it took. His parents fondly repeated: "The important thing was to be together as a family." When his birthday approached, he asked as a gift to travel to that charming island. However, his parents were limited to answering: "Son, be satisfied with what we give to you; it is not enough for more." And then George had no choice but to put away his magazine and look at it sometimes, to dream that he was there between the waves and the sea.

As he reached teens after thinking so much about his trip, he vowed to visit it one day. For this, he worked hard and raised money to achieve his goal. In the course of his life, he had different jobs, always as an apprentice giving his greatest commitment and determined to master what he set out to do.

His first job was the most influential in his life, collecting manure on a farm. Despite being an unpleasant job he tried to do his best and took some positive aspects out of it. The best part of his job was the afternoons after work when at the end of the day he would have lunch on a bench under a large, cool tree. From there, he could see a large part of the farm, its large barnyard full of cows, which sometimes amused him. The gate of the farm was full of various flowers. It was a beautiful garden filled with many colors that matched the whole place and conveyed a relaxing feeling. When passing by, he always took a big breath of air and when he let it out he felt how his body was released. Even through his pores, those delicious scents were accompanied by a sigh. It was his main delight.

After some time his boss assigned him to work in one of his houses as an assistant to a gardener who had been working there for years. In that house, the garden was immense and full of a variety of plants, both ornamental and fruit. George had the opportunity to learn another trade that he loved. The plants calmed him and gave him a sense of peace, plus he had a good teacher; his name was Harry, a septuagenarian with a young spirit. This kind gentleman taught him all the basic principles of gardening with much patience and dedication. This created a good friendship between them; this wise man gave him excellent advice.

What George loved most about this work was the wonder of seeing the butterflies up close drinking the nectar of the flowers and seeing how their wings flapped slightly, tasting that with joy, it was a mesmerizing scene. Slow and colorful ladybugs adorned the plants with their cuteness; he took them on his finger and played with them. But hummingbirds on the other hand, managed to distract him in such a way when they perched on a branch to rest. It was extraordinary to see such a fast bird at rest.

For a long time, he had different jobs, and when he was about to reach his goal, he had some mishaps with his parents. So being the older brother and the only one working at the time, he had to take responsibility for the expenses. He felt no discomfort; it was his family who needed him. He was mindful of the loving teachings he had.

George continued to work and slowly he recovered what he had invested in health. Years went by and he still maintained his goal. On his thirty-second birthday, his family decided to give him a surprise. They gave him some cash among all of them, which would be enough to complete the money and travel. When he received it, he hugged them all and only managed to say "thank you so much," in tears. His parents wished him success and that he would return home healthy and with many pictures of the place.

At last, he was able to book the flight and prepare everything to leave. Dreaming of traveling for so long and not knowing what to bring, he laughed at the nerves and excitement he felt. He made a list and over two days had everything organized.

At the airport, to his surprise, his old and great friend Harry was waiting for him to wish him a good trip and also gave him a small envelope that he asked to open while on the island. They said goodbye and George left for the plane.

During the flight, he slept a little, but he woke up and when he touched the pocket of the jacket he was wearing. He remembered the envelope his friend had given him. He couldn't resist his curiosity and opened it. When he saw its contents he smiled and felt a lot of tenderness. Inside was a keychain carved in wood with a wide tree that reminded him of his first job and when he used to eat under one similar to that. It also had a handwritten note that read, "Dear friend, I wish you success on your journey, always remember, not the journey, but all that you learned trying to reach your goal and think also of those who were there to support you. You made it."

These words touched his soul and he felt great joy. As he looked out the window, he thought about his friend's note and felt very lucky; he was absolutely right, pursuing his dream led him to make decisions, new learnings. He had a great teacher who brought him closer to nature and was able to appreciate his wonders.

His trip around the island began and during this, the keychain accompanied him as if all his loved ones were with him. Everything was better than he expected. The island was like a fantasy; it had the attention of kind people and very comfortable accommodations. Valparaiso Island had this name that meant, "Come to paradise." And this was because of a virgin beach; you could only go there to visit since it was preserved for its biodiversity. Upon arrival, you could hear the sea. The sand was white and its crystal clear waters were warm; in it there were reefs and fish of different colors. The sky was clear blue and the breeze was blowing softly. This was the best part of the trip. He felt like he was dreaming in that place and kept repeating to himself "Thank you universe."

Satisfied, he returned home. When the years passed and he had his children, who curiously asked about the keychain he always carried with him wherever he went, he would tell them his anecdote that concluded by saying, "If you fight for what you dream of, you will achieve it and knowledge you will obtain."

The New Awakening of a Young Man

There was once a boy named Jacob, who was always connected to social networks. His social life turned from the phone to the computer and vice versa.

Over time he got increasingly further away from the people around him. He had a job that did not matter much to him; he would go, do what he had to do and return home by bus. He entered his world when he arrived at his house. His classmates realized that he was not very sociable and tried to include him in their groups of friends. However, he would simply reply: "No, thanks, I'm busy." That situation led him to be totally alone and live an automaton life.

One day, with so much insistence on the part of his classmates, he got tired and decided to say yes. They always wanted to play basketball with him. That same afternoon after work, he went with his colleagues to the place where they were going to play.

While there, the boys made teams and included Jacob in one of them. After a while of playing, they realized how little performance he had in the game. On the other hand, he felt disappointed in himself. His arms and legs did not give him the necessary strength for the effort he had to make; he got tired very quickly and had to stop to rest at times. Jacob said to himself, "I can't believe how bad a performance I am. I thought it would be easy to shoot like in video games, but it doesn't really come close to playing in real life."

To his surprise when he finished, his classmates were happy to play with him, and one of them asked him, "How are you feeling Jacob? You had fun?" To which Jacob replies, "I feel tired, but fine, even though I'm not good at playing." He was a bit embarrassed about how little experience he has played. "Yeah, I didn't know how much fun playing basketball was." The friends were very happy to hear him say those words, to which another boy replied: "Jacob, you can come whenever you want to play with us, after work or in the afternoons off. We can teach you to play basketball; don't worry about that. You just need to practice and train a little." Jacob was glad to hear that. The last sentence left him thoughtful, "Train a little." He said in his mind. And he said goodbye to his friends.

After such an exhausting day, he realized how much fun and how good it feels to play sports and interact with other people. He arrived home in high spirits, even though he was physically tired. It felt great to let off some of that pent-up energy. He thought, "I should train and exercise a lot, I feel very weak. The way I am I won't be able to give my best." So he decided that the next day he would start an exercise routine.

The next day he did what he said. It was a weekend morning, and Jacob, after breakfast, was getting ready to go jogging. He put on a jumpsuit, a sports flannel, put some good music on his phone, put on his headphones and went out for a jog motivated, thinking about how good he felt the day he played with his teammates.

About 5 minutes later: "Oh my God, I can't do it anymore! I think I'm out of air!" He said panting as he pauses for a moment. Just then one of his coworkers named Willy walks by, looked at him, and said, "Hey Jacob, how are you? Training? That's great!" To which Jacob replied, "Yeah, it's really hard though! I get tired really fast." Willy said, "Easy mate I recommend you jog slowly at first, then you get used to it. I know it will get easier to trot, but you must train every day if you want to stop getting tired fast. I recommend you go to the park four blocks ahead and cross to the right. It's a great place to train and take advantage of the good views." Jacob, motivated, replied: "I will! And I will go there. Thanks for your recommendations, Willy." They said goodbye and Jacob trotted off to the park.

When he got there, he was surprised at how huge the park was. "How come I've never seen this park so big?" He said to himself as he entered through an archway that said "Welcome to Rumdel Park." He was stunned by the beauty of such large green areas. He felt the fresh wind blowing through those huge trees, the oxygen that this place was able to provide. The path was wide of bricks with beautiful mosaics. It ended in a path of sand and small stones comfortable for walking and jogging. It also had a large artificial lake in the middle of the park and some people were trotting, others exercising in an area with exercise machines. It was like a paradise just around the corner that he had never noticed before.

After walking and admiring the place for a while, he thought about how much he had been lost locked up at home, unable to admire life with his own eyes, and regretted all the time invested in something that did not make him happy and that in the end, they were only tools. But now he had the opportunity to live, enjoy his life, run, share and have new friends. He felt refreshed and proud to take the helm of his ship.

Then without further regrets, he began to jog and enjoy the cool weather, the leaves falling from the trees, finally appreciating life with his own eyes, feeling really free, and spending his energy on something worthwhile. A while later he stopped to rest on one of the park benches and had an idea: "I would like to share on my social networks for people who always connect, what it really is to enjoy life." He said to himself. He took out his cell phone and took a selfie with a beautiful view between trees and the lake, edited it, and wrote.

"Hey! You! You are looking at this, get out of here and live your own life!"

166

And from that day on he moved further away from the virtual world and closer to the real world.

From Accountant to Drummer

Roger was a brilliant accountant who worked in one of the largest financial services companies in the country, he was an excellent professional who managed a portfolio of very selected clients who generated a lot of money. His bosses were delighted with him, and they thought he was a money-making machine. Thanks to his job he was a wealthy man but the excess of responsibilities kept him stressed and moody.

He was married to Sarah and they had two children. Giselle, 16 years old, and Robert, 14 years old. They lived in a comfortable house located in an elegant urbanization with green gardens and impeccable streets.

Roger was happy with his life, but he felt the enormous weight of stress on his shoulders and this made him nostalgic for his youth; he thought how carefree he was when he was just a young student and was part of a rock band where he was the drummer.

One day in his office after lunch, he settled down to rest, and memories of the band and how happy he was playing drums came to mind. He thought how good it would be to have a drum set and be able to play it when he was feeling stressed. He meditated on that and laughed quietly and noticed that he felt much better. He was no longer angry, on the contrary, he felt happy and concluded that the solution to his problems was to buy a set of drums and vent all his anger on it.

When he got home he had dinner with his family and hardly spoke. The idea of the drums had him absorbed. He got up and went around his house looking for the best place to locate it. He walked around the living room, the guest room and the garage, but he understood that he would have to explain why he bought it and felt ashamed of the criticism. So he decided to buy it secretly from his family, and thinking aloud he said to himself, "But where do I put it? In the office? It would be excellent because that's where all my stress is generated. But they will think that I went completely crazy if they see me madly playing the drums, hahaha!!! Not in the office!"

Very concentrated looking for an answer, he remembered the warehouse that he has rented near his office, where he keeps the old files, and excitedly exclaimed aloud, "I have it! It will be in the warehouse!"

Sarah listened to him and, surprised, asked him, "What will be in the warehouse darling?"

"Nothing sweetie!" He replied mischievously. "I have days looking for some papers and they are sure to be in the warehouse."

"Ok!" Sarah replied and Roger said to himself, "I have to be careful, I don't want to be discovered because tomorrow will be my big concert."

The next day Roger left early for work, but first, he would buy his drums from a prestigious store that sells the best instruments in town. Excited, he entered the large store and observed the instruments, and saw between guitars and basses a beautiful black and gold drums and his heart jumped. It was love at first sight!; and said to the seller: "That's perfect! I'll take it."

They placed the disassembled battery in several boxes in his car and he left excited. He felt he was about to start a great adventure!

He arrived at his office and his day was difficult; Roger couldn't wait to go play his new drums. The stressful day passed and he quickly left the office and drove to the warehouse, immediately assembled his drums, and played it with great enthusiasm. He felt great, he felt like a carefree and happy young man.

Without realizing it, the hours passed and he went home but it was already late; Sarah was waiting and worriedly asked him: "Why are you arriving at this time?"

"Oh, don't worry. I just stayed in the office getting work done." He replied to his wife.

"Please don't do that! You work a lot throughout the day; don't stay at night too, think about your health." Sarah said to her husband worriedly.

He looked at her in silence and thought, "Now what do I do?" He did not want to cheat on his wife but he was ashamed to tell her the truth. Then he said to her: "I'll try to get there earlier but I'll have to stay the occasional night."

The next day he had a strenuous day's work and ran to his refuge, his cellar, and there he completely unloaded for a long time. Going to his place became his new routine and within two weeks the basement now looked like a stage. He had installed microphones, a sound system, and lots of lights.

His family had already noticed his frequent absences and Sarah confronted him one night saying: "What are you hiding from me?" I have called you on your mobile and the office's phone and I have not been able to reach you. "

"Nothing! I already told you that I have a lot of work! I don't answer at the office and I turn off my mobile so they don't bother me." And he went to sleep.

The next day Sarah was willing to find out the truth. She waited for him when he left the office and followed him in the car. Roger drove to the warehouse without noticing that he was being followed and when he opened the door Sarah sneaked in and observed everything without understanding anything. Roger was surprised and ashamed! With a broken voice, he explained everything to her and she told him: "You didn't have to hide it from me, love. I support you unconditionally; dreams are not a cause for shame among the family."

He told her that he had been invited to enter a talent show organized by the store where he had bought his drums, but he already felt very old and was afraid of making a fool of himself. Sarah encouraged him to sign up on the condition that he go home and tell his children, who were worried about him too.

Very happy, Roger signed up for the contest and dedicated himself to practicing several hours a day when leaving his office. He did it with great enthusiasm and in a couple of weeks, the day of the big event arrived. Roger enthusiastically played his drums. He played with the support of his wife and children and deeply realized he won first place.

Holidays in Lake Auyahú

William was a very successful contractor. He was the owner of a company dedicated to the remodeling and construction of houses; he was a very dedicated and passionate professional about his work to which he devoted much of his time. But despite working hard, he was always aware of all the affairs of his home and the boys' school; in short, he was a loving father and exemplary husband who sought the best for his children and his loving wife, Claire.

William had two sons: 15-year-old Zack and 13-year-old Tim; both boys were affectionate, cheerful, and good students. He was proud of his children and showed his affection for them by showering them with comforts and many attentions.

William worked very hard but knew how to make good use of his free time, he organized constant walks and trips with his family. Sometimes they traveled to very distant places but they always did so surrounded by luxuries and all the comforts that money could guarantee.

In one of his trips to a beautiful beach, he observed a lovely sunset with Claire and remembered the beautiful sunsets of Lake Auyahú, where, as a child, he spent many of his vacations with his parents. Every summer he helped his father clean, repair, and paint the little house on the lake and he loved that, but after many years doing the same, the holidays were tedious to the point of never wanting to return to the lake and he vowed to vacation to everyone when he had his family.

Deep in thought, he heard Claire's voice, "Dear, why are you so quiet and thoughtful? Is everything okay?"

William answered quite absent-mindedly, "Ah! Everything is fine! I'm just remembering the endless vacations with my parents in that old house on Lake Auyahú."

"Was that the lake house your late father talked about so much? You never wanted to take us to!" Claire said to him.

He replied to her, "Exactly that house! Is that we went so many times during my childhood that I got bored of always doing the same thing; it was always painting, repairing, and cleaning the house and we hardly had time to swim and play in the lake. There my father taught me everything he knew about repairing houses."

"Sounds wonderful!" Exclaimed Claire and then added: "That's where your career in construction began."

William jumped in his chair; it was true! Those tedious vacations had been the beginning of his passion for construction. Thanks to his father and that old house he learned to enjoy family vacations and discovered his true vocation.

As night fell they returned to the hotel, and during dinner William watched his children, realizing that they too needed to learn that the best things in life come with discipline, dedication, and love. At that precise moment, he understood what he had to do and happily told them: "Kids! I am already planning our next vacation. I will take you to a very beautiful place that you have never been to!"

"Where are we going, Dad?" Asked Tim.

"To a beautiful lake with crystalline waters and white sand, where I used to go with my parents when I was a kid." Answered William.

His children were very happy because their father always took them to the best places. Meanwhile, Claire listened quite confused to her husband without saying a word.

At the end of dinner, they went to their rooms, and privately Claire told her husband, "I don't understand you! Just a while ago you said that those vacations were the worst for you, and now you want us to go! Please explain to me."

William replied with a big smile. "You were right in what you told me on the beach: that's where it all started! Thanks to my father, those vacations, and that house, I am who I am. I want my children to also understand the value of work and to learn that the fruits that are harvested with dedication are the best."

And so he continued telling Claire about his plans and she excitedly offered her full support.

The months quickly passed and summer arrived. It was time to go on vacation and the boys were very excited. They had not the remotest idea of what awaited them and William looked at them mischievously because he had everything planned. Finally, the long-awaited day arrived and very early in the morning everyone boarded the large truck and began the long journey that took them almost two days.

When they got to the lake, Zack and Tim were amazed. It was very beautiful and they practiced all kinds of water sports; there were also nice houses that caught their attention but when they got to the front of a dilapidated house William said: "Done! We have arrived." And his children gaped at the place. It was the ugliest house on the whole lake!

Zack said in amazement: "But dad this is embarrassing! How are we going to stay here? This place is infested with mice. I want to go back to our house!

William told him: "Son, this is a wonderful lake and this is our house! It just needs dedication, love, and that we work together as a family and you will see that in a short time it will look very different. Summer is just beginning and we will have time to enjoy when we are done."

178

Tim, still not out of his amazement, told him, "I support you, dad," and Claire added, "Me too my love". William stared at Zack and he said: "Well, I'll also help you repair your awful house."

"Thanks, champion! I have sent to bring everything necessary and a couple of my best workers to give us a hand." William said.

William was very happy to assign each one of them their tasks and they all started the titanic work together. After a few days of intense effort, William was moved to see the performance of his sons and after three weeks the house was ready. It looked really lovely; they all hugged and stared at it and Zack said to his father: "You were right, dad, it just needed our love and dedication; it is the most beautiful house on the lake."

Back to the Region

It was a cold winter morning. The station said it would be a cool day, without excesses, with a temperature of no less than 15 degrees, but they were not at all right with their invented forecast. When they started their trip, Austin and his friends, who intended to see their families in the old county where they grew up, were wearing perhaps more than ten clothes, not counting the respective raincoats in case it snowed or rained. It was barely 9:30 a.m. and it did not seem that the day could get better, to tell the truth. The idea of suspending the trip had already sounded to go at Easter or perhaps during the following summer. However, they could not turn back; their families were already waiting for them, they had everything ready and well packed; and despite the inconveniences presented by the season, the trip undoubtedly had to go on.

Austin traveled with his best friends from childhood, who growing up all made the same decision to go together to the state capital, because in their town they felt stagnant, even depressed. In their way of seeing things, that place lacked opportunities; spending more time in that place was a synonym of slow death due to absence of activity. Their relatives continued there and although they had already become city people for some time, fate forced them to go to the place where it all began.

Once started, the temperature began to decline once more, reaching limits where not even the most experts in that environment could be comfortable. "What liars those of the station, with this climate we could freeze a ball of fire," Jack said. The view of the pavement slowly began to undergo a kind of metamorphosis to become a real ice rink. "Soon we will see the athletes skating, others playing curling, suddenly others practicing hockey and if we are lucky we will be able to see Santa's sleigh practicing his landings; you know, which is in case they see a small red nose-shaped light," added Charlie.

The trip was getting long and it didn't look like they were going to get to a good point, because everything they saw was white. The snow as they advanced was getting thicker and although they wanted to stop, to rest or eat something, it was a risky task, Austin was driving and he didn't want to arrive at his father's house with the car he was given as a present last Christmas in pieces. "Drive carefully, not that way, remember it's not a toy, you are responsible not only for you but also for everyone who goes with you," was all that was going through Austin's head at the time. "I'm bored, we should listen to music, relax a little don't you think?" Asked Lucy. They all agreed and slowly the melodies made an appearance; soft and delicate notes pleased the guys' ears, making everything stop mattering for that instant. They sang at pleasure and each song served as a perfect stimulant to tune more with themselves, forgetting their problems, thinking about the fantastic and the implausible. In a sense, they didn't need a bed to feel pleasure; they climaxed only using their ears.

Meanwhile, the road remained the same, white as the pearls hidden at the bottom of the sea. The hours kept running, the music kept playing. They really did not know very clearly what happened at that moment. They lost all sense of direction because from one moment to another they were completely lost at the mercy of the hostility of their environment and the cold of the night. "How did this happen to us?" Jack said in a very morose tone. "It was all your fault, Austin," Lucy said. "Mine? I was distracted by the music you played. Everyone had to be attentive, for the way the day was, it was possible to get lost," Austin replied. "You insisted on continuing the trip, now look how well it turned out," Lucy stated. "You must keep quiet both of you. This is tragic, but it is not the end of the world and if it is to blame someone, we must all take responsibility, Lucy, stop reproaching Austin and you, my friend do the same with her. Remember, more than friends, we are family and if we got here as one, we must leave the same way. So, I ask you please to be quiet." Jack said to their friends.

Now with the tension decelerated and with a clearer mind, Austin told her, "Hey Lucy, I'm sorry, I shouldn't have spoken to you that way. Jack is right, I will never speak to you that way again." In the same way, she replied, "I was also a fool. You don't have to apologize, now we must concentrate on finding a way to get out of here alive."

With the situation resolved, the 3 best friends got down to work. They all had little battery and a lousy internet signal on their cell phones. It was too cold to go out even though they were well wrapped up, they still did not want to take that kind of risk. They spent the night in the car, hoping that in the morning they could be better located with the help of sunlight. They slept like sardines in a can but beating the low temperatures. When they woke up, they got back to their feet as best they could, rattling as many bones and joints as possible. If anyone could hear them, the sounds were indescribable but very funny.

Out of nowhere, hidden under the driver's seat, the guys found an old map that had their destination marked. They were able to locate themselves thanks to the snow that spread. They saw that they were more or less close, just about 90 kilometers from their destination. They had to accelerate, go in a hurry because they had to arrive in time to start the preparations for the Christmas party. When they started, they all worked like a machine: Lucy looking at the map to see the accesses, Jake showing Austin where to go, and the latter doing his job like a professional, and in less time than expected, they arrived at their destination, finally meeting with the rest of their families.

The Day I Met You

It was during the magical night of that summer where for the first time Joel felt what poets feel when they are in love. It was simple, like the sting of a bee, but in a certain sense, it enlightened his mind, invading every part of his body until he found the rest he needed in his heart. Marcus, his best friend, was present that day and asked him about what was happening to him, "What is it that you have? Or did you see a dead person?" The question was intended to make him laugh a little because Joel had already a long time looking into the void in complete silence. His answer, far from being fatalistic, brought a passive smile to Marcus who felt relieved after hearing his friend's voice again. It was after rejoining his gaze that he said, "Hey Marcus, did you ever feel in love?" Marcus puzzled by the question, said, "I guess so Joel, I don't understand why you ask that."

Again distracted, this time with his gaze fixed on the wheel of fortune Joel replied, "I just feel that way right now or at least I think I do, I've never had a girlfriend. I think my last date was two years ago, but this time it's something different or at least that's what my chest says." Puzzled by that statement, his friend inferred, "In love? What do you say, Joel? Hahaha!!! Who is the girl, what's her name?" After the laughter, the playfulness, and the reciprocated questions, Joel looked at him again and replied, "I have no idea who she is. I don't know the first letter of her name, but I guarantee she will be the love of my life." More laughter accompanied that summer night, the wind blowing the peaks of that valley gave its own soundtrack to the moment, which gradually became perfect for the intentions of our Joel.

The hours passed slowly and both friends to the beat dictated by the moon, the wind, and the stars, began to look for her, after losing track of her after dinner. "The hot dogs were good, although next time I will avoid putting so much mustard on it," Marcus added. A little disoriented, Joel, who slowly felt his quest was becoming more and more difficult, responded, "They were incredible, but we were able to eat later. Now I can no longer find her and perhaps I have already lost her forever." Marcus responded with a half-laugh, "Haha, to begin with, it was you who wanted to eat, I was planning to go home, I'll work tomorrow, but I accepted this because it's fun and because I love you."

Joel responded like this, "Is this funny to you?" Without thinking, Marcus said, "Of course, don't berate yourself. The night has been fun, that we haven't found your girl is your stomach's fault, not mine. We must have faith that something good will come out of all this, and if this is not the case, then you will have a nice anecdote to tell your grandchildren. Of course, as long as you have them."

The night began to sing. The melody was played by the wind, the owls, and the circus music that sounded on each side of that fair. The stars shone like the morning sun, signaling that perhaps the best was yet to come, giving the warning they needed to end the intrepid search. That place was gigantic. Two roller coasters welcomed you, among more colossal attractions that were left and right. It was easy to get lost just because of how large the enclosure turned out to be and that without counting that on that Saturday, the place was full of people.

Within seconds of passing through the horror house for the fifth time in a row and after eating their tenth cotton candy, a bright light showed them the way. Maybe it was the moon, a badly positioned reflector, or was just maybe it could have been some divine act that showed him where they should go. Joel, with an air of hope and the impetus of a champion said, "There it is! It's her, she's eating cotton candy too." Marcus replied, "Joel, look around buddy, everyone is eating cotton candy. Are you sure it's your girl?"

Calm, and determined he responded: "It has to be; by God, it must be her. My eyes cannot be deceiving me; at least I hope so. Otherwise, please put me in a mental hospital." Marcus hilariously answered, "Definitely you are crazy, hahaha! but I swear that if the girl calls the police when you approach, I will tell them this and see if they will take pity on you." Joel answered with irony: "Friend, if she calls the police we will go to jail both. In any case, you are like my accomplice, don't you think?" Marcus stopped laughing and responded, "We are fried. Don't waste your time anymore and go before she leaves."

With no time to lose, at full speed both friends ran in search of what they had been looking for. Joel would get to talk to that mysterious girl and Marcus, a smile on the face of his dear friend. The night continued to collaborate; as if by magic, they could make their way through the huge crowd present in the park. Before reaching the vicinity of one of the roller coasters, Joel stopped to buy a rose. According to him, it was to appear less threatening and more empathetic. Marcus stayed away so that his friend could get into action when he reached the girl. The nerves were dispersed everywhere in his body. He could talk to her, but at the moment of finishing the first sentence, all that environment crumbled like a stack of cards. Everything colorful became black and white, until everything disappeared leaving nothing but silence.

A charming voice whispered to Joel in his ears, "Wake up dear, even if it's Sunday you shouldn't sleep so much." It was the girl in the park who spoke, "What were you dreaming about, sleepyhead?" And Joel, seeing her in love, replied, "With the day I met you."

190

A Journey through the Mind

The drops fell slowly and very closely. He could not touch them, because Rick wanted to avoid a cold, but the smell of freshwater with divine spring brought back memories of the most fantastic moments of his life. During that spring, little rain had been forecast. In fact, it had been a warmer season than usual, sometimes giving the notion that it was already summer. Rick had been at his sister's house for a few years, after ending a marriage that did not go well. She lived alone so she did not mind sharing the roof with her brother. They had not lived together for more than six years. However, being together again was the same as when they were children.

In silence, she approached him and said, "Brother, it's time to eat. Are you coming or not?" Rick responded, "Sure, even if your food is terrible." Raquel replied, "I've been calling you for hours, and you looked like a fool watching the drops fall. It made me remember how when we were kids and I caught you in the bathroom with dad's magazines." Rick immediately said, "I don't know what you're talking about, I never dug into dad's stuff." "Don't play dumb, I'll never forget your face when you saw me. They could even use it for a horror movie," said Raquel.

The rain did not stop and consolidated in time, making them lose the notion of the hours and space. While they ate, Rick continued with his gaze fixed on the window that was in front of the kitchen. The sound of the water hitting the ceiling, the grass, and the walls became something hypnotic, causing Rick to gradually lose himself in that one-rhythm orchestra. Dinner, his sister, and all his surroundings slowly seemed to be more distant. Meanwhile he, or perhaps his mind was swimming in the rain that Sunday afternoon.

The mind tends to be a mysterious place, and as deep as the ocean itself, full of unpublished rooms, where memories of past lives hide, of what we were and what we could be, but, giving some clues of what we can become. Rick awoke in a site, a place that he knew with homey smells, freshly toasted bread, recently squeezed oranges, honey, and butter, all nicely accompanied by laughter he hadn't heard in years. The grass was green, and the sun was shining uniquely. It was then when he saw the place where he was and could not believe it until his heart gave him the confirmation that he was not hallucinating.

It was the country house, where he grew up with Raquel and his parents. The same place where he learned to put his boots on, where he rode for the first time on horseback, where for the first time he kissed, and where they also broke his heart. The place was intact, clean, magnificent, the grass freshly cut and most importantly, there were people, it was inhabited.

In the distance he heard voices, discussing whether to use ham or pastrami, whether to bring cola or orange juice. They could not see him, and confused, he tried to find the purpose of why the rain had brought him there. Everything was still confusing and although he clearly remembered that day, there were some forgotten details. Fear seized him. He was afraid to continue. He didn't want to cry, getting tears out was a waste of time. He looked for exits, hit himself, pinched himself, even washed his face with the water from a pond, but nothing worked. Rick was slow to realize that if he really wanted to return, the only thing he had in his power was to continue the journey of that family.

Since the divorce everything had become a little gray. Rick had lost his hopes, his motivations, even though he was still a young man, with a whole career and life ahead of him. That event had marked him; he was nowhere to be found. He went through hundreds of changes; he did everything to try to recover what he had lost. However, he did not realize that the more he tried, the more he got lost inside himself. It was then when the idea of going with Raquel seemed good, after a walk in the rain. Being close to a loved one made him regain a lot of confidence, but Rick had to learn an important lesson from someone he could only find in his memories.

The family was going to an old castle that was in the surrounding areas of their house in the countryside. It was an old medieval fortress, which, despite the corrosion provided by time, maintained a comfortable aesthetic. The plan was to spend the day there, have a picnic, get to know the place and learn about its history, and the truth is that it was fully accomplished.

Already with a sunset in progress that gave with its light a different contrast to the valley, filling it with satin colors, that dizzy to the eye just by looking at them. Suddenly a boy ran and fell into a well. His sister was the first to notice and looked for the father with fear for the life of her brother, Rick never left the boy behind, he saw in his eyes, the fear, the hopelessness that he felt in recent times, the feeling that all was lost. Both cried and then, his redemption presented itself. The father, with a rope, went down as he could to the well and with a smile took his son, looked at him and said, "How great you are. You are a champ; these things happen to you and will continue to happen to you. Falling is very important, in this or whatever during life, because it is the only way to learn to get up. Come back home son, let's go back."

Suddenly, his sister's voice sounded and everything cleared up again, "Brother, it's time to eat. Are you coming or not?" Rick responded instantly, "Sure, I wouldn't miss it for the world." At that moment they both felt that something had changed and that everything was going to be better.

The Art of Being Persistent

Billy was a kind boy, a lover of adventure, photography, and world travel, however, he was the kind of person who started with a dream but never persisted to make it come true.

One day, while having lunch with his family, Billy's mother asked her oldest son, "Honey, how's work going?"

His brother answered his mother, "Great, mother, many patients in the office."

"I am proud of you, love, I love being the mother of the best doctor in town. You see it, Billy, you should be more like your brother." His mother told him.

The boy, hearing his mother's comparative comments, tried to ignore them until his father asked him, "How do you plan to make a living Billy? Look at your brother, in two weeks you will reach the age of majority and it is time to look for a place to live, and we will not be able to continue carrying you."

From a hit, Billy took his things and got up from the table, without speaking to his family. As he walked quickly down the hall, his brother took his arm, "Hey! Don't pay attention to our parents. If you want you can go live with me, my apartment is always alone and..."

"Not! I'm sick of being compared to you. I may not be as successful as you, but I do follow my heart. Not like all of you, who pretend to be happy and are not." Billy replied angrily.

His brother tried to speak, but Billy quickly made his way to his room, slamming the door shut. Leaning his back from the door he released all the air that was compressed in him. Full of rage he took all his things and put them in a suitcase. After several hours, he quietly left the house, loaded his things into the vehicle, and quickly left the property.

After touring the streets of the city, Billy decided to go to his favorite coffee shop. He took a seat in his usual place and suddenly a girl sat at the table, "Can't you see it's occupied?" Billy told her, to which she replied to him: "Yes, but that doesn't mean you can't share the place with me."

The boy stared at her and tried to ignore her, but the girl asked, "What's got you in a bad mood? Can I help you with something?"

"Only if you have the power to become me in my brother, then yes." The boy answered her.

The girl widened her eyes and rubbed her chin as if she were coming up with a plan, "Sorry, I didn't mean that."

The girl said, "Come on, tell me what happened to you. Sharing sorrows relieves sadness."

Billy sighed, called the waitress, ordered two large chocolates, and began to tell the girl everything that had happened to him. The girl looked at him attentively to each word, smiled every time he told her that he had had a dream, but saddened when it ended without results.

"My parents have always wanted me to be like my brother, but that's not who I am. Yes, I want to be successful, but in something that I really like, not in what they want."

The girl looked at him thoughtfully and said, "You're looking for a house, right? Today is your lucky day. I offer you a house and a job, but you must be responsible, okay?"

The boy, surprised by the words of his new friend, smiled and accepted. Together they went to a cozy little apartment in the center of the city.

"The job consists of selling pastry items to cake chefs. It's easy, you just have to sell. You start tomorrow, so go to sleep. We'll get up very early," said the girl.

Billy paid attention. Entering his new room, he laid back on his bed and in seconds he was awakened by a loud noise. He jumped up, grabbed his phone, and noticed that it was five in the morning. "A while longer please."

His new friend replied. "No, Billy! It's time to work."

Without spirits and with his eyes still closed, he headed to the bathroom to take a shower. After an hour, they were both ready to go out on a tour of the big city. Billy had never thought of becoming a salesman; yet he knew that if he didn't succeed, he would have to live on the streets.

The first place where they stopped was a luxurious bakery that had all kinds of sweets everywhere, chocolate fountains, candies, and cakes of all colors. The girl greeted them and suddenly a beautiful woman started to serve them. "Good morning, what the...Billy? Billy Elliot? How have you been? I'm the girl with braces from high school."

Billy in seconds remembered the woman in front of him, greeting her with a warm hug and explaining why he had come to that place. Billy's companion explained to her about their products and the woman, happy to receive them, agreed to buy them all the material that the place would need.

The second stop was a bakery that sold gluten-free sweets. The salesgirl had always wanted to be able to sell products to that place, but the manager never agreed to serve her. However, that day was different. Upon entering, the first thing that was heard was, "Elliot! What are you doing on this side of the world?"

The manager came over to say hello, offering his hand to both of them. Billy recognized him immediately, as he was one of his adventure friends in high school, both of whom had traveled most of the world on vacation.

Billy said, "Now I am a seller of pastry items. My partner and I have come to offer you the best products for your sweets"

His friend smiled, refusing and explaining what kind of product he was selling.

Billy replied, "No problem, we also sell gluten-free items. Come on, give me one last chance to be successful and you won't regret it."

The manager thought for a few seconds and then with a smile agreed. The girl who accompanied him was happy. Day after day, they both woke up eager to meet their goals and get the best customers in the market. From that moment, Billy understood the importance of being persistent with his dreams.

The Dragon and the Hunter

Marcus was a veteran hunter, full of energy and fascinated by nature. He lived in a small house on the highest mountain in the forest, surrounded by pine trees and beautiful flowers. One day, while he was in the kitchen having a cup of coffee, the sound of the door called his attention. He slowly placed his cup on the table, got up from his seat, took his ax and asked very close to the door, "Who is it?"

The person on the other side did not answer. However, he knocked harder on the door again. Angry at not getting an answer, he opened the door with a bang. A man dressed in black stood with his fist raised, about to knock again.

"What do you want?" Marcus asked at the man that was about to knock on the door again.

The man introduced himself. "My name is Ares, I come to request your services."

Marcus was silent for a few seconds until he replied, "I don't do that kind of work anymore. I just take care of my forest now."

At that moment a heavy bag crashed against the porch. The hunter turned to see what it was and some shiny coins appeared. "You must go to the dark mountains in search of the creature that lives there and the rest of the payment will be yours. I know you need it." Ares said.

The stranger turned around, got on his horse, and rode away. Marcus had not received that kind of work for months, but the little money he had accumulated over the last few years had been spent on alcohol and gambling in nearby towns. He took the bag and went into the house.

As the hunter prepared himself, his horse whinnied loudly before, "Easy buddy, I've got a bad feeling too."

He hugged the horse until he calmed it down, picked up his pack, and together they started the journey. The first stop was in a small village near the waterfalls. A beautiful but disheveled young woman appeared in the middle of the road, approached the horse and began to caress it, "Be careful, my horse doesn't like everybody." Marcus warned the young woman.

But in that instant, the horse watched as if before it stood a beautiful apple, "I think we're even friends." The girl told him.

Marcus paid no attention to the situation. The next day, again the girl appeared, "Didn't you hear me when I said not to touch my horse?"

The young woman asked, "Can I join your trip?" To which he answered, "No."

She insisted, "I promise I won't bother, just let me accompany you."

Marcus replied, "You don't even know where I'm going."

The girl said, "I bet it's much better than here."

The hunter determinedly studied all around him. He nodded and the girl with a smile on her face started walking.

The young woman asked, "Where are we headed?" To which he replied, "To the dark mountains."

The girl did not gesture a single word. When the three of them were close, the girl asked, "What are we here for? Don't you think it's too dangerous a place for a lumberjack like you?"

Marcus answered, "I am a hunter. If you are too afraid you can go. You are free."

At that moment, the whole place became dark. Several shadows passed through the trees and the girl began to tremble. Marcus took a box of matches and together with a stone he managed to light the lamp he kept among his things. "Don't move away from us, if you want to get out of here." He said at her.

The girl nodded. After a long walk, the three of them came upon a cold cave. The hunter told her to wait at her post, while he entered the place. He firmly took his lantern and as he entered, beautiful colored lights began to illuminate everything. To his surprise, at the bottom of the cave, a small dragon was resting. Its scales were purple and its chest had the perfect combination of dark colors. Slowly he approached it and placed a shackle on one of its limbs, took several steps away, and then pulled on it. The dragon hit so hard as it fell out of place that it was knocked unconscious, making Marcus' job easier.

As he came out of the cave with his creature in tow, he attracted the attention of the girl, who petrified the hunter with a scream.

The young woman said, "Let it go, it's not to blame. If you're looking for someone it's me. Just let it go."

However, Marcus didn't understand anything, until Ares appeared behind the trees. Taking the girl by surprise. He said, "All right hunter, take it. Now leave the girl and the dragon with me."

Marcus was confused, "What's going on?"

At that moment something hit the hunter's head very hard, causing him to lose consciousness for a few minutes. When he woke up, he and his horse were tied to one of the trees. He carefully pulled himself together, put his boot to the tree and pulled out a knife that allowed him to free himself. Quickly he got on his horse and began the journey in search of the girl. A few meters away, the screams caught his attention. He hid behind the bushes and listened while Ares tried to convince the girl to give him her powers. Marcus waited until everyone was resting to approach and free them.

The girl said to him, "Please release my friend. Don't let them hurt it."

The hunter, after releasing her tried to run towards the dragon, when an arrow hit his chest. The girl tried to get closer and he indicated her to go after her friend. The girl ran to her dragon and began to recite some words in an ancient language, causing the dragon's scales to light up and suddenly a strong light flooded the whole place, undoing all the souls with evil intentions. Marcus opened his eyes slowly and when he met the girl, he noticed that they were in another place. Now they were at home.

Marcus asked her, "Who are you?" To which she replied, "I am the queen of the forest. Thank you for saving us. For that reason I will give you a gift."

The girl smiled waving her hand. Suddenly, behind her a huge bag of money appeared. Again she thanked and quickly her friend emerged to take her with him. From that moment on, Marcus dedicated himself to saving magical creatures in the forest.

The Power of the Mind

Noah was a hard-working man, full of dreams and eager to fulfill them. He worked for an insurance company, had an important job, earned enough to live well, had a wonderful wife and a pet that adored him.

One day, while having lunch in the company coffee shop, he received an unexpected message, "Hi, Noah. Please stop by the office I need to talk to you."

He finished his lunch, grabbed his things, and headed for his boss's office. His boss said, "Welcome Noah, nice to have you here. I'd really like to call you for other reasons, but I have to tell you that we are downsizing. You worked here until today."

Noah replied, "But why? All those years of hard work didn't pay off?"

The boss said, "We're very sorry. You know how these company things are."

Slowly he got up from his seat, took his things and left the company. When he arrived home, the atmosphere was strange. Everything was dark and the only sound that could be heard was the barking of the dog who was happy to see his owner. Noah, turning on the light in the kitchen, saw a note on the counter, next to a heart-shaped candy, "Dear Noah, I am so sorry. I can't take it anymore. You always come home late and never have time for me. Please don't look for me, it's better to go our separate ways."

With tears in his eyes, the man opened the fridge and took a bottle of beer, the kind he only drank on special occasions. The dog, seeing him so sad, climbed onto the furniture and laid down on it. The next day, when Noah woke up, he realized that he had not slept in his bed. He got up from the couch and went to the kitchen to get something to eat.

Noah said, "What are we going to do now dog? You're the only thing I have left in my life."

The dog barked as if to encourage the man and together they ate reheated burgers for breakfast. When they finished, the loud ringing of the phone flooded the house and Noah rushed out to answer it, "Hello?"

A manly voice answered, "What are you doing at this hour in your house man?"

Noah replied, "Hi Flavio, I've been fired and my wife has left me. I don't think it's a good time for any of your invitations to those weird events."

Flavio responded, "What! What happened? I'll be right to your home."

But before the man could refuse his friend had hung up the phone. After several hours, the door rang. Noah got up from the couch where he had spent most of the time since he had arrived home and opened the door half-heartedly. His best friend Flavio burst in, demanding an explanation for everything he had told him on the phone. Noah slowly opened the refrigerator door again, taking the last of his beer.

Noah said, "Great, we're out of beers. But, just as you heard it, my friend, the only thing I have is my dog."

Flavio replied, "No way! You have me, I am your best friend and I will never leave you. Why don't you come with me to one of my events? You no longer have the excuse of working all day. You must distract yourself."

Noah sighed deeply and finally agreed. Flavio said goodbye and promised to pick up his friend at five in the afternoon. The hours passed quickly and two minutes before the appointed time Flavio's horn sounded outside the house. Noah came out wearing sweatpants and a worn sweatshirt and Flavio saw him and sent him back to the dressing room.

His friend told him, "I know you're going through a tough time, but you have to buck up. Look at this as an opportunity; you never know when things can change."

Noah said to his friend, "No, everything has collapsed. I have no more life, Flavio."

Flavio replied, "Come on! Fix yourself up. My best friend isn't that depressive."

Noah said, "I'm not even a quarter of what I was a week ago."

Flavio took a big breath of air and began to remind him of all the good things Noah was before his wife and his old job. Somewhat more encouraged, the man decided to change his attire to something more formal and they both left for the big event.

The event was about personal growth. Many people around the city gathered once a week to tell their stories and how after many tragedies, they decided to grow as people and everything else in their lives made sense.

"You know I hate coming to this kind of place. I'm suffering from being a failure." Noah complained.

"Calm down, follow me." Flavio said to his friend.

They both entered a huge room; at the back was a podium and a man began to speak. The man was talking about meditation and how important it is for the human being. He was explaining all the benefits of growing as a person and the successes that it brought.

Noah, at first he was not happy. He looked at everyone with hatred, but as he continued to listen to him, his anger disappeared. He felt motivated and eager to be successful.

When Flavio finished, he left his friend at home, waited for him to enter through the door and went on his way.

Noah entered his home, his cute dog greeted him happily and he thanked him, petted him, and began to walk around the house. The place was a mess, beer bottles everywhere and food wrappers on the floor. With encouragement, he began to pick up all the garbage, cleaned and reorganized the house. He set up a space to meditate and bought a bunch of books that would help him become aware of the universe.

Weeks went by and day after day, Noah got into the habit of meditating, training for an hour a day and attending courses to improve his knowledge. One day, while he was drinking his coffee, the phone rang.

An insurance company wanted to hire him, offered him a good position and an excellent salary. Happily, he accepted and from that moment on, Noah was no longer afraid of losing everything.

Between Love, Chocolate and Madness

Alexa was a renowned pastry chef, she loved sweets, spent most of her time in the kitchen, and had a dream of opening her own chocolate shop. At a very young age, she began her cooking studies all over Europe, until one day while she was walking the streets of Spain, a huge shop caught her attention. The site was decorated with lights and plants, all in a minimalist style. However, what was most abundant were the chocolates in all their presentations. Without thinking about it, Alexa entered the place enchanted, looking at the display cases. An older man, behind the counter, saw her so enchanted and asked her, "Which is your favorite chocolate?"

The girl did not know what words to say to that question, for she had never stopped to look for a favorite kind of chocolate. "It's my first time in a place like this."

The older man said, "Congratulations! Come, I'll give you a tour."

After giving her a tour of the place and lovingly explaining to her all about chocolate, Alexa fell in love, and from there she wanted to become a pastry chef and open her own chocolate shop.

One day, while on her way to her baking classes, she received an email that read, "Chef Lewis will not be able to continue the course with you. Chef Morgan will now be your new teacher."

Alexa took it lightly, so she packed her things and made her way to the classroom. Once most of the students were at their desks, a tall, strikingly handsome man with gray eyes entered. His expression denoted power as if he were a god walking among mortals.

The Chef said, "If you don't want to be a failure, you have to do everything as I say, got it?"

In a soundless chorus, everyone responded, "Yes, Chef!"

The first class was hard, as most of the students were frightened by the Chef's shouting and demands. The week went on the same way, full of shouting, phrases that lowered everyone's spirits, and every day the students were leaving. When Friday arrived, the chef entered the classroom and saw only three people, he applauded, "Now we can begin, tell me your names and why you enrolled in this subject."

The last to speak was Alexa, "I'm Alexa. One day while I was walking..."

The chef interrupted her by saying, "Get to the point Alexa."

To which she replied, "I stumbled upon a chocolate shop and since then my dream has been to open one."

The man, upon hearing the last sentence, took his marker and began to write on the blackboard, telling them all about chocolate. The three students were in their places paying attention to everything their teacher was saying, until one second he stopped and asked them to start preparing a delicious chocolate. The three of them froze.

"Are you guys deaf?" The Chef said. They all jumped up and ran to their work tables, grabbed portions of chocolate, and began to work on their creation. One of the guys was nervous and from fright he let his chocolate burn. The other girl was so focused on not failing that she forgot to prepare the mold where she would pour her result, causing her chocolate to break completely when she unmolded it. However, Alexa looked calmer, she worked patiently and without despair, moving in place as if she were a professional.

At the end of the time established by the Chef, he was in charge of passing by each counter, "This is horrible! Your chocolate is burnt...What happened to this? I told you a bonbon, not a soup...and you Alexa, what kind of mess have you prepared?"

The moment the Chef took the small bonbon to his mouth, his words melted and his hard expression relaxed for a few seconds, almost a smile escaped from his face, but without further ado he just added, "That's terrible! All of you, get out here and you Alexa, I'll see you early here."

Alexa opened her eyes like a plate and only nodded in response. The next day, very early the girl arrived at the agreed place, and without greeting the chef just said, "Follow me."

Before Alexa could respond, the grumpy man was walking toward the parking lot. With a slight gesture he motioned for her to get into the car and she accepted. After a few hours, the car stopped at a mountain and finally the driver spoke.

The Chef asked her, "Do you know what the difference is between a successful person and a normal person?"

To which she replied, "No, Chef"

The Chef said, "The love and madness you devote to your dreams."

They both got out of the vehicle and in front of them was a large sign that read, "Bridge Jumping."

Alexa tried to say something when she read it, and Chef Morgan said, "If you really love chocolate, you'll need a little bit of craziness for all the road ahead. Do you dare to jump in?"

Offering his hand to continue, the girl somewhat trembling accepted. Together they made a long line and when it was almost their turn Alexa said, "I don't think I can do it, I..."

The Chef took her by the hand, some people started to put the harness on her and before the girl ran away, he said, "In cooking, in desserts and love, a little craziness never hurts."

At that moment they both jumped and adrenaline took over their bodies. The next day, upon arriving back to class, the Chef asked the three students to prepare a bar of chocolate, unlike anything he had ever tasted, something full of love and madness, the best would pass the course. Alexa happily started her bonbon, taking different ingredients from the fridges and preparing a bar of chocolate full of love and madness.

At the end of the time, the Chef walked around the tables, and when he reached Alexa's place, he took the bonbon and put it in his mouth. A smile came to his face and he said, "Love, chocolate and madness, my favorite."

The Wonderful Power of Self-control

Once upon a time there was a worm that lived happily in a garden full of vigorous plants with fragrant and beautiful flowers, and an endless number of beetles, butterflies and birds.

Life here seemed wonderful, but the worm often felt some anxiety and fear for the possibility of being pecked by birds, the heavy blow of huge raindrops, the attacks of other insects where he rested, or worse, the fatality of being eaten by some animal such as a frog.

Worried about this uncertain situation, the worm went for a walk outside his garden one day, where he accidentally stumbled upon a river inhabited by an enormous alligator.

"What's the matter with you, why are you wearing such a distressed face?" The alligator asked the little insect.

"It's just that I live worried about what might happen to me as a result of what surrounds me on a daily routine." Replied the worm.

"But don't you know the famous law of mentalism that says that fear attracts that which is most feared?" Asked the alligator.

"No, I've never heard that statement before." The worm replied intrigued.

The alligator said, "For this law affirms that fear is like a powerful magnet that attracts, by the forces of thought and feeling, everything that has a certain affinity with the cause that generated it."

"Well, what should I do then to feel more at ease?" The worm asked curiously.

"Well, for that there is another expression that says 'don't worry, get busy.'" Replied the smiling alligator, and then continued, "If I lived worrying about everything around me, I would be more anxious than you are now."

"Why?" Asked the worm. And the alligator answered, "Let me explain. I live in the waters of this river along with others of my own species that are fierce and sometimes attack me for various reasons. Also, sometimes hunters come to capture us to take our skin and sell it, which causes us a lot of stress."

"That's terrible!" Exclaimed the worm. "And how do they manage all that?" He asked.

"With a positive attitude. You should know that ships don't sink because of the water around them, but because of the water that enters them, something that will only happen if you allow it." The crocodile added.

"But sometimes, bad things still happen to us, even if we do everything to avoid it." Said the worm, still saddened.

"In that case, rest assured that these vicissitudes constitute tests or experiences that we must undergo to become stronger." The alligator wisely said.

And so these two animals continued to talk for a long time, until the worm had to return to his garden because it was getting dark.

As he crept silently along the ground in the darkness, the worm felt a certain fear, but his conversation with the alligator had given him the courage to face any circumstance.

Suddenly, as he passed near a pond, a frog with a very unpleasant appearance and a threatening attitude looked at the insect with interest, who, with a calm but agile attitude, entered the hole of a dry trunk close to him.

The frog tried obstinately to capture the worm, but all his attempts were unsuccessful, because the worm was well sheltered in the bark of this tree.

"Positive mind!" The worm kept repeating to himself as he waited hidden in the log.

When at last the frog gave up his plan and withdrew, the worm went out carefully and continued on his way, now among stems, branches and leaves.

Not much time had elapsed when the worm saw, at some distance, one of those lizards that have bulging eyes and a huge tongue that shoots out like arrows. The lizard was on a branch parallel to the worm's, so he had no choice but to move on.

"Oh, don't let it see me!" The worm said to himself as he walked stealthily trying to go unnoticed.

But the lizard was very clever, so it immediately became aware of the worm's presence and tried to catch it by throwing its sticky tongue at it several times.

Agitated, the worm looked around and saw under him a plant with beautiful pot-shaped flowers. "This is my chance to survive," he thought. But then he reflected, "But what if that pot flower turns out to be an insect trap? I'll be lost! No matter, I'll still take the risk."

Then, without thinking about it, the worm jumped from the branch where it was, towards the flower below and reached it in one go.

Indeed, the flower where the worm fell was a trap, but not one of those so-called carnivorous plants that have specialized glands to digest the bodies of trapped insects, but one of those that have certain adaptations that encourage the insect, in its attempt to get out, to pass through certain places where the sexual organs containing pollen are located.

"I think I can get out through that hole over there." Said the worm to himself, as he walked along the inner surface of the flower pot. And indeed, the little insect managed to get out through the hole in the flower without any difficulty.

While walking again through the branches and leaves of other trees, the worm was thinking, "Certainly day-by-day we are exposed to countless dangerous situations, shocks or calamities, but the important thing is how we face them. How grateful I am for the alligator's words! Thanks to them, I am now able to see things differently, I feel I have been reborn internally and I have greater strength to face external conditions."

At last the worm managed to reach his garden unharmed, but the insect that had just arrived was no longer that fearful and disturbed worm that had left several hours ago, but a confident, daring, determined and happy individual.

And this transformation of the worm did not only occur internally because soon this animal turned into a beautiful and spectacular butterfly.

Jade's Interesting Experience

Jade was a beautiful girl who worked as a physical therapist in a rehabilitation center for the disabled. As the young woman was very efficient in her work and quite affectionate towards the inmates, all the personnel of the institution had a lot of affection and respect for her.

One day, when entering a room to do her daily work, Jade found that the woman she had to attend to was not in her bed. This woman's name was Vivian, and she was unable to walk due to damage to her legs from an accident several years ago, so Jade was surprised when she couldn't find her in her usual place.

"Where is Mrs. Vivian? Did her relatives transfer her to another care center?" Wondered Jade. She then decided to inquire about her at the institute's administration offices.

"Could you please let me know if Ms. Vivian Clayton was transferred to another care center?" The therapist asked when she was in front of the receptionist.

"No, Mrs. Clayton should be in her room as usual." The employee replied.

Jade, puzzled, returned again to Mrs. Vivian's room, and what would not be her surprise when she found her, as usual, sitting on her bed quietly reading her favorite novel.

"Mrs. Vivian, a moment ago I came to this room to attend to you and I didn't find you in your bed. Could you explain to me how this could have happened." Asked the young woman.

The lady smiled mischievously, gently tapped the side of the bed with the palm of her right hand, and then said to the girl, "Come, sit here so I can tell you my secret."

Jade's curiosity was at its peak. She immediately sat down next to Mrs. Clayton and brought her ears as close to the lady as she could.

"You know, thousands of years ago there existed a civilization endowed with great beauty, well-being and wealth where the land was fertile, the climate very pleasant, and the vegetation lush. That's where I was born and that's where I was a few moments ago when you came," said the old lady.

"You are kidding me, Mrs. Vivian?" Asked Jade half disappointed.

"Of course not!" Replied the lady. Then she added, "Do you see this beautiful jewel hanging around my neck?"

"Yes." Replied the young physical therapist.

"Well, sometimes, my gem glows brightly on my chest as if it comes to life, and when it does, it immediately transports me to the world where I once lived and I am known as Artemis." The lady narrated.

Jade could not believe what she had just heard. She tried to say something to the lady, but she interrupted her to say, "I know you're not going to believe me, so I'll prove it to you."

"How?" Asked Jade, incredulous and ready to play along with Vivian.

"The next time my gem glows, I will call you to place it on you to see if you too can see what I have seen. But you must be very alert, because this could happen any day and any time!" Exclaimed Vivian with great seriousness.

The girl did not know what to say. After giving Mrs. Clayton her phone number, so that she could call her at any time, and after giving her massages as usual, Jade left the room more confused than ever.

"Could it be that Mrs. Clayton has lost her mind, poor lady!" She thought as she left the room.

Then it happened that one morning when Jade was about to finish her day's work at the center, she received a call from Mrs. Clayton.

227

"Are you ready to travel, Miss Jade?" Asked Vivian on the other end of the phone line.

"I guess so." The girl replied. And she quickly made her way to the lady's room.

Upon entering the room, Jade immediately noticed the gem on Vivian's chest flashed brightly. Then, the restless lady stripped off her necklace and quickly hung it around Jade's neck.

The skeptical girl felt a halo of light envelop her completely and made her close her eyes. When she opened them, Jade was stunned. She was in the most beautiful city she had ever seen.

All the buildings in this city were covered with gold leaf, which gave it an appearance of great magnificence. In addition, a gigantic rainbow bathed everything with its lovely colored lights. Some rivers of crystalline waters harmoniously crossed this place, and countless springs and fountains abutted with exquisitely decorated architectural works.

As for the inhabitants, they were all good-looking, tall, with shapely bodies, large blue eyes and golden hair. They wore long colorful robes made of fine fabrics, with a sash tied at the waist and ornaments made of emeralds, diamonds and other precious stones, as well as delicate sandals, completed the attire.

In this stunning setting, Jade encountered a very beautiful woman resembling Vivian.

"Welcome, I am Rhea, and who are you?" The woman asked the self-absorbed girl.

"My name is Jade." The young woman replied.

The beautiful Rhea took Jade's hand as if in an attitude of greeting, and instantly, she opened her large eyes and said, "I see you know my mother, Artemis, but in another city and in another time."

"How do you know that?" Asked Jade in amazement.

"I saw it in your mind when I touched your hand; besides, you are wearing her jewel with the family gem." The woman replied kindly.

Jade did not know what to say. She was overwhelmed with awe and fascination. Then, her interlocutor added, "Don't be afraid, I know you care for her and are helping her to regain her ability to walk. If she entrusted you with her charm and you were able to reach our world, it is because you are a worthy person. Therefore, I will give you a gift before you leave."

Then Rhea gave Jade a very beautiful gem similar to Vivian's, while saying, "With it, you will also be able to come and visit us."

And so, Jade returned to Vivian filled with beautiful feelings.

The Sweet Chains of Love

This is the story of a young man named Lewis, a professional and hardworking man, who dreamed of the freedom of being able to travel all over the world whenever he wanted. So, one day when Lewis was fast asleep, a fairy came to him and whispered in his ear, "I will grant you your greatest wish." And then she immediately transformed the young man into a beautifully colored bird.

When Lewis woke up and noticed what he had become, he was afraid at first, but then he said to himself, "Since I am now a bird, I can finally realize my dream of traveling and going everywhere I want to go."

So Lewis took flight and began to look down upon all the wonders of nature, its towering mountains, the lush vegetation of varied hues and colors, the beautiful lakes, rivers and waterfalls, and countless animals of the most varied and amazing species.

He also toured numerous countries, enjoying the sight of impressive statues and architectural monuments such as the Great Pyramid of Giza, the Parthenon in Athens, the Statue of Liberty, the guardians of Easter Island, the Taj Majal in India, the Red Palace in Russia, among many others.

Then, one day when Lewis was tired of traveling and perched on the branch of a tree, he thought, "I have already traveled much of the world and felt free, but why do I feel that something is still missing?"

When Lewis observed a mother bird on the branch of an adjoining tree cooing tenderly to her chicks, he said to himself seriously, "I have no children and no one to care for or coo to." But his musing did not last long, for soon Lewis spotted a flock of wild ducks quacking merrily past and decided to follow them.

These ducks, after much flying, stopped at a pond to rest and swim, while Lewis watched them from his perch on the top edge of a farm gate. Suddenly, huge hands encircled the little bird's body, seized it and transferred it to the inside of a cage.

"So end my rides around the world!" Thought Lewis.

Thereupon, the captor took the cage, placed a huge pink ribbon on its top and took it to the room of a beautiful young woman, to whom he said, "Bianca, look what I have brought you as a birthday present."

The young girl opened her huge green eyes and upon seeing the beautiful multicolored bird inside the cage, exclaimed, "Oh, it's beautiful daddy, thank you so much!"

From that day on, Bianca never left her new companion's side. Every day, before feeding him birdseed or other appetizing seed, she would say, "Good morning, dear friend, how did you wake up today?"

As the months passed, when Bianca noticed that her bird was tame, she took him out of his cage and placed him on her shoulder, where the animal remained silent and calm for a long time.

One day when Bianca was very distressed trying to solve a math homework assignment she had been given at the university, Lewis, from the girl's shoulder, noticed that he was able to do it. Then, at a moment when Bianca fell asleep, the bird took a bottle of ink that was on the girl's desk, inserted one of his paws, and with his fingers soaked in ink, began to solve, on a sheet of paper, the difficult numerical task.

After a while, when Bianca awoke and observed the ink strokes in her notebook, along with Lewis's colored paws, she exclaimed in alarm, "Oh, Lewis, what have you done?" However, upon taking a closer look and noticing how her math homework seemed to have been solved, Bianca dumbfoundedly cried out, "Daddy, come look at this!"

Bianca's father, having seen the sheets of paper with a large amount of numbers scribbled on it and Lewis' paws smudged, asked the girl, "Did he do this?"

The young girl replied, "It looks like he did, Dad."

Her dad said, "So if what is embodied there is correct, this bird is very intelligent."

The girl then decided to transcribe the information scribbled by Lewis on the sheet of paper and take it to her math teacher the next day. The teacher, upon reviewing it, said with satisfaction, "Excellent, Bianca, you correctly solved every problem I assigned you."

Bianca couldn't believe what she had just heard, she ran quickly home and when she stood in front of Lewis, placing a blank sheet of paper and some ink in front of him, she asked, "Who are you?"

The bird flew to the ink, dipped his right paw in it, and wrote on the paper, "I'm Lewis, I was captured on your birthday."

"Oh, I'm so sorry, my friend." Bianca announced. Then, taking the bird in her hands and before throwing him out of the window, she said sadly, "Please forgive us for having kept you, prisoner, for so long, you can now go peacefully to enjoy your flight, as it should be."

Lewis didn't know what to think, he was very puzzled. He flew to a nearby tree and from there, with some sadness, flew away from the girl.

A year passed. Lewis, after traveling intensely, decided to return to Bianca's house. When he landed at her bedroom window, Bianca looked at him with her beautiful green eyes

234

and exclaimed, "Lewis, you're back at last." Then, rushing hurriedly to the window, the young woman took the bird in her hands and gave it a gentle kiss on his head.

Immediately, the bird transformed into the handsome young boy he once was, and looking at Bianca he said sweetly, "I came back because I love you."

From then on, Lewis and Bianca have never separated again. Lewis's longing for freedom had been transformed into sweet chains of love.

A Special House by the Sea

When old Bob Morse moved into his old house by the sea, he never imagined the interesting events that awaited him there.

Bob had inherited the house from his mother and only considered moving in when he got his pension.

So, once settled in their new home, the Morse couple gradually began to get used to it.

Almost every morning, Bob and his wife got up early to go and buy the latest of their catch from the nearby fishermen. This included not only a wide variety of fish, but also some mollusks such as squid, shrimp and octopus with which Mrs. Morse prepared some exquisite menus.

In the afternoons, Bob would lie down to rest in a hammock hung in the wide corridor of his house, where he would sometimes fall asleep peacefully listening to the sound of the waves.

It was also common for the old man to bathe at sunset in the crystalline waters of the sea with his wife, while they both enjoyed an exquisite fruit cocktail prepared by this excellent cook. Indeed, Barbara's cocktails were a delight to the palate. She made them by mixing some common or exotic fruits with certain liquors, and then served them in glasses made from the shells of pineapples, watermelons and tender coconuts.

"Cheers, my beloved." Bob would say to Barbara as he clinked his drink with hers.

At night, when the temperature of the sea became warmer, old Bob and his wife would stroll hand in hand with their feet touching the warm waters that swayed gently back and forth to the shore.

Thus passed the days of the Morse family in this earthly aquatic paradise, when suddenly one night a violent storm broke out. It seemed as if the sea had suddenly become enraged, the great waves rose and fell heavily, crashing against the rocks and buildings on the shore.

Bob and his neighbors spent the whole night in anguish because of this gale. None of them could sleep a wink that night, but the next morning, everything dawned as if nothing had happened, the sea looked incredibly serene and flat and the wind was barely audible.

Only one event seemed to the people of this place very unusual. Since that day, very strange fish began to appear on the shore and in shallow waters.

That same afternoon, taking advantage of the stillness of the ocean, Bob started the engines of his boat and went out to fish in moderately deep water. Quickly and nimbly the man set his hook and sat patiently waiting for a fish to bite.

Not much time had elapsed when suddenly Bob noticed a very strange being slowly emerging from the waters. It was a half-man, half-fish creature that timidly approached the boat where the old man stood motionless and dumbfounded.

"Sir, I have a problem and I need your help." The creature said to the man.

Bob answered nothing, for he was still not out of his astonishment. The strange being continued, "Do you remember yesterday's storm? Well, that strong movement of the sea moved the wreckage of an old shipwreck, and my companion was trapped in it."

"Oh, how sorry I am." The old man replied at last.

The creature said, "Yes, I believe that if you lend me your ropes and with them, I manage to tie up the wreck of the sunken vessel, you may be able to move it using the force exerted by the engines of your moving boat."

"Let's try it then." Bob quickly replied.

And so they did. Bob gradually released his ropes to the strange being, while the submerged one carefully tugged at them. Then, at a signal from the creature, the old man started his boat's engines and advanced some distance out to sea.

239

After a few minutes, Bob began to worry as he saw that he had no news of his companion. Suddenly, a couple of fantastic beings emerged happily from the water, jumping nimbly like dolphins and revealing their shiny tails full of colorful and shiny scales. It was a beautiful sight that Bob would remember forever.

The pair then approached the old man, and there, amid the fading sunlight, Bob witnessed the image of a siren whose beauty would be the envy of any woman. Her face was of delicate features and porcelain-like skin, with oval eyes framed by long lashes, while long reddish hair, streaked with blue and green fell across the shoulders and breasts of this marvelous creature.

"Thank you, for helping my partner to save my life." The siren said to the man.

"We will be eternally grateful to you." The other being added.

And so, as quickly as they arrived, these two mythological beings disappeared from the man's sight.

Bob, excited and grateful for having had the joy of witnessing such creatures, returned home as quickly as he could. There he told his wife everything he had seen, and she, as excited as he was, said, "I wish I could have been there."

Several months passed. The days had gone by uneventfully, but one day Barbara began to become unstoppably ill without showing any improvement. Bob was devastated. In an attempt to get away from it all and relax for a moment, the old man took his boat and sailed it some distance from home.

Then, that couple of beautiful and fantastic beings that the man had once seen and helped appeared before him and said, "Take this pearl and give it to your wife, it is a powerful medicine and a gift to you."

Bob could not believe it, gratefully took the pearl and immediately returned home, where once in front of his wife, he gave her the pearl to drink and waited patiently until she was completely healed.

Travel to a Distant Past

Silvester and Agatha were two archaeologists who had had the opportunity to study the Pyramid of Giza in Egypt.

"Now I see why they call it the Great Pyramid, it is more immense than others we studied before." Agatha said very surprised, looking at the pyramid from the outside.

"Yes, it is so majestic, besides being the largest in Egypt, it is the oldest of the seven wonders of the ancient world." Silvester said.

"Look at how immense each stone block is, it must weigh more than two tons each." Agatha said.

"It's hard to imagine, what was the technology they used to move these blocks." Silvester noted.

"It is thought that they were Egyptians with great technical knowledge, where they used wood, sleds, ramps and traps, in addition to the strength of thousands of free men or slaves." Agatha complemented.

"Currently there are some theories, where it is thought that they had the technical assistance of beings from other worlds, although I don't share that idea." Said Silvester.

"I'm not that skeptical about it, because they are actually very large works for the time." Agatha commented.

243

They continued their advance through the great structure, passed into the interior, and descended through a passage to the subterranean chamber, then went up to the Queen's chamber, from there through the great gallery until they reached the King's chamber.

Throughout this journey, they observed how majestic the long interior passages were, especially the passage of the great gallery with staggered stones, forming a false vault. They also highlighted the two rooms, like sarcophagi, a well and a small gallery, in the subway chamber; while in the Queen's chamber, the smooth walls were distinguished, without decoration, with a niche and sloping ceiling; and in the King's chamber, the granite slabs and an empty sarcophagus, without inscriptions, were also appreciated.

"Touch the texture of this sarcophagus. It is still in good condition." Agatha said to Silvester.

When they had both touched the sarcophagus at the same time, a mysterious whirlpool formed inside and swept them away.

A portal had been created, through which they traveled for a long time until they fell back to about 2500 B.C., at which time the sarcophagus was in the process of being pulled down. B.C., at which time the pyramid was being built.

Both were wearing period clothing and were at the worksite

with some unknown construction tools in their hands. "What happened to us, I don't understand where we are and why we are dressed like this." Agatha asked very confused.

To which Silvester couldn't explain either, "This is crazy!" He said very perplexed.

"Let's keep calm and go with the flow in this mysterious world. Let's see how far this all leads." Said Agatha, recovering a little.

They observed that, indeed, there was a considerable amount of people of the time working on the construction. But, in addition, they had very advanced technology for the moment, with excavating machines and small ships that moved in the air, from one side to the other, from which a blue light was projected that made the heavy blocks levitate and were transported to the pyramid under construction, where it was placing them with great precision.

One of these ships stopped its work and a humanoid figure got off, but it was too distant from the archaeologists to detail them; but they could perceive that they were workers who operated these small ships to help the humans in the mobilization of the blocks. In fact, humans and these extraterrestrial beings were working together in the elaboration of such an impressive work of art.

All this made it evident, before Silvester and Agatha's eyes, that theories such as the use of sand ramps and others known until then, to move those blocks, were not correct since they were mobilized by those flying objects.

"We now know how they moved such heavy boulders." Agatha said.

"Incredible, and I was in denial about this possibility." Exclaimed Silvester, still in awe.

After a while of observing the whole extraterrestrial technological panorama, together with the work of many humans, a large flying ship appeared from the sky, with a slightly blinding glow. It had a pyramidal shape, similar to the shape of the Great Pyramid of Giza of today, but it was very metallic, bluish-green in color, with a relief similar to the blocks of the pyramid.

The ship landed a short distance from the construction site, a kind of hatch opening through which several humanoid figures descended. They were tall, white beings, with long, grayish or silver hair, with eyes a little wider apart than those of humans. Their clothing was golden, decorated with precious stones, which refracted many colored lights as they moved.

A few humans, those who ruled the construction, met with these extraterrestrial beings. Agatha and Silvester, though a bit fearful, also crept closer to try to listen. These beings spoke in a strange language, but one that was mysteriously intelligible to the archaeologists.

"We already have this construction quite advanced, when we finish we will make the others, to be able to return promptly to our plants." Said one of them.

"As we indicated to them, internally we will place certain devices, in some chambers, with which they will be able to communicate through time with our worlds." Indicated the other one.

"That is why it must be a very strong construction, which can withstand the ravages of time and natural phenomena." Continued the first one.

"Moreover, these constructions will be perfectly aligned with Orion's belt, which for you are only distant stars, but they are our planets; such alignments can strategically allow such communication." Said the other.

Thus, Silvester and Agatha stayed a while longer, eavesdropping on the conversation between humans and aliens, until the latter boarded their ships. Then, the archaeologists walked to a chamber, quite advanced in construction, which looked like what would currently be the King's chamber. There, the portal opened again, taking them back to their own time.

Both were still perplexed by what had happened, but after a

while they felt very happy for having had the opportunity to take a look at that distant and wonderful past, where they knew a little of the great mystery of the construction of the pyramid.

Field Trip with Students

At the University, Professor Samuel, from the Botany Department, was to conduct a field trip with his fifth-semester students. He told them that it was necessary to carry out this activity outside the university campus, to collect plant samples, which they should preserve and then study in the laboratory.

"The field trip will take place next Saturday; we will go to a location approximately 30 minutes from the college; we will go in a campus bus; there we will be received at his house. The employee who is in charge of reproducing the reading material here, is Mr. Francis, who kindly offered his house. He says that the vegetation in that area is lush, with many flowers, and that near his house there is a river." Explained the professor.

"What should we bring for this outing, professor?" Asked one of the students.

"You should bring clothes that cover your body well and boots to protect yourselves from rubbing against the vegetation or insect bites; also, you can bring some food and water, since we will be spending the whole day in that area." Answered Samuel.

"Is it mandatory for all of us to attend that tour?" Asked another student.

"It is not, since you can go to another country site that you know, near your homes, where you can find plants, but they are not food crops or garden plants; you should consult the book I recommended to help you in the activity." Indicated the teacher.

Once the explanation was finished and all the doubts were clarified, the class ended and they said goodbye until the day of the trip.

When the day arrived, they met early at the agreed place, where the transport picked them up. Not everyone attended, but those who were present were very excited, because they would go out to visit natural sites and put into practice the things they only knew in books and by explanation of their teachers.

They departed to their destination. They left towards the outskirts of the city, until they reached a highway; then they took a small road that ascended a little, heading towards the programmed locality.

Soon they arrived at the scheduled area. The driver knew Mr. Francis' house location. There, he and his family received them very kindly. One of Francis' sons, Gregory, would serve as his guide in the field, along with other young locals.

"Welcome to my humble home, this is my family." Francis said.

"Thank you very much and nice to meet you." Said Professor Samuel, as he greeted and introduced himself to the Francis' family and the young locals.

All the students thanked and greeted politely. After a while, they were ready to start the walking tour.

They crossed the small road and began the ascent into a steep, wooded area. The air was pure, the soil fertile, the climate pleasant. Next to the leafy trees, there were small grasses and bushes, and on these trees could be seen, vines and orchids with beautiful flowers that emitted rich fragrances; in addition, there was a great variety of insects, reptiles, worms and birds, whose songs turned the environment into a small paradise of harmony.

They had not gone very far, when one of the students, being a little overweight, felt a little fatigued, and asked, "Professor, is it much farther to finish this trip?"

One of the guides, seeing that neither the professor nor the other students, including the girls, were so exhausted and complaining, said, "There is still a long way to go, we must climb this and other hills." And all the others laughed, because of the funny face that the aforementioned student made when he heard the answer.

The students looked very excitedly at the various plants, the teacher explained many things about them while indicating that they should collect only a portion of 30 cm of the branches with flowers and fruits; as for the herbs, they could collect them whole, pulling them from the roots.

"Remember that everyone should collect different plants." Samuel said.

The students were ecstatic with the work, especially because of the rarity and scent of the different flowers, never seen around their homes.

They had already collected many plants when they reached the top of the hill, "What a wonderful place, from here you can see the whole panorama." Said the student who was complaining before.

They stayed there for a while contemplating the landscape and taking pictures, then they went down to the house, where Mr. Francis was waiting for them while he prepared a barbecue for everyone. They all helped and then tasted the delicious food as if they were with family.

Then Gregory made them an invitation, "We have a river nearby, with warm water, if you like we can go for a while." They all agreed and went.

When they arrived, they were fascinated by how crystal clear and pleasant the water was, "Let's jump in at once." Said one of the girls. They didn't think twice and dived into the water. There they swam, played and had a lot of fun.

The teacher was sharing with them, while observing some flowering plants that were on the banks of the river, "Here you can take advantage and collect some missing plants." He said.

When they were about to return to Francis' house, they collected some more plants, "Let's go, our transportation will arrive soon." Said the professor.

When the bus arrived, they said goodbye very grateful and fascinated by the wonderful outing; they left that place very comforted, with a lot of joy and a feeling of rest and tranquility, besides learning many things about plants, directly in the field.

"You can come back whenever you like." Said Mr. Francis, and all the students wished they could come back someday.

When they returned the following week to their botany lab to study the preserved plants, they told their classmates who did not attend how wonderful the field trip was, and they regretted not attending.

"Professor, will we have another field trip during the rest of the course?" They asked anxiously.

"Indeed, we will have another field trip in a month, this time to an experimental station located on the coast." Said Samuel, and everyone shouted with joy.

The Color of Amethyst

Amethyst was a beautiful maiden who lived in a wooded region. This girl used to go out in the evenings with her friends to roam the fields for fun and to look for beautiful flowers.

"Let's go down to the river for a little swim." Proposed her friend Margaret.

"That's a good idea since it's getting pretty hot." Agreed Christina.

"Let's see who gets there first." Said Amethyst as she started a race.

They ran until they reached the riverbank; this one had crystal clear and very calm waters. They bathed and swam for a long time.

At that moment a very attractive young man passed by the river. He stopped in his tracks when he looked at the girls, but he was more impressed by the beauty of Amethyst; he even felt true love.

The girls noticed the boy's presence and shyly hid behind some bushes. But from that moment on, he kept thinking about the image of that pretty girl, so he always used to pass by the same place, hoping to see her again.

Amethyst and her friends were very busy during those days, so they went out a little to walk in the countryside and swim in the river.

One day he went to a well to fetch water for his home; coincidentally, at that moment the young man, whom they had seen at the river, also happened to be there. When they looked at each other, they kindled a spark of love for one another.

"Hello, I had been begging for some time to meet you again, can you tell me your name?" The boy asked. To which she replied to him, "I'm Amethyst; yes I already remember your face, but I don't know your name either."

He answered to her, "My name is Eugene, I have my home a bit distant from here, I am in these lands visiting some family members, whom I haven't seen since I was a very young boy."

They talked for a long time and agreed to meet, and from that moment on their love grew deeper.

One day, when she was again with her friends in the countryside, a god observed her and was captivated by her beauty. It was the god Dionysus, who at that moment did not try to approach her because she was with her friends. Amethyst and her friends did not notice his presence.

The next day, while Amethyst was on her way alone to a neighboring village for supplies, the god intercepted her.

He was kind to her and tried to seduce her but she did not reciprocate, for in her heart there was only love for Eugene. The god was a bit insistent, to the point that the beautiful young woman was afraid and begged the gods to help her get rid of that guy, not knowing that he was also a god.

The goddess of hunting, who was near that place in her hunting day, heard her prayers, moved to the place and seeing that it was another god who was harassing the beautiful maiden, she could only transform her into a white quartz crystal rock, so she could escape from that being.

Seeing her thus metamorphosed, Dionysus burst into tears, magically created a cup of wine, which he poured over the white rock, staining it with the characteristic purple of the amethyst stone. After a while he left, a little frustrated and disconsolate for not having been able to have such a beautiful maiden.

For his part, Eugene searched for a long time for his beloved, without having an answer for her disappearance, until one day Dionysus found him very sad, at the side of a road.

"What is the matter with you? Why are you so distressed?" He said to Eugene.

"I have lost my adored one, I have looked for her in many places and I have not been able to find her, my happiness is by her side." Said the young man crestfallen, and then he gave more details to the god.

Dionysus understood that it was the same girl transformed by his fault, and deplored his behavior, "I am sorry for what happened, I know who it is because I am the god responsible for her disappearance."

Eugene, seeing the deity's true regret, said to him, "If you are a god, you can immediately take me to the place where my beloved turned to stone is and reverse that condition so that we can be happy."

"I can take you to that place, but I cannot restore her original form, for I do not have the power to undo what was initially performed by another god." The god said to him.

"Oh, so nothing can be done to reverse the damage anymore?" Asked Eugene sadly.

"Calm down, there is always something that can be done. Let's go to the site and invoke the goddess of the hunt, who was the one who transformed her to rid her of me." Dionysius said as he took Eugene by the arm. And they immediately moved magically to the site.

Eugene tightly embraced the beautiful stone into which his beloved had been transformed, while he invoked the goddess. She appeared and was earnestly requested to return the maiden to her original form.

"I have reconsidered the mistake I made and I will no longer bother this girl if you turn her back into a human; besides, I have realized that these two beings love each other deeply." Dionysus told her.

The goddess reversed her magic and the girl gradually resumed her human form; however, the girl's body was adorned with a beautiful dress, shining purple like that of the precise amethyst stone, a garment she did not have when she was transformed into a rock.

Amethyst and Eugene hugged each other tightly, then Eugene looked at her and said, "How beautiful is that dress you are wearing, I have never seen it on you before."

"I don't know where it came from either." She replied very strangely.

"I am sorry for what happened, I hope you can forgive me; as for your dress, it is the product of the cup of wine I spilled on you when you were a rock. Only I can change it, but I would like you to keep it like that, for it looks very nice on you and it would be a gift to redeem my mistake a little." The god said to her.

Amethyst and Eugene smiled and accepted with pleasure. Since then, they have been close friends with these gods, who were the first guests at their wedding. Nowadays, in that place, there shine many precious violet gems, known as amethysts, which are used as a symbol of peace, tranquility and protection.

Joseph and the Fascinating Orchids

Joseph was a university student of Administration. However, he did not like that career, he was only there to please his father, who wanted him to be in charge of managing his company in the future. In reality, he did not like that or any other career. He did not want to study anything, but to lead a young man's life without obligations.

One day while he was walking with his friend Alice, she had convinced him to study for some upcoming exams, "Come to my house on Saturday, we can study there and you will improve your grades because you run the risk of failing the subjects."

"I was planning to go out with some friends to go fishing, but that's okay, I'll go with you to study." Joseph told her.

That day, he woke up late and did not remember the commitment he had made with Alice, then he saw a notebook lying on the floor and fell into the matter; he fixed himself and left for her home.

"You're a little late, I'm already ahead on the topics, but never mind, we can go back to the beginning." Alice told him.

He smiled and, without much interest, opened his books. After a few hours, they decided to take a break and went out to the girl's father's garden. As they entered that place, a great variety of rich fragrances invaded their sense of smell. Then, their sight was enraptured with the most beautiful colors and with the various floral forms.

"What a beautiful place, I've never seen anything like this. It's so relaxing that you could even sleep peacefully." Joseph said very delightedly.

Alice's father, Ezekiel, was there doing his gardening work, which he did very often, as it was his fascination.

Alice introduced him to her friend and they greeted each other. Joseph began to take an interest in this fascinating world of growing beautiful flowering plants and began to talk with Ezekiel, who taught him a few things about this beautiful and relaxing work, while the boy became more and more enthusiastic about the plants.

"In this other area of the garden, you can observe my small collection of orchids. Smell this flower, it is really exquisite smelling," Ezekiel said.

"Oh, what a rich fragrance; there's a hint of orange!" Exclaimed the young man.

"Yes, and if you smell these others, you can tell the difference in their rich scents, plus, as you see, their colors are really beautiful and of various shades." Explained the gentleman.

"I think that among all these plants, I like the orchids the best." Joseph said.

"In that case, I'm going to give you these two plants as gifts to include in your mom's garden." Ezekiel said.

Joseph took the beautiful gifts with great pleasure and went back to study with Alice. "Now I am clear about what I want to study, I am going to change my career to be a botanist." He told the girl. Indeed, he managed his change and soon began to study that science.

From that time on, the young man took great interest in his studies, always got good grades, learned much more about plants, and always sought to orient himself towards the study of orchids.

The two plants that Mr. Ezekiel had given him prospered under his care at his mother's house; he acquired new orchids in some establishments, multiplied many of them, and increased their quantity and variety.

After some time he obtained his degree as a botanist, began to work as a teacher in his area, bought a house, where he promptly designed a beautiful garden.

"Mom, I'm going to take some of these orchids with me, the rest of them, I'm going to leave for you to take care of." He said as he moved out.

"How nice my son, I am already used to them and I like their beautiful flowers very much." His mother remarked.

After a while, he had the most beautiful garden in the area, all the neighbors and passersby, admired and stopped to appreciate his gorgeous and rare plants. Many of them visited him to have more contact and to see them more closely. On certain occasions he gave away some and sold others, as he had an abundance of them.

Every morning he would go out to his garden, with a hot cup of coffee or an exquisite chocolate, to contemplate his orchids; for those moments brought him a lot of peace and tranquility. He would spend a long time there, multiplying them, placing them in new substrates, watering them, etc.

One day his friend Alice came to visit, accompanied by Mr. Ezekiel, because although he had taken another major in college, they remained good friends.

"Hi Joseph, you look great today." Alice said.

"Yes, the ambiance of my garden and the rich scent of its flowers keep me looking good." He replied, and they all laughed.

"I see you have many more orchids than I have, and very varied." Ezekiel said.

"It has been the fruit of great labor, but very rewarding."

Joseph replied.

"Look at these rare insects that land on the flowers dad!" Exclaimed Alice.

"Yes, in my garden too many of these and more to come, I don't know why it likes these flowers so much." Ezekiel said.

"I have learned many things while studying. One of them is that many orchids have adopted forms similar to these rare insects, so that they, believing they are in front of possible mates, try to copulate with them. At the end of their failed attempt at reproduction, these animals move away with the pollen stuck to their heads, to visit other flowers of the same species and pollinate them." Explained Joseph.

"How interesting!" Exclaimed Alice.

"I have also managed to pollinate them manually and, moreover, cross-pollinate orchids of different species." Joseph complimented.

After much time chatting inside the garden and explaining to it, many other things learned about the fascinating world of orchids, Alice and Ezekiel were to leave.

"I am very impressed by your magnificent garden and all your explanations about things I didn't know, even though I have been growing orchids for years." Ezekiel said.

"I am very grateful to you for being the one who initiated me into this spectacular and relaxing world of orchids; that is why I am the one who now wants to give you these beautiful plants." Said Joseph as he took some orchids and gave them to Ezekiel.

Good Actions

Jason was a very cheerful young boy, he was known by everyone in the small community where he lived because he liked to do good and help anyone who needed a hand. His favorite pastime was to ride through the streets on the bicycle his mother gave him when he was just a child.

He had an incredible affection for that object, because it was the most precious thing he owned. He said that its wheels were the fastest in the world and that its small seat was the most comfortable of all. He always took great care of it, until one day everything changed.

One sunny morning, Jason woke up very early to do the homework he had pending. He got out of his bed and went to the kitchen to start the day with a full stomach.

When he was ready, he was finally able to leave his house in the company of his beloved dog named Gio. He walked to the garage of his house to get his bike, and when he had it with him, he set off on his way.

The day was wonderful. The sky was full of clouds of different shapes and the birds were reciting beautiful melodies that were sneaking through the ear canal of the young boy. All that made Jason take a deep breath in gratitude for everything that surrounded him, no doubt he was someone very happy.

After several hours doing various tasks, Jason and his dog decided it was time to go back. They were both very hungry and his mother must have food ready. But when the boy got on his bike, Gio looked at the sky and started barking as a sign that something was not right.

The young man looked at the sky and immediately knew something wasn't right. He tried to calm his pet so he could get back as soon as possible and said, "Gio, take it easy. The weather won't hurt you; don't worry." Having said this, they returned to their home.

Moments before the companions arrived at their home, they heard a loud rumble coming from the sky and everything lit up for a few seconds. That sound made the two companions panic causing them to pick up their pace.

When they were about to arrive, it started to rain very hard. Jason looked at Gio and told him, "Run home! Now!" The intelligent dog ran as fast as he could, leaving behind the young boy, who was fighting against the strong winds because he refused to leave his beloved bike in the middle of the road.

After several minutes of struggle, the boy decided that the best thing would be to leave it on the sidewalk. He did not want to do it but he had no other choice, he watched it for a few seconds. He felt that time stopped for a few moments as all the memories he had with that object passed through his head as if it were a great lightning bolt.

"Thank you for everything." He said wistfully as he placed it on the ground and then ran home. That had been the hardest thing he had ever done in his life because he knew there was little chance that he would be in that place when it all happened.

When he arrived home, his mother was waiting for him in the living room next to Gio, who was soaking wet from the fierce rain. "Honey, you're finally here! I was so worried about you." Said the relieved woman as she approached him to hug him.

"I had to leave the bicycle on the street; I couldn't bring it all the way here." His mother looked him straight in the eyes and said, "Son, there are situations where we have to make sacrifices. Life teaches us that material things are not so important." She paused to stroke his hair and continued, "I'm sure wonderful things are waiting for you. Don't worry, honey." Mother and son melted into a warm embrace and set out to wait for the deluge to end.

The next day, the sun reigned again in the small community. Jason got out of his bed and went to the place where he had left his beloved bicycle. When he arrived at the site he realized his suspicions were true. There was no trace of the precious object, making the young boy feel a little sad.

Several seconds later Gio arrived and kept him company. The boy stood next to his beloved pet and immediately remembered the words his mother had said to him, "There are more important things than a bicycle, I have you and my mom, you are everything to me." Jason said while caressing his faithful friend's fur.

Days passed and everyone in the community had heard about what happened to the young boy. With the help of his mother, they decided to plan a surprise for him. The boy knew nothing of what his neighbors and friends were planning. They kept the secret very well until the big day arrived.

One Sunday morning, Jason was sleeping peacefully in his room. His mother knocked on the door and the sleepy boy mumbled, "Come in, Mom." And then the woman entered the room.

"Hello, sweetheart. The neighbors have a surprise for you." said his mother. Those words had aroused the boy's curiosity, so he quickly walked to the bathroom to get dressed and leave his house.

Minutes later, the boy was ready to leave his home, but his mother blindfolded him. When she was sure her son couldn't see anything, she guided him towards the front yard. They both stopped and the woman moved a little away from him. "Ready, you can take off the blindfold." Jason followed the instructions he had been given and was very surprised to see what his neighbors did for him.

They found his bike and had repaired it. That gesture on everyone's part made the young boy moved and he let out a few happy tears. "Thank you all for doing this for me, I am so grateful to have such good people in my life." And his mother told him, "You are a good person."

After the Storm

Jackson was a very happy man. He had a beautiful family and a good job. He got everything he had always wanted thanks to his precious lucky charm, that little object had helped him throughout his life. Nowhere else he had gotten the good vibes that it gave him; that was the reason why he treasured it so much. It was the most precious thing he had until one day everything changed.

One very rainy morning, Jackson woke up at his usual time. The noisy alarm clock resting on his nightstand had interrupted his sleep of relaxation, so he turned it off and got out of bed to start getting ready.

When he was finally ready to leave, he said goodbye to his adoring wife and cute daughter, but as he opened the door he noticed that the amount of water falling from the sky prevented him from walking freely to his vehicle, so he went to the kitchen where his family was and said, "The weather is crazy! Susan, where's the umbrella?" And received a simple reply, "In the cupboard, honey." The man thanked her and headed to where his wife had indicated.

When he had the umbrella in his hands, he was finally able to leave his house, but the wind almost blew the object out of control. He entered the car, started the engine, and set off for his work.

The roads were clear, there were not so many vehicles in the lanes because the water lashed every corner of the city. The noise caused by the falling drops was very relaxing but Jackson turned on the heater as the cold outside hit his body.

Arriving at the company he owned, he walked to his desk while taking the small amulet in the pocket of his pants, deposited it in his usual drawer, and finally he could start his workday.

The rain was still having its way in the small town, but this was not an impediment for Jackson to do his work. He had his eyes fixed on the computer, nothing could distract him from what he was doing, but suddenly everything went dark.

It was a blackout. The busy man did not know what was causing of this, but he suspected that it must have something to do with the rain that was falling with great fury. After several minutes of thinking, he decided that it would be best for him and all the workers to return to their homes until the weather improved.

He took his belongings and walked back to his car, completely forgetting the little amulet that had always accompanied him. When he reached the car, he started it up again and headed for home.

After a while of driving, Jackson was stuck in traffic, which seemed a little strange to him since the streets had been clear for several minutes, but he had no choice but to wait for everything to return to normal.

The hours passed and the impatient man was still in the same place. The drops fell on the small roof of the car causing a relaxing sound that managed to distract him at times. The heater was still on and Jackson was craving for a delicious hot chocolate that would help him with the wait, but unfortunately he was far from getting it.

A few hours later, the vehicles around Jackson began to move. Finally, he could start the engine and head for home, it was rare for that kind of thing to happen to him. He had always had very good luck, but that day a series of situations happened that had never occurred to him before.

After he had meditated a bit on why his day was the way it was, he remembered that he had left his precious amulet in his office, "That's why I've had such bad luck!" He said to himself, but something didn't make sense. "I had my amulet when the blackout happened; I don't understand what's going on."

He continued driving for a couple more minutes until after so long he had arrived at his home. He got out of his car and ran towards the entrance of his cozy home. The water drops fell on him making his suit totally soaked "Great, that's what I needed." He expressed as he walked through the door.

Susan heard her dear husband's voice and quickly made her way to where he was to find out what had happened. When she was in front of him she didn't hesitate to ask, "What happened to you, Jackson?" His suit was soaked thanks to the fierce rain; his shoes were covered by a dark puddle and his hair was a mess. Small branches and leaves decorated it nonchalantly.

Jackson knew the reason why all that had happened to him. "Honey, I think my amulet stopped working." He said a little discouraged. His wife heard his words and smiled as she shook her head, "Honey, your amulet didn't stop working. What happens is that there are days that will be very good and others not so good." She paused a little while she approached him to try to fix his hair a little. "Bad days give us many lessons. They serve to see life from another point of view, and let us know that the next morning will be better."

It continued to rain for the rest of the day. Susan's words played over and over again in Jackson's mind and he realized that his wife was quite right. The example that had helped him to accept it had been when the blackout occurred, since at that time he had his precious amulet under his possession.

The next morning, the man woke up at the same time as usual. When he got out of bed he walked to the window that was in his room. When he opened it, the bright rays of the sun came through. He smiled broadly to see the sky was adorned by a beautiful rainbow. The different colors managed to fill him with good energies and finally said, "Today will be a wonderful day."

Forest Fairies

Megan was an exemplary teenager. Her family was one of the wealthiest in the city. This was because Carl, her father, owned the largest textile company in Europe, was recognized worldwide for the excellent quality of its products and the speed with which they were delivered.

Megan and her sisters were raised under the doctrine of their parents, "Success is the answer to happiness." That phrase accompanied them since they were very small, but the three young women thought that there must be something else that would generate happiness. They doubted that ideology and were willing to change many things in their family for the good of all.

Her past had been very troubled. From a very young age she knew that in her family there was a great lack of happiness. She knew something was missing despite all the hard work and success her parents had. They were missing that last piece to complete the puzzle.

One sunny day, the three girls were having breakfast in the large kitchen of their mansion, Megan noticed that their parents had gone out very early, leaving them alone without a guardian to be near them. She said, "This can't go on; even though I am close to turning eighteen, I am still a child and have grown up without the love of our parents."

Stacy, the youngest of three sisters, asked, "What do you plan to do, sister?" This made Megan freeze. Although she was very clear about her ideas, she didn't have the necessary tools to face such a complex situation. In an attempt to show calm she said, "Calm down, girls, trust me. We will get our parents back and we can be a very happy family."

Megan went to her room to think more clearly. She analyzed each of the possibilities she had so that her parents could see the big mistake they were making and concluded that the best thing to do would be to talk directly to them, but she had the great fear of not being heard because of her age and how they would take her words.

She was a very brave girl. She took it upon herself to do good and always saw to it. When she knew what she had to do, she waited patiently for her parents to come home from their long day's work.

A few hours later, Megan heard the engine of her father's vehicle; she left her room and went to the living room to greet them. When they opened the door, the two adults were very excited to see their oldest daughter, and Carl decided to greet her first, "My princess, how was your day?" Megan was quick to respond, "Not so good, Dad. You guys are never home. My sisters and I, we never hear from both of you all day. We want to be a normal family for a day."

Her mother listened intently to every word her daughter uttered and replied in a very gruff manner, "We're doing this for your future, because we want to give you the best. You are still a child, so go up to your room." She paused for a breath and finally said, "When you grow up you will understand each of our sacrifices."

Megan went up to her bedroom very sad. When she opened the door she met her two sisters, who supported her and tried to cheer her up a little. They were also affected by everything that happened and felt their older sister's regret. "What can we do?" Asked Stacy, and Sky, her other sister, answered her, "I think we should teach our parents a lesson."

Both girls looked her straight in the eyes and she continued talking, "We should leave here and go to the forest in front. They will see that something is not right and we will finally be heard." That idea was not very wise but Megan liked it and she decided to carry it out, "We will leave at midnight. This way nobody will know we left and they will find out the next morning." Said the oldest of them all; and then they went to sleep.

At midnight an alarm began to sound. Megan hurried to turn it off while saying, "It's time." And her sisters obeyed her. After getting everything ready, the girls, very cautiously, left their home, made sure no one saw them leave, and when they were finally outside, they found themselves in front of the immense forest.

They went in little by little. They did not feel any fear. It was quite the opposite; they experienced very nice sensations. They felt protected, relaxed and very happy. They kept walking, and they were all sure they would feel better as they went increasingly deeper into the trees.

After walking a few more minutes, Megan noticed something very small, but at the same time very bright near them. When she observed it more carefully, she realized it was a fairy inviting them to follow her. That tiny person made the sisters incredulous at what their eyes were seeing, and without thinking much, they decided to follow her.

After a short walk, they arrived at a beautiful meadow filled with thousands of fantasy creatures. The fairies began to communicate with them and explained their parents had already found out about their escape and their other fairy friends had been in charge of guiding them to where they were.

When both parents arrived at that place, they ran to their daughters to melt in a warm hug. After that touching moment, the girls and all the fairies began to explain the reason why they had planned to leave their home. They made them understand what was bothering them and told them that success is not the key to happiness, since there were many other things with which they could achieve those feelings. In this case, it was the love of the family.

Sam's Dream

Some years ago in New York City, there lived a young communications student named Sam. His life was very complicated and boring. He only thought about doing all his homework and his future.

He lived with his parents, who were very professional people and made the boy study non-stop so that one day he would be as recognized as they were. But his dream was to become an astronaut. He loved everything related to the universe and the planets, and he was very curious to know what was behind the black holes.

His parents prevented him from making his dream come true. They believed that this desire lacked logic and Sam knew it. But although he had never confronted them he worked in secret to be able to enter one of the most prestigious space institutions.

One sunny day, Sam was designing a prototype of space rockets, his cell phone began to ring and when he took it in his hands he realized his friend was calling him "Hey, man, what's up?" His partner answered very excitedly. "In two months there will be an admission test in the school of space studies. You should try your luck."

That news managed to surprise Sam. For the first time in a long time he had the opportunity to do something he really liked, but he knew it would be very difficult because his parents would not be happy about his choice. "I'm not too sure, my parents won't like me getting in." Said the boy a little discouraged.

His friend was annoyed by that answer and he said, "Are you crazy? Brother, this is the opportunity you've been waiting for so long. You don't have to let it pass. Things like this won't happen twice in your life." Sam knew he was right and decided to tell him, "Okay, I'll think about it. I'll call you on Sunday to let you know my decision."

The boy accepted his proposal and finally they said goodbye. Sam leaned his whole body back on his desk chair. He was excited about the news, but the odds of something going wrong were present in his head.

The minutes passed and Sam felt calmer, he put on relaxing music and laid down on his comfortable bed to imagine tropical countries. When he did that he remembered many happy moments of his childhood. That was the place he used to escape from the world.

While he was on that trip, he imagined what it would be like to be in space and to see the Earth from above. He wondered if there was noise in that immense place. He began to wonder about many things were related to the galaxy, and that led him to decide to follow his dream. "I have to do it, I want to be happy and that is the only way to achieve it." Sam said as he fixed his bed so he could sleep.

The next morning, the boy woke up very early because he wanted to practice what he would tell his parents. When he knew what he had to tell them, he decided it was time to go to the kitchen to wait for them.

A couple of minutes later, they were all gathered in the kitchen, Sam greeted them warmly and then invited them to sit down because he had some very important news to tell them. "I decided to leave the communications university, I want to be a scientist and later become an astronaut."

His parents could not believe what their ears had heard. Their son's words had left them stunned. They began to dialogue with him to make him think things a little better. Sam denied all the options they gave him because he was tired of doing what they wanted. His life had become a movie that repeated itself endlessly, and he needed a change.

Both adults looked at each other for a few moments. They finally understood they were not looking out for their son's happiness because they were only worried about what their acquaintances would say if the boy failed. His dad said, "I am so proud to be your father. You are willing to give up everything just to be happy. That is the greatest act of bravery I have ever seen. I love you, son."

His parents approached him and they all melted into a warm hug. They were finally walking the same path. All this made Sam feel very happy because for the first time in a long time he felt supported by the most important people in his life.

The days went by and finally, Sunday had arrived. Sam called his best friend to let him know what had happened. When he told him he would be taking the test, the young boy got very excited dropping his cell phone in the bathtub.

Sam studied like crazy for two months. Although he knew he had a lot of advantage because he had always studied advanced sciences independently, he did not want to leave his destiny in the hands of luck: "I am close to getting it, in a few days I will have the opportunity of my life." Sam told his dear friend, who had never left him alone.

When the long-awaited day arrived, everyone was in that place. Before Sam crossed the classroom door, his parents stopped him to tell him a few words: "Remember that you have to watch over your happiness above all. Nothing matters more than that; understood, champion?" The boy nodded his head and finally entered the classroom to take the admission test.

The following hours were the longest of Sam's entire life, but he left the institution very happy. His tutor told him that he had entered and that he would have the opportunity to become a professional astronaut. His parents and his faithful friend were very happy to hear the news. It was the best thing they had ever heard.

So after several years, Sam managed to make his first trip into space and became the most awarded scientist in history. His capabilities had no limit, and his next big goal was to develop a technology that would allow him to enter a black hole to investigate it.

Time and Its Whims

Chris was an elderly gentleman who had dedicated his whole life to fishing. He was in great demand in the town where he lived because the quality of his products was very good. His goal was to get as much money as possible in a short time, so he could retire and enjoy the beautiful views of what would be his country house, which would be located in one of the most magical mountains in the area.

Time had always been a problem for him. Since he was very young, his parents had put him to work. That was the reason why at the age of fifteen he was working in different constructions. That was how he got money and could have the job from which he lived. All that effort brought him a lot of stress, sleepless nights, and anxiety problems, but he managed to solve them on the high seas: fishing became his best friend.

One sunny day, he was preparing everything he would use the next day, but he realized that something was missing in him. He thought about the last time he had taken a vacation and said, "I feel very tired, I think it's time to rest for a few days."

But after thinking several seconds he said, "No way, I have a goal and I won't be able to meet it if I take a rest. Then I'll have time to relax," and continued packing all his tools in the boat.

When he had everything ready, he set an alarm that would help him wake up very early to start working. He settled his bed and finally he could sleep peacefully.

The alarm clock interrupted his sleep and Chris did not take long to get out of bed. He went to the kitchen to have breakfast, and while eating he said to himself, "Today will be a wonderful day." After several minutes in silence, he felt a slight pain in his chest, but he did not give it importance because time was very valuable and he had to leave his house as soon as possible. When he finished eating, he left to the port to begin his adventure.

It was a very quiet day, he used the road to relax. When he drove, he appreciated the beautiful views that surrounded him, that transported him to a place that only he knew, a magical place where nothing and no one could negatively affect him. There was no room for stress. "Although life is a little difficult, it gives us lovely moments we must learn to enjoy." Chris said marveled as he continued driving.

When he arrived at the port, the pain he felt in his chest increased, which made him stop for a moment to think if it was a good idea to set sail in those conditions. He took his pocket watch to check the time because he needed to study the situation. When he noticed that much period had passed he said, "No way, I have to work one way or another. I have to stop making excuses; they won't get me on the right track." He said as he grabbed his belongings so he could start sailing.

When he was fishing, he wondered again if all the work he was doing was necessary. He had enough money to retire quietly, and for the first time in a long period a feeling of satisfaction filled him completely. His work had paid off and he was beginning to believe that the countless hours under the sun were affecting his way of thinking.

"Maybe this will be my last year of work. When I get back I'll start looking for a cottage; it's a good time to do it." Chris said very cheerfully as he put away the nets so he could return to the mainland.

On the way to the port, the pain that had accompanied him increased a little more, which made him speed up the course to go to the hospital as soon as possible. When he arrived at the dock, Chris tried to calm down a bit to ask someone he knew if he could take him to the nearest medical center to make sure that everything was all right with his body.

When he arrived at the place, he sat patiently waiting his turn because there were several people in the emergency room. After several minutes the person in charge appeared in front of Chris and asked him to follow him to do a few tests. That way they could diagnose what was happening to him.

After several tests, the doctor approached Chris. He watched him very carefully because he had the results in his hands. Finally, the internist said, "You are starting to develop some heart problems. This is due to the high levels of stress you have been under. The best thing you can do is take a vacation, so you can rest and your body will stop straining."

Those words made Chris very surprised. After a long time he understood that health and happiness were the most important things in life. The goal he had was close to taking him towards its end. "Unbelievable, time can be very capricious. All my life I worked so hard believing that time would not catch up with me, but what I was doing was taking time away from my life, and the moments of rest were going to disappear completely."

Chris thanked his doctor for treating him, then left the clinic and headed home. He was going to sell everything to take advantage of the opportunity he had. He wanted to live the life he had worked for many years.

A couple of months later, Chris managed to buy the country house he had longed for. It was a place away from civilization, where he could enjoy the imposing mountains while savoring a delicious cup of coffee.

After all he had lived through, he was able to enjoy the small pleasures of life. He stopped thinking about the passing of time to be able to walk with it. He was grateful for the pleasures that nature offered him and began to be part of it.

The Trip

Some years ago in a nomadic community, there lived a woman named Ang. She was someone with a big heart, a good person with whom it was impossible to be bored, but those virtues were not enough for the other villagers. They did not have much appreciation for her because they believed that she was someone incapable of giving thanks for the good moments of life.

For them, that was something unforgivable in their community, because being a nomadic tribe, one of their principles was to thank Mother Nature for every blessing she bestowed on them, no matter how big or how small.

Ang knew what everyone thought about her, and she also knew that if she wanted to have a much happier life she should be a more grateful person. One day she decided to go and talk to the wisest man in the whole tribe; he could give her some answer to all the doubts she had in her head.

When she arrived at the place, he was waiting for her with his doors open, "Come in and make yourself comfortable, Ang." The gentleman told her holding a cup of hot tea, which he handed her when they were face to face. She trusted him and his abilities, the old man's reputation was very good and she knew he would succeed in putting an end to her complicated situation.

"I want to give my life a change, I would like to feel loved by all the people in the tribe." Said the desperate woman as she watched the shaman take a mysterious drink to prepare a ritual.

After a couple of minutes in silence, the man said, "There is nothing I can do. You must learn to love yourself as you are, that is the only way that will lead you to happiness." Those words left Ang deep in thought and she decided to ask, "How can I achieve that?"

The shaman said to her, "Have you heard the story about the forest that can teach people the path they need to follow?" The woman shook her head and the man continued, "You have to follow the song of the eagles that are found in the mountains. Their frequency is heard only by people who have a pure heart."

Ang could not believe what she had heard was real, but she trusted the man. She took her belongings and thanked the old man for everything he had told her, and then ran out of that place in a hurry because she needed to start her adventure as soon as possible.

When she arrived at her hut, she noticed all her neighbors were gathering everything to go to a new location. This was because they were running out of the crops they had, besides the cattle had devoured all the grass that was in that area; they needed to get away from there.

"What is the next resting point?" Ang asked one of her neighbors, who in a very nonchalant way answered her, "We will go to the highest mountain in this area." The woman was stressed when she heard those words. She knew that she could not take too long because she could lose her tribe forever. Without giving explanations she decided to start her journey.

The route was wonderful. Ang was surrounded by beautiful nature and was accompanied by the good-looking views of the imposing Alps adorned by a delicate layer of snow. "I think this is what the man meant when he said that nature teaches the lessons of life. How is it possible that I have never stopped to admire all this?" Ang said as she continued her journey.

After a couple of hours walking, she started to get discouraged. She didn't hear the eagles singing and she knew that could mean she wasn't worthy of visiting that forest, so she decided to stop for a moment to try to clear her mind.

Meditation made all her senses sharpen, which made her able to hear the sound she wanted so much. The eagles were singing for her because she deserved it more than anyone else, so she started running in the direction of the beautiful melody.

She knew she was close because the noise was getting increasingly louder. As she ran she decided to close her eyes to enjoy the moment. She was going to make it and fate would tell her when to open them.

Suddenly she crashed into a huge tree, and was surprised to find that she was already in front of the legendary forest. Nature invited her to pass. Ang knew she had nothing to fear because everything around her had a totally spiritual reason; everything would give her a little more wisdom so that she would come back a much more complete person.

After walking a little bit, she realized she was in the middle of a meadow and that she was only accompanied by an ancient tree. She thought she had taken the wrong path, but a voice told her, "Calm down, little one, you are in the right place. I am very happy that you are here." Ang was very confused and she decided to ask, "Who are you? Are you the tree?" Receiving as an answer, "No, my dear, I am everything, I am the whole forest. I am here to congratulate you because you managed to find the absolute truth. This rewarding journey made you understand how necessary it is to value what surrounds you and enjoy every moment, just as you did when you were in front of the beautiful views of the Alps."

Ang was very happy because she had changed many things inside her, besides she felt more complete from the moment the forest talked to her. She knew that its magic had affected her soul.

She thanked the mysterious voice very happily while she let herself fall on the soft snow because of the exhaustion that reigned in her body, making her lose consciousness for a few hours.

When she opened her eyes she noticed that she was with her people. They treated her with much love because they felt that something had changed in her; they felt her positivity. At last, Ang was one more of the tribe; she was someone different and much happier.

The Busiest City

In a kingdom far away, there lived a very arrogant king who loved to spend all his money on new clothes. He had dresses, capes, and crowns for every occasion. The small town where the kingdom was located was very cheerful and fun. The villagers every night held fairs and parties that turned the whole place into a real carnival.

The city had one of the most important yarn markets in the world, as weavers from all over the world came in search of the best merchandise to weave enchanting costumes.

One day a group of vandals posed as weavers, assuring the merchants that they would weave beautiful fabrics, with colors and designs unique in the whole kingdom. The emperor, upon hearing about these weavers, was delighted and immediately gave the group of vandals a good deal of money in advance so that they could work faster and make their weavings in less time.

The bandits, eager for profit, set up looms and pretended to work day and night for the king's commission, demanding fine, expensive cloth and as much gold as possible. But the king, desperate to try on his new suit, decided to send one of his workers. When the young man arrived at the place, he went in and got a big surprise.

303

"Good Lord, what's the meaning of this? There's nothing here!" He said surprised.

The group of men greeted him with a warm welcome and asked, "Can't you see it? What do you think you see on the loom? Aren't these colors magnificent?"

The young man was getting very closer to the loom, but he still could not see anything, the men around him kept insisting, "Don't you like what you see?"

The poor young man, frightened by the looks of the bandits and the answer that the king could give him, ended up affirming and approving the work of the strangers.

He said to them, "Everything is wonderful, very beautiful those colors, yes it has been unique and impressive. I will tell my king what I have seen."

The group of men, happy for what they had done, continued to ask the king for more money, more gold, high quantities of fine fabrics, and slowly the king granted them. After a few days, the ruler wanted to know more about the wonderful work the weavers were doing, and this time he sent one of the wisest elders in the kingdom and the same thing happened again.

They said to the old man, "Come closer, aren't these clothes unique?"

The old man surprised and intimidated by the bandits affirmed and left the place just as convinced as the previous one. When he returned to the king he commented, "The cloths these weavers are making are unique, magnificent, I have no words to describe them."

Weeks later the king wanted to see with his own eyes the wonders that his friends had told them about. He wanted to appreciate those vivid colors that they had mentioned. In minutes he summoned the royal guard and a group of soldiers went to the house of the swindlers, opening the way to the highest authority. When the king arrived at the place he saw nothing. The bandits greeted him with sympathy and welcoming him and asked, "What do you think of our splendid work?"

The emperor could not believe that he could not see anything and think, "Shall I be so foolish as not to see what is truly before me, or am I no longer serving as a king? That would be truly dreadful!"

So in fear of losing his throne he affirmed in the face of the bandits' questions, "They are magnificent! I like them very much, everyone will envy me when I'm showing them off to society."

The group of men was amazed at the attitude and the compliments that the king threw at the costumes and fabrics that he could not see. While clarifying doubts with the weavers, he proposed to premiere the new dresses for the following festivities that would be held throughout the kingdom.

The king congratulated the bandits and told them, "Today I celebrate all of you for making the most beautiful fabrics and costumes in the city. Thanks to you all, I will be the envy of all the kingdoms. From today on you guys will be the official weavers of the kingdom."

The bandits were happy and enjoyed the whole spectacle that had been formed for them. The king, while preparing for the upcoming festivities, began to measure the new costumes that had been made for them and without being able to see anything he approved and disapproved of some of them. "I don't like this one, it makes me look fat...this one suits me very well, it makes me look taller...I love this one it has a unique color..."

The people around him didn't understand, but just nodded and replied, "Very nice! Those outfits look great on you."

The great day arrived and the kingdom's festivities began happily. The king's time had come, for he wore nothing and believed that the suit he carried was a deep blue. The bells rang and the king looked out from the balcony.

"Welcome everyone to the best festivities of the kingdom. We thank the new weavers, who have made me the beautiful costume I carry today and we tell all the weavers of the world that they are welcome to create more costumes like these!" He said to his subjects.

The people shouted with excitement and as the king gave his tour through the streets of the kingdom, some children approached him and asked, "Why are you naked?"

The guards accompanying the king watched them carefully and tried to stop them from continuing to talk when another of the little ones exclaimed, "It can't be, the king is naked!"

A group of people crowded the place, some shouted that it was a beautiful suit and others shouted how naked the king looked before his people. For an instant the king confirmed what he had wondered sometime before. However, feeling that his people supported him with his imaginary clothing, he continued his tour of the kingdom and offering to give away a variety of suits to those who thought that the king's clothing was magnificent.

Andrew's Sudden Peace

One evening when young Andrew was strolling alone in a park, he came upon a very strange-looking old man.

"What is your name?" Asked the old man.

"My name is Andrew." Replied the young man.

"And what is a person like you doing all alone in a park at this hour?" The old man asked again.

"I might as well ask the same question of you." Andrew answered.

The old man smiled and said nothing. Then Andrew began to tell him, "I am a medical student. Months ago I lost my parents and was left with no place to live and no money to pay for my studies, I don't know what to do."

The old man said, "I can offer you a place to go, but it is a long way from here, deep in the forest."

Andrew didn't know what to say. On the one hand, the old man's appearance instilled a certain fear in him, but on the other hand, the man's words made him feel comforted. Then, after a moment's thought, he answered, "All right, I accept your offer, but first tell me what I should do and how much it would cost me."

"You don't have to pay anything, just go to this address," said the old man, handing Andrew a piece of paper with a kind of map traced on it.

Then the old man added, "Also, let me give you something." And then he took the palm of the young man's right hand and traced on it, with his index finger, the imaginary figure of a triangle.

The young man was confused. When he looked up to ask the old man what he had done meant, the old man had disappeared.

Andrew was more puzzled, but he plucked up his courage and set off for the place marked on his map. He walked through the forest along a rather dark trail and sometimes felt like turning back.

He even went over a suspension bridge, something he never thought he would do, as he was very afraid of heights.

Suddenly, amid all the darkness, the young man saw a faint light. As he looked up, he noticed before him the figure of a kind of temple.

Andrew felt a certain relief in his heart, for he was already tired of walking in the cold and darkness. He quickened his pace and soon found himself in front of the temple. As he approached the door, some children opened it just before he touched it.

"My name is Karim, are you looking for the master?" Asked one of the kids. To which Andrew replied, "I actually came all the way here because I have nowhere to go, and an old man invited me. He just handed me this map and..." The young man didn't have time to explain further, because the other boy immediately said, "Show us the palms of your hands."

Andrew showed them his hands, as the two kids looked at each other and smilingly exclaimed animatedly, "Welcome to your home, young master!"

The young man was now indeed more confused. Then from one of the rooms in the temple, a girl's voice was heard saying, "What's the matter, who's there?"

"It's our new teacher." Karim replied.

The girl then approached the door and looked at the young man curiously.

"He has the mark on his right hand, we saw it." Karim informed.

The girl then led the young man inside the house and asked him how he had acquired the mark. Andrew saw no mark on his hand but told his companions that an old man had drawn an imaginary triangle with his finger.

"Then that's all there is to talk about, you are our new master." The girl said.

311

"Could you explain a little more about this, please?" Andrew implored.

"Of course. This is a healing temple, here villagers and people from many places come from time to time to seek help to heal their physical, mental, or spiritual wounds." The young girl explained.

"Yes, Master Munt was the one who was in charge of this, but now we suppose it will be you who will do it." Karim said.

"By the way, I am Leila, the master's assistant and these are my brothers Karim and Kurt. I imagine you already know them." Said the girl.

Andrew was surprised. So he was quick to say, "But I'm just a medical student who was almost finishing his degree, and I'm not yet allowed to practice my profession."

"Don't worry, most people who come here are quickly filled with a great spiritual peace, and soon begin to heal all the wounds or illnesses in their body." Kurt said.

The young man was so tired and hungry that he hardly listened to what was being said. The children, noticing this, invited him to sit in a comfortable chair while they prepared a delicious dinner for him.

After dinner, Andrew was taken to a beautiful and comfortable room where he fell asleep peacefully.

The next morning, after a great stretch of arms, the young man could see how the sunlight streamed into the room through a huge window that allowed observing much of the nature surrounding the temple. He was indeed in a lovely place that inspired much peace and tranquility.

"Good morning." Karim said very excitedly, as he peeked his face through the door of Andrew's room.

"Ready to take care of your first patient?" Asked Kurt.

So the boys helped Andrew get cleaned up and dressed and then took him to the office where Leila was waiting for him.

"Oh, how beautiful you look!" Exclaimed Andrew as he saw his new assistant dressed in a beautiful, impeccable white suit.

Then Andrew, in the middle of a beautiful temple surrounded by nature, began to practice medicine almost without charging anything to his patients, since in this place he had everything he needed, a lush orchard from which he obtained his food, wonderful life companions, and patients who, by helping them, made him feel more and more useful and fulfilled.

Relaxing Meditations and Positive Affirmations for Adults

A Wonderful Blue

Welcome, dear friend. In this special meeting, you and I will start a wonderful journey, where you can calm all the noise in your mind, become aware of the great power that balance has in you. You will remember that feeling of harmony that your mind has gradually forgotten, and you will be filled with full happiness. I want you to keep in mind that you are a majestic, special being, full of light and with an incomparable essence. You deserve a space of intimacy where you can let go of all those ties that do not allow you to rest. You can clear your mind and recharge yourself with the best positive energy in the universe.

(Short pause)

Before starting our trip, the first thing we will do is find a calm and harmonious place, where you can isolate yourself from any noise or loud sound that does not allow you to remain calm. Lie gently on the surface of your choice, it may be the most comfortable sofa you have, or if it is in your bed, much better. Lay your head on a padded pillow, letting your neck rest from all that tension you may be building up. Stretch your arms and legs to clear your muscles of whatever weights you may be holding. Little by little, allow your whole body to fall onto the surface of the mattress. When you feel ready, close your eyes and trust the sound of my voice.

(Short pause)

Inhale slowly, absorbing all the positive energies and enjoying the moment. Then exhale. Your mind has begun to free itself of all those negative thoughts and the charges that you have accumulated over time. The noise and fear have completely disappeared. Here there is only tranquility, well-being, and prosperity. Do not worry if at some point in our trip the dream wants to take you with it, allow yourself to flow like the universe, and accept its invitation to tranquility. You deserve to be happy. Now you are experiencing new sensations, your senses have become acute and have reconnected with your natural essence, achieving a perfect harmonic balance.

(Short pause)

Now, you will begin to recognize each sensation of your body, how the energy runs through you, how your nerves work simultaneously, and how you begin to release the restlessness in yourself. Do not put resistance to your feelings, accept them without changing anything, pay attention to it as someone listen to the sound of the wind. Inhale deeply, allowing yourself to be free of any thoughts, then exhale and release all that noise that by nature does not belong to you. Very well, identify all the points of tension in your body, in your legs, in your arms, in the low of your back, in the shoulders, and your neck. Begin to release yourself little by little, and let yourself flow.

(Short pause)

You are infinite light

Your whole being is united with the universe

Everything you want you can have it

You are happiness

You are at the right time

You are passionate

You are a being flexible to situations

You are a being with beautiful feelings

You are the most special being in the universe

(Long pause)

A gentle breeze begins to caress all your skin, running through your feet, your legs, your torso, and your arms. Above you appears a wonderful sky full of pastel tones, you can notice the dominant blue in it. The sun is resting in the sky, giving you warm rays that fill you with new energy. Inhale slowly and then exhale. Beneath your body is a silky surface that gently hugs you. Your hands begin to touch it, you notice that it is a wonderful soil that embraces you with a light cover of green grass. You feel at peace, full of confidence, and happy to be in that place.

(Short pause)

You feel different, a feeling of well-being invades your body, and you begin to vibrate differently, in harmony with the place that surrounds you. You breathe in slowly, observing every detail of the paradise before you, and then you exhale. You stand up and receive the call of nature. You realize that you are in front of a beautiful forest. Around you, many pines and plants add thickness to the landscape. You start to walk all over the place, you enjoy the gentle wind that caresses your face and the softness of the plants that caress you when you walk. A soft smell begins to take over your nose. The smell of roses becomes stronger and stronger, until your eyes are delighted with huge red roses in the middle of the forest. Inhale calmly, feel the energy of the flowers in front of you, absorb their power and courage, then exhale.

(Short pause)

You keep traveling all over the space. You hear the wonderful song of birds above your head and you can feel the magical energy of nature surrounding you. You notice that the pines begin to make their way towards some magnificent mountains. Your body begins to move magically as if it knew the place. Breathe in. Feel the energy of harmony in your body, and then breathe out. Huge mountains and a magical turquoise lake begin to appear before you. The image before you seems to be unique, here, everything is perfectly balanced.

(Short pause)

As you keep moving, you reach the shore. You visualize the perfect details of the mountains before you and see how the snow is falling from them. They are imposing beings and they make you feel calm. Your soul understands nature, now both are connected by the energy of the universe. Inhale slowly, feeling the power within you and the well-being that being in the present causes you. Your mind begins to free itself; you begin to heal from the depths of yourself. A delicate wind runs through your skin, increasing relaxation in you, love takes hold of you and you feel like you are melting into the soft mattress that supports you. Finally, you manage to fall asleep completely. Good night, dear friend.

A Walk through the Heights

Welcome, dear friend. In this meeting, we will immerse ourselves in a wonderful journey. You and I will delve into the depths of your mind. Today we will connect to the purest energies of love, harmony, and prosperity. In this trip I will help you balance your thoughts so that you can give yourself that rest that you want so much. We will put the noisy thoughts aside and you will allow peace to begin to reign in your being. You are an incredible, wonderful, and unique being, filled with an infinite light that illuminates the entire universe. For that reason you deserve to dedicate a space of tranquility just for you, where you can free yourself from all that energy and annoying thoughts that don't let you rest. You can achieve that revitalizing and pleasant dream you want so much. Your body and mind will align to release your worries.

(Short pause)

To begin with our meeting, the first thing you should do is search for a serene, calm space away from annoying noises, where your mind can find calm and your body can let itself be carried away by the healing energies. If you feel that special place in the comfort of your room it will be much better. The place should have good air circulation, cool weather, and comfort as much as possible. Once you have found it, slowly lie down on a comfortable surface, it can be your sofa of choice or in the softness of your bed. Lay your back straight on the mattress, making your shoulders and head relax completely. Rest your arms on each side of your body, letting them release all those tensions that accumulate daily. When you feel ready close your eyes slowly and let yourself be carried away by the sweet sound of my voice. The time has come to begin.

(Short pause)

Inhale slowly, becoming aware of the here and now, then exhale. Feel how the air goes through you, caressing each part of your interior. Direct your attention to the natural movements of your body, begin to understand how it works innately. Pay attention to all the points of support, such as the soles of your feet in contact with the ground, your back on the mattress, or simply the contact of the clothes on your skin. You are doing it very well.

(Short pause)

More and more you are disconnecting from everything around you. Breathe deeply, holding the air for a few seconds inside you, let it go through your lungs, and then exhale all that is no longer part of you. Your body and mind become completely calm; your senses find the perfect balance. Enjoy the new sensations that run through your skin. The climate that surrounds us is pleasant, you do not feel fear, the fears are gone, the tensions are gone and everything around you begins to disappear. The dream has taken over you, there are no bad thoughts, doubts, or problems in this space. There is only you and your harmony.

(Middle pause)

You are a valuable being

You are a being with unique abilities

You are strong

You are a complete being

You have wonderful value to the universe

You are a grateful being

You are a wonderful, rich, and successful being

You have an incredible talent to love

You are a being full of love and balance

(Long pause)

Relaxation becomes part of your being; you begin to let yourself be carried away by the energy of the universe and you let yourself fall completely on the surface where you are. Your molecules have begun to vibrate at the frequency of abundance. The dream has been drawing you into a calm and balanced space. The feeling of complete relaxation increases more and more. Now it runs through your hips, your torso, your shoulders and finally settles in your mind. All the resistances that existed have disappeared. The fears are gone and the negative thoughts were drained from your mind.

(Short pause)

You feel completely free, your body, your mind, and your soul have begun to flow with the energy of the universe; you feel grateful and full of harmony. In front of you appears a beautiful sky decorated with shades of pink, violet, and orange. Inhale slowly, feeling the new energy travel through your body, moving from your feet to your head, then exhale. You stand up and notice you are in a wonderful field; the ground is soft, the view is refreshing and your soul feels connected to nature.

(Short pause)

You look around you, enjoying all the details until you notice that in the distance there is a hot air balloon waiting for you. You start walking through the beautiful countryside, feeling the wonderful caresses of the ground under your feet. You feel complete, full of love and tranquility. When you arrive in front of the vehicle that awaits you, you slowly open the door and step into it. Little by little the hot air balloon begins to rise from the ground until you finally find yourself flying.

(Short pause)

The wind is caressing every part of you. You feel how it recharges your energy and fills your soul with life. You slowly inhale the delicious aromas that begin to appear in the sky and then exhale. You feel free and light. The balloon each time rises a little more until it reaches the clouds. The view is incredible; the clouds are arranged in such a way that they create a path for only you to travel. You feel happy and grateful to the universe; you enjoy the connection you have with it. Now you understand your place in the world and how important you are to it. You feel the delicious caresses of the wind on your face, making you relax more and more. Tranquility takes hold of you and you feel how your whole body begins to sink into the mattress that supports you. Finally, you manage to fall asleep. Good night, dear friend.

An Adventure through Nature

Welcome, dear friend. In this new session, you and I will enter a majestic journey, allowing your soul and your mind to be charged with positive, harmonious, and prosperous energies so that you can reconnect with the universe. You are a magical, splendid being, with a united essence, full of love, optimism, and healthy. Today, I am here to help you achieve a pleasant and invigorating sleep. Your mind and body will achieve perfect balance, allowing fears, worries, and negative thoughts to disappear.

(Short pause)

To begin our meeting, we must find a comfortable place away from distractions. Where silence can follow us throughout our pleasant journey. The place must be cool, with good air circulation and a pleasant climate. Place your body on a padded surface; find the most comfortable position for you, allowing all the tensions in your body to disappear and for tranquility to begin to become part of you. Rest your head on a soft pillow that allows your body to feel comfortable. Inhale calmly, letting yourself go and then exhale. When you feel ready, slowly close your eyes and let yourself be enveloped by the powerful healing energy of the universe.

(Short pause)

Silence begins to take over your mind, emptying itself of all those things that are taking up space inside. Breathe gently, enjoying the sensations your body is experiencing, and then exhale as calmly as you can. The noise, fear, and worries are gone. Your body is a sanctuary of peace, where only well-being and positive thoughts abound. All the tensions and excess weight disappear from you; now you are a light and clean being. You breathe in through your nose slowly, then exhale, and allow yourself to flow, without blocks or ties. Remember that you are free as the wind.

(Short pause)

In this instance you have begun to flow, freeing yourself of all those thoughts that filled your mind with incessant noises. Breathe little by little, enjoying the caresses of the air on your skin, then exhale and let yourself go. Allow the tensions in your muscles to disappear and your soul to feel the power of the cosmos within. You notice effervescent energy running through your body; it is pleasant. In these moments your mind begins to travel to another plane, transcending in a perfect and balanced way. You can feel that you are now part of something bigger than your whole being. The calm passing through all the places of your being. It walks through your legs, through your hips, and your chest. Allow yourself to be aware of each emotion you are experiencing. Little by little you begin to connect with the universe. Your body and mind are separating and restful sleep is taking over you. The resistances and fears are gone.

(Middle pause)

Your whole being is perfect

You are a free person like the wind

You are a valuable and important being

You are pure and sincere love

You are a skillful being

You are kind

You are a healthy being

Your whole being is full of wonderful energy

You are a being full of love

(Long pause)

A relaxing tingle begins to flow through you, going from your chest to your shoulders. Your whole body has fallen completely on the surface of the pleasant mattress that supports it. You have been carried away by tranquility, allowing yourself that deep desire to be free. The tingling continues to rise, now you feel it in your neck, your jaw, and your forehead until it finally takes over your mind. The resistances have disappeared, in the same way, the insecurities and the problems. You find yourself swimming in the sea of balance.

(Short pause)

A slight breeze moves through your legs, slowly rises to your chest, and runs through your arms. Before you, a beautiful sky welcomes you, the sun's rays warm your skin, balancing the climate around you. Inhale slowly, feeling your body filled with positive and vigorous energies, then exhale, expelling any thoughts that remain in your mind. From where you are, you visualize that around you are beautiful trees full of pink flowers; the whole place is full of those flowers and they form a wonderful path. Nature wants to communicate with you and your soul opens to receive the wisdom of the universe.

(Short pause)

Slowly you stand up and start walking down the path formed by the beautiful flowers. You can feel the softness of the bushes around you and how comfortable the earth is under your feet. You breathe calmly, delighting in the wonderful smell that envelops the entire place, then exhale. At the end of your tour, you see an incredible lake, it is in total calm and from afar it transmits an amazing serenity. Your feet begin to move in that direction and, as you get closer, you notice there is a bridge for you. You slowly walk across the bridge and take a seat in front of the wonderful paradise.

(Short pause)

You detail every inch of the landscape before you. You feel protected by the trees, your soul begins the connection with nature and its energy begins to be part of you. Today you are becoming aware of the great power you have as a human being and as a creative figure in this universe. You feel grateful, full of hope, peace, love, and tranquility. A slight wind begins to caress you, making you feel that delicious floral aroma that is behind you, relaxing you completely. Now you are aware of the great power of nature and the universe, you remembered your essence and your unity with what surrounds you. Little by little, your body becomes lighter, completely melting into the soft surface that receives it, and finally, you manage to fall asleep. Good night, dear friend.

An Enchanted Path

Welcome, partner, to our meditation session, a beautiful moment of calm and relaxation in which you can clear your mind and connect with the Universe to find the peace you need. From this moment you are closer and closer to reaching a pleasant dream with which you will be filled with life and good energy so that you can happily continue your passage through this world, a world that awaits you with open arms so that you shine and dazzle everyone with your light.

(Middle pause)

Before starting our meditation, I want to invite you to find a quiet place where you can sit on a chair or lie on your bed, feeling comfortable and focusing only on the feeling of relaxation that will come to your body when you stretch it fully, keeping your back straight, relaxing your neck, and releasing all the tensions within you.

(Long pause)

Now is the time to close your eyes and empty your mind of all thoughts. Imagine your spirit as a great bird that enters your head and, with the flapping of its wings, it drives away thoughts to discard them and make them go very far from you. Each time it flies it manages to reach further into your depths, where everything that makes you worried or stressed is found and the strength of its wings is so great that what previously seemed enormous becomes tiny and finally leaves.

(Long pause)

This is a moment of relaxation and peace, a pause from the outside world and all the problems that come with it. With the beautiful journey we will undertake, you will be able to find your North and heal your spirit while I will be in charge of guiding you through a magical place where you can find yourself and recognize the great virtues in you and that need to come out to the light.

(Short pause)

You are light and you are full of love

Your purpose in this life is only to be happy and you will be happy because that is what you are destined for

You transmit peace, love, and cordiality

You are getting rid of everything negative in your life and building a positive attitude towards the world.

You are the key that opens all the doors so that happiness comes to your life.

(Long pause)

The positivity that surrounds you begins to provide you with a state of tranquility that fills you and allows you to observe a sphere of light that moves around you, illuminating the emptiness in which you find yourself. Slowly, the little sphere begins to grow, and with it, the feeling of calm in your heart. Before continuing with this experience, I want you to know that there is no problem if you want to sleep instead of ending our meditation because that is exactly what we are looking for. Simply focus on letting yourself be carried away by what your soul dictates. You see how the light begins to enter your chest and you feel your spirit begins to fly freely, starting your journey.

(Short pause)

You begin to feel you are back on the ground and by inhaling deeply to enjoy the delicious aroma of wet earth, you understand that you are back in control of your body. Slowly you perceive how the exquisite smell spreads through your body, leaving you with an amazing sensation of fullness and purification that you allow yourself to enjoy for a moment when you feel completely abstracted from the world.

(Middle pause)

When you feel satisfied, you begin to observe everything around you and discover that it could not be more fantastic. You are standing right in front of a wonderful path of lights of the most beautiful white color you have seen and they are strategically placed to grant the light to an impressive forest full of endless lines of huge bamboo that reach as far as the eye can see.

(Short pause)

The landscape turns out to be so captivating that you begin to make your way through the lights and you start to feel yourself in the middle of a surprising dream that envelops you and fills you with joy. Your walk is slow because you want to enjoy every inch of the space you are in and with each step you take, you feel in greater contact with nature.

(Middle pause)

The extreme softness of the dirt road makes you feel Mother Nature gives you the balm that heals any wound that may be in your soul and the love you need to love yourself. In addition, the delicate surface takes you as if you were walking on the clouds and that thought makes you look up to see the sky but you are surprised to see that the green leaves of the gigantic bamboos almost completely cover the sky. However, you manage to notice a beautiful starry sky, and together with the beautiful lights, they give the magical illumination of the place.

(Middle pause)

The wind that blows slightly making your hair move in its direction feels different from the one you know as if its air were gently spraying you, completely covering you with tranquility, love, and a feeling of peace that shelters your heart, making you feel a happy and renewed person.

(Middle pause)

After a while, you see how little by little the path of lights begins to narrow, and when you reach the end of it, you come across a beautiful bed made of the same bamboos that have been with you during this fascinating experience. Inside you there is a strong feeling that invites you to lie down on the bed and following your instincts you do it calmly, surprising you with its softness and with the feeling of calm that you find yourself on that delicate surface.

(Short pause)

The huge bamboo lightly collides with each other, generating together with the wind an exquisite whisper with which you begin to feel hypnotized and you let yourself be carried away to end up letting sleep finally reach you, to take you on a delicious journey of tranquility.

(Middle pause)

Sweet dreams, mate.

The Inner Light

Hello, friend, welcome to our meditation session, this moment of calm that will be destined for the encounter of the relaxation you need to feel someone healthy and happy with yourself. Today, through this trip, you will be able to know a new and wonderful world that the Universe has destined for you and it will be in that beautiful place, where you will be able to achieve a pleasant dream that will make you feel full.

(Middle pause)

I want to invite you to find a quiet place where you can feel comfortable and away from the outside world. There you must sit on a chair or lie on your bed, stretching your body, keeping your back straight, and relaxing your neck so that you release all your tensions. In that way, you are prepared for everything you will soon be able to live and above all things so that you can enjoy the sleep that you will finally get.

(Long pause)

It is time to close your eyes slowly, allow yourself to listen to the silence that surrounds my voice, and enjoy the tranquility that exists in the space where you are. Now begin to enter your mind and calmly analyze everything in it, so that you begin to let it go. Remove all your thoughts, problems, concerns, and anything that may disturb you because from this moment, that no longer exists, and only your peace of mind matters.

(Long pause)

Remember, my friend, that this is a moment of relaxation and peace where you give yourself a well-deserved break from all the thoughts that may upset you. In this incredible visit to the fantastic space you will be lucky enough to know, you will be able to find your North and heal your spirit with the help of the Universe that will use your inner beauty to recreate that of the place you will soon arrive, so you can understand the wonderful things that are within you.

(Short pause)

Your soul is open for all good energies to enter and flow freely

Your heart abounds with love, tranquility, and forgiveness for others and even for yourself

All the wonders of life follow you, find you and stay with you to make you someone completely happy

You are someone who attracts all the good that is in the Universe because you deserve it

(Long pause)

You begin to feel how your spirit is freed from everything that connects you with the physical world, to give space to a feeling of joy that shelters your soul as you begin the journey that will take you to the place that has been prepared for you. Before continuing with our experience, I want you to know that there is no problem if you want to sleep instead of finishing this meditation because that is what we hope to achieve and there will always be another moment for you to continue. Slowly you feel that a soft tickle runs through your body and this is how you can know you have reached your destination.

(Middle pause)

When you notice that you are in the place you were hoping to get to, you become aware that you are sitting on a beautiful wooden bench located in the middle of what seems to be nowhere. The only thing you can see near you are some beautiful trees with many branches from which small buds protrude that for some unknown reason, attract your attention.

(Short pause)

The smell of fresh nature that unfolds around the place is delicious and the tranquility that it makes you feel could not be compared to anything other than the wonder itself. The blue sky gives you the most beautiful view when a cloud begins to cover the sun, letting only some of its rays escape from it to give that fascinating touch of gold to the fabulous space full of small leaves that are scattered on the ground, making it look more captivating.

(Middle pause)

The wind brushes your skin in a soft caress that leaves you completely mesmerized as it lifts some leaves from the ground to make them move through space in a delicate natural dance that could not be more fascinating.

(Middle pause)

The soft golden light of the rays of the great star gives the perfect light that harmoniously combines with the tranquility that is breathed in the place where you are. All the beauty generates in your heart a feeling of peace never before experienced, that spreads through your chest filling you with happiness as you inhale the pure air and look up at the sky which, with the contrast of its beautiful blue, and its elegant white clouds, makes you feel grateful to the Universe for allowing you to feel as good as at this moment.

(Middle pause)

At the same moment in which gratitude towards life fills your body, the beautiful buds on the branches of the trees begin to slowly open, revealing a multitude of flowers with beautiful shades from the purest white, a tender pink and even reaching on some occasions, to an intense red that evokes the great love that fills you right now.

(Middle pause)

The change between the landscape is as fleeting as it is wonderful and the feeling that the nature you are in is reflecting the growth that your soul is living, makes you deeply happy and that is exactly what is happening with this peaceful moment. The light within you blooms like the same flowers and begins to come out to illuminate the path of your life and become a being full of joy.

(Long pause)

The happiness you currently feel leads you to enter a trance that doesn't allow you to notice that as if by magic, the bench where you were sitting is gone and that now you find yourself in a huge bed as soft and delicious as the clouds of the sky that you observe as you begin to let yourself be carried away by the floral scent of space and suddenly, your eyes begin to close so that you fall into a deep sleep.

(Middle pause)

Sweet Dreams, friend.

Floating with the Wind

Hello, friend. I welcome you to our meditation session in which you can feel how calm and relaxation takes over you on a fabulous journey full of magic and the tranquility that you have been looking for. In a few minutes, you will experience how your spirit begins to fly freely towards peace and extraordinary things that will allow you to be happy, and achieve deep and pleasant sleep.

(Short pause)

At this moment I want to ask you to find a quiet place where you can sit on a chair or lie on your bed so that you can stretch your body, keep your back straight, relax your neck and free yourself from the tensions inside you. You should be prepared so that serenity fills you completely and, when the moment comes, you can enter that dream you have sought so much.

(Long pause)

It is time to slowly close your eyes and prepare your mind for all that is to come. Let yourself be guided by the darkness you can appreciate within you and enter your mind calmly and with great security, begin to empty all the thoughts that do not allow your soul to find the relaxation you want. Take your time to discard any ideas that may disturb you in this moment of relaxation.

(Middle pause)

I want you to remember that taking this time was a great decision. This is a break that is dedicated to you, to the peace and relaxation you have always wanted to have for your life. Every second of this moment has been created so that you can find your North and heal the wounds of your spirit, those that do not allow you to advance towards the encounter of the peace and happiness you deserve.

(Middle pause)

You are grateful for the life you have and it is that gratitude that attracts all the good vibes of the Universe

You love and value yourself

You want, you can and you deserve to be happy

You are love and there is love in everything around you

You invite good and let it enter your life

You have a great light that illuminates your path and guides you to the right place to be happy

(Long pause)

You begin to feel how a sense of calm begins to spread through your body, letting you enjoy the tranquility you now experience. Suddenly, a light begins to come out of nowhere to approach you. Before continuing with our meditation, I want to clarify that if you want to sleep without having finished our experience, you can do it freely because that is what we are looking for. When the light has reached you, it begins to cover you completely and all you see is a beautiful glow that fills you with peace and slowly takes you to your destination.

(Middle pause)

From one moment to another, the beautiful light that previously covered the space where you were, moves away to give space to the golden rays of the precious sun that adorns the beautiful sky above you. The majesty of the sky before you powerfully awakens the curiosity to observe much more of the place where you are and when you do, you notice you are in a place that could only have been drawn by the wonderful artist that is Mother Nature.

(Short pause)

In front of you, there is a great lake with water so clear that it reflects the clouds above it and so calm that it causes your soul immense peace. The beauty of the space makes you want to get closer to the water. When you start to do it, you notice that you are barefoot. The delicacy of the grains of sun-hot sand that sneak between your toes is simply delicious, so you decide to stop a moment to bury your feet in it and cover them completely to enjoy that feeling of warmth that it generates in you.

(Long pause)

After a few minutes you decide to continue your way to the lake and when you get there your face is perfectly reflected in it, causing you to begin to detail yourself completely. Your hair looks delicate and soft, your skin shines thanks to the beautiful sun while your eyes look so alive as never before because in them the joy of your soul is reflected when experiencing something so sensational. This is how you begin to see yourself for what you are, someone beautiful, full of life and vitality. Someone who deserves to be happy and who has within himself a brightness as beautiful as that of the sun that now shelters you with its rays.

(Middle pause)

The complete security you feel when you are aware of what you are is something surprising and almost imperceptible details are remarkable for you now that you are so calm. That is why you begin to feel how your blood flows through your veins carrying in it a new factor, the tranquility that you have always longed for. As that happens, you fully perceive how that serenity flows from your head, through your arms, down to your legs, and down to your feet, causing you to become as light as a feather and begin to float through the place.

(Middle pause)

The happiness in your heart is infinite and your chest shows it by vibrating with the beats of that organ that reminds you that you are alive. Those exquisite beats within you fill you with joy, which makes you smile as you observe your reflection in the water and then laugh when you realize that now you are like a bird that flies freely, without ties and dislikes, but only carrying an immense joy of living.

(Middle pause)

Slowly, that calm you feel begins to take over even more and you start to feel tired. Your body continues to float in the wind while your eyes begin to close at the moment when you find yourself so enthralled with the experience, you begin to let yourself go and then fall into the warm arms of the dream that now welcomes you.

(Middle pause)

Rest, my friend.

A Magical Place

Welcome, dear friend, this is our meditation session, a moment in which I will go with you and guide you through a beautiful place, where you can experience deeply wonderful things that will allow you to obtain the calm and relaxation you need to feel full and achieve that pleasant dream that you have longed for.

(Short pause)

I want to invite you to find a quiet place away from all the noise and distractions of the outside world, where you can feel comfortable and sit on a chair or lie on your bed so that you keep your back straight, stretch your body, relax your neck and release all the tensions that are inside you.

(Long pause)

Now you must calmly close your eyes, let yourself be carried away by the delicious silence that takes over the space in which you find yourself, filling you with calm. Under that calm, inspect your mind and observe all the thoughts that are in it and then invite them to leave and get away from you, opening all the space within you towards good vibes and happiness.

(Middle pause)

This is a moment of relaxation, a pause in which you seek to fill yourself with peace, as well as find your North and heal your spirit, making it erase all the memories of pain and regrets that may be within you so that they are replaced by the feeling of joy and calm that will fill your soul, making you feel happy to be alive.

(Short pause)

You enjoy your life in the here and now

The love and light that is within you, have the power to heal any wound

The Universe says yes to what you believe and accepts you as one of its best children

You have wonderful things in you waiting to be enjoyed

You have the conviction to be happy and to live your life to the fullest

(Long pause)

The tranquility that exists in you, makes your spirit begin to feel free and that sensation provides you with the strength you need to take the flight that will take you directly to your destination. Before continuing, I want you to know that there is no problem if you want to fall asleep instead of finishing the experience because that is precisely the goal we are looking for and you can always come back at another time to finish it.

Slowly, you feel that you step on the ground. That is the signal you needed to know you are in the place that has been prepared for you.

(Short pause)

By looking at where you are, you notice that everything as far as your eye can see can only be classified as a masterpiece of Mother Nature. Around you, a stone path is surrounded by orange meadows and in the distance, a collection of tiny green mountains seem to emerge from the earth returning to the place where you are, an almost magical space that fills you with great astonishment.

(Middle pause)

As you continue to see everything, the inevitable feeling that you are entering another world is within you. That is why you begin to walk slowly between the mounds surrounded by green bushes loaded with striking flowers with bright colors, which fill the place with a delicious smell of cinnamon that delights your nostrils while you breathe slowly to enjoy that sensation.

(Long pause)

When you admire the bushes, you begin to see a kind of lights or flashes of the most beautiful colors that go from one side to the other floating through the air and moving calmly like small lanterns created by magic and that seek to make this fascinating experience something much more incredible and relaxing for you. Watching those lights slowly give a surprising touch of color to space, it completely envelops you and when they start to climb a nearby hill, something inside you invites you to follow them to have the pleasure of continuing to witness something so pleasant.

(Middle pause)

As you walk behind the colorful lights, you delight with beautiful sheeps that look like pretty clouds on the ground while just like you, they cross the hill looking for some grass. Later, you have the pleasure of spotting some fascinating rabbits that make quick happy jumps when they find themselves enjoying this magical place.

(Short pause)

The lights seem to have reached their destination when you arrive at a place that seems to have come out of the most beautiful dream. In the middle of the road there is a beautiful river with calm waters that slowly descends the hill and over it, a wonderful stone bridge is decorated with some transparent quartz that sticks out of it and makes it look like the most perfect creation. There the lights begin to disappear into the water as if they had taken you through space so that you could enjoy the incredible place that you can now see.

(Middle pause)

The tranquility that a place like that gives you is something that goes beyond what you could ever wish for and your heart beats joyfully as you feel as full as never before. The rhythm of your breathing is becoming smoother due to the relaxation you can feel and how your chest swells every time you allow yourself to inhale the pure air of space that again makes you feel in awe.

(Long pause)

The calm that are now experiencing leads you to cross to the other side of the bridge to find a large place full of small tulips with different colors that invite you to lie on them to find the rest you want so much. When you lean on the flowers, your lungs are flooded with that wonderful smell of honey that only nature could provide you, and it is that aroma that makes you enter into deep hypnosis, that leads you to close your eyes slowly and enjoy it much more. In this way, your body relaxes more and more while you breathe slowly and this is how your consciousness begins to mix with the wind to leave you wrapped in a deep and pleasant sleep.

(Middle pause)

Rest, dear friend.

Exploring the Sea

Hi friend! Welcome back to another adventure. Today I promise you that we will live experiences you have never experienced before. To have a healthy life, have energy, and face new challenges, it is very important to sleep. I know it costs you a bit, but don't worry, you can count on me to compensate for that difficulty. After a tiring day, it is time to relax, breathe calmly, and achieve the peace only you deserve.

(Short pause)

When you do something, you must make sure you live it fully, this is no exception. Search the place in your home, where you feel most comfortable. Preferably where you can lay your back, your neck is free from all the stresses of the day and your feet are straight. You will need to help your imagination and grant it the facilities so that it enters the adventure. Just like that, you are ready for the wonders of today!

(Short pause)

Imagine the sea in all its splendor, leagues full of mysteries, treasures, wonders, and species that you have never imagined before. An intense sun, which reflects the arrival of summer. Heat, sand, and an excellent beach, undoubtedly the best to enjoy a relaxing day. Remember to soften yourself, let go of everything that stresses you, and only let good energies flow.

You are a free person! You have a wonderful fighting spirit; you are always ready to face challenges with a smile.

(Short pause)

You always pursue and achieve your dreams. Despite the difficulties, you struggle to reach each goal. You motivate everyone around you. You are a being of light and you illuminate any situation, no matter how dark it may be. I admire you very much, for your bravery, persistence, but especially for never giving up. I am sure that you will succeed in everything you set out to do!

(Middle pause)

Inhale, exhale, until your breath calms completely, then close your eyes and imagine your ideal vacation, on a great sunny day and a beautiful beach, full of many surprises. Your feet in the warm sand, an umbrella protects you from sun rays and also gives you an excellent view of the landscape. The waves of the sea collide with the shore, demanding that you enter the beach and enjoy the water. It is possible that at some point during the adventure, you feel so tired that you want to go to sleep. Don't worry, dear friend; that is completely normal it is what I am looking for. When you want an adventure, I am here for you!

(Long pause)

Summer arrives and with it, your time to take some time off. What better place than the beach! People are happiest on the beach. When you arrive, you hear only laughter. You see many people enjoying themselves and in the background an immense blue sea, which looks like a painting made by the best artist in the world. Not only are you going to see, but you can also hear how the sea calls you, "Come here, let's enjoy!" It's all you hear. No one can refuse such a wonderful invitation.

The end of the wave covers your feet, with warm and crystalline water, which makes you close your eyes. But no, it is not a dream, that feeling is real. As you enter the sea, you become one with the beautiful beach. You dive in and see the beautiful corals, small fish, and strangely shaped stones. The most unusual thing is that you do not need oxygen, it is as if the sea is giving you the power to explore it, without having to rise to the surface to take a breath.

You are free, you stretch both arms and legs to swim and accept the adventure that the sea offers you. It did not take long and the dolphins begin to surround you, you do not hesitate to caress them and play with them, they are as cute as you always thought. You see fish that you have never seen before, their colors, sizes, and shapes are very varied, so much so that you hardly analyze one and another appears, totally different and wonderful.

Turtles, algae, sea rocks. The marine world captivates you! You never thought to go so deep and see the diversity of that, which humans consider, another world. Right now, that's your world! The limit arrives, you feel that little by little the power that the sea gives you expires. The whales accompany you to the surface and you finally look back at the land. You understand that always carrying everything is not the solution. The sea world is made up of many species and each one contributes something to form that wonderful marine ecosystem.

Thanks to everything that happens, you realize how important it is to take a break from time to time. You overextend yourself and push your body and mind to the limit; however, you are not entirely happy. Rest not only restores but also provides new opportunities to improve. Your experience at sea made you a new person. One that trusts its environment and does its work, but does not overload itself with the full weight of responsibility, since in society everyone must fulfill their activities, such as the marine world.

You only outlined a smile, which is going to be your secret and your tool to help others, but also to help yourself. You return to your umbrella, and the afternoon is ending. The sunset gives a wonderful view, which makes you hallucinate, lie down on the sand, get drunk with the sound of the sea. Put on your glasses, and look like the sun, very slowly it sets on the horizon very slowly.

The next time the sun rises, you will be a more confident person, able to understand that rest is essential for the success of all your pending tasks. Despite spending all day swimming, under great depths, your body is fresher than ever, but it is your mind that is like new. Slowly, and to the rhythm of the sun, your eyes close gently. You think about all your adventures and how pleasant the rest is. Finally, you can let go of all the negative charges and fall asleep.

Eagle Eyes

Hello dear friend! Today I extend my hand to you, together we can make a fantastic journey, through your imagination, that will relax you and lead you to sleep. Breathe deeply and calmly and let peace take over your body and mind. Forget all your barriers at this moment and let yourself go.

(Short pause)

The best way to relax and achieve your peace before sleeping is to take a journey through your imagination. Find the comfort of a place where you like to fall asleep in a calm, deep and relaxed way. I invite you to imagine an environment of dim light, where the spectacular aromas of spring wildflowers enter your body through your slow breathing and make you float into a deep sleep. Inhale, exhale, and lie down with your back straight, in a position where you feel completely comfortable and free of tension.

(Short pause)

While your breathing is slow and calm, your eyelids are closing and becoming heavy. Are you sleepy? Do you want to sleep? It's my mission to make you sleep. Sleep friend. I will wait for you as long as it takes. Relax, empty your mind. Leave only space to imagine that you are flying and that the gentle spring breeze caresses your face and gives an almost divine inner peace that makes you reach your maximum rest. Remember that you are the owner of your feelings and your imagination and that no one can usurp that moment or that dimension.

(Short pause)

In your inner world, everything is balanced and in an orderly manner. You are a fair leader. A being with wonderful feelings where confidence in yourself and your great kindness towards others stand out. You are endowed with great wisdom and immense willpower. Surrender will never be in your plans, on the contrary, winning is your flag! The force is within you. You are capable of solving any situation!

(Middle pause)

You are in your best moment of the day. Your body is as light as a feather. For that reason, you can see everything from above. You are privileged to fly and observe the wonders that spring does when it arrives. Look at the beautiful colors of nature, breathe fresh air, and feel with your senses the different textures and greens of the mountains and meadows. The hum of the wind reaching your ears is like the music of a great symphony orchestra. Allow all this wonder to lead you to the ecstasy of total relaxation and you can heal your spirit.

(Long pause)

Since you are already relaxed and at peace, allow yourself to imagine that you are a great eagle. Its eyes and ears will now be yours; its wings will be your outstretched arms. You will be the guide; the flight itinerary is yours. Surrender to adventure, enjoy the climate, the colors, the breeze, the aromas, and the natural landscapes. Touring from the sky, the wonderful natural landscapes is a sublime fact that will elevate your relaxation, your calm, your tranquility, your rest, your peace and everything will take you to sleep soundly.

Standing on the flake of a large tree, look carefully around you and see how spring takes all of nature and makes it shine before your eyes. Standing almost on top of the world, feel the warm breeze caress your face. Watch as the green leaves of the trees begin their new cycle. The large trees and shrubs move their spikes, from one side to the other, warning the rest of the living beings that spring has begun and that all the green and multicolored beauty of the forest will be restored.

From the top, you can watch the animals come out of their burrows with their new young. You feel full and happy seeing how animals form their families and protect them until nature itself tells them to. You may be sleepy. Let the smell of the fresh forest flood your senses. Take a deep breath. This air is very pure and comforting. Everything is beautiful. You feel free and happily relaxed! You begin to understand the days ahead will bring new expectations and rewarding moments in the life of every living being.

You decide to take your flight and start exploring the most intrinsic natural beauties of the mountains, to the beat of a slow but detailed flight. You realize that you are already flying over the majestic blue river, where you can see through its crystalline and pristine waters the wide range of colorful fish that aimlessly prowl every corner of the immense river. You look closely as the wind creates tiny circles on the surface of the water, which from your height look like a classical ballet show.

Your flight is very smooth. You are enjoying it a lot. You feel in your arms the continuous currents of warm air that run throughout your body and allow you to recharge your batteries and move on, awakening your explorer spirit in you. You take a gentle walk through the meadows where you see a large number of living species and endless colors from the flowers, shrubs, and grasses that feed the animals. The silence is only broken by the harmonious chirping of the birds that take you to a magical relaxation, where you can close your eyes and rest knowing that each cycle has a hopeful purpose that balances nature and each living being.

All you look at is flourishing life, which makes you passionate and fills you with optimism. It relaxes you to know that life is full of details and unique moments, where you can change the perspective for your own and common benefit. Seeing and feeling through the eyes of the eagle, all that natural beauty, in perfect harmony, living together without distinction of races, gives you the feeling of security, happiness, and confidence. That relaxes you, calms you down, and makes you sleep deeply.

A Trip to Pluto

Welcome my friend! As always I am happy to have your company. Today we have a very special meeting, I will take your imagination very far from this planet. Remember to have your mind and body at rest. You and I will make a great team and we will make you fall asleep. Take your time, breathe in and out calmly, many times. Repeat this process until you are totally calm.

(Short pause)

Comfort is essential to get into today's adventure. Make sure to find a place to rest your body, a sofa, your bed, or your favorite chair. Preferably where your body is completely stretched and free of tension. After a tiring day, you deserve the best of deals, so I'll make sure of it.

(Short pause)

Inhale. Hold your breath for a few seconds and release it, close your eyes and imagine the incredible things that can exist in the far reaches of the galaxy. Planets of all kinds, but especially one, Pluto, where the snow falls permanently. Remember that if you feel tired and want to sleep, you must. My job is to help you with that and nothing makes me happier than seeing you rest.

(Short pause)

There is no one like you. You can bring joy to others, endure difficult moments and overcome them with flying colors. You have support from your loved ones and they are proud of you. Your dreams will come true, never doubt it, just work hard and help others. Remember, there is no one like you, you are a unique being.

(Middle pause)

Keep your eyes closed, feel how your body can rise to leave planet Earth. You can walk in space, the planets look wonderful, when you walk on the moon, you feel like you are walking on cotton rugs. It is an incredible feeling! Without a doubt, your experience should not stop there. Your objective is that planet called Pluto. Do you feel sleepy? Then go rest, remember, your dream is non-negotiable. Pluto will always be there; we will visit it anytime you want.

(Long pause)

Stars, spaceships, the moon, and many planets are on your horizon. It is difficult to decide where to start, but among everything, there is a small planet that shines with its own light, one that undoubtedly catches your attention. Pluto attracts you visually, it is the one chosen for your adventure, that's why you approach and observe its great glaciers that surround the whole place. It is a very cold environment, however, the planet seemed to wait for you.

In that cabin you see, there is the correct cloth for low temperatures, so change yourself. Now is the time to explore! Your first steps on Pluto are very delicate since the floor is frozen. Observe in the distance; that polar bear is three times the size of bears on Earth. This one is harmless. It is playing with its young; it looks at you with tenderness. You feel calm, relaxed, calm, at home. You are also curious about that animal species, so you cheer up and go to meet it. A baby licks your face and lies down on your body; its fur is soft. You hug it. It's like hugging a stuffed animal!

The company is nice, but you want to see more. You go a little further and look at large constructions made of ice. Buildings, houses, parks, even vehicles are made of ice. Although many people always said that life did not exist on other planets, you can see with your eyes that all those people are wrong. Everyone on Pluto helps each other, smiles, and is in a good mood. They are also very welcoming and they like your visit.

The inhabitants share with you a delicious hot chocolate, while they tell you their wonderful stories. They also promise to teach you something fascinating. You can't miss the opportunity to make figures with the snow that constantly fell. You make snowmen, angels, and even a small castle. You learn quickly how to shape snow! Taking advantage of your

373

company, all the people, assemble their snowballs and begin to play. You have never witnessed anything like this: everyone leaves their occupations and plays with you. It is the coldest planet, but with the warmest and most wonderful people of all.

Pluto begins to get dark, the days last longer, but coincidentally, you have arrived at the right time. You walk to the big fire. Everyone surrounds you and points out that the surprise is right above you, in the sky. The beautiful northern lights illuminate everything. There are no words to describe its beauty and perfection! You look with great pleasure and amazement. You close your eyes and feel like one of them envelops you and gives you a light walk through the beautifully lit sky.

It is just at that moment when you realize how important the union of family and friends is. When you step on Pluto, you do not feel cold, because of the warmth of the people who live there; you feel covered and protected at all times. In front of your eyes, you have the most beautiful auroras in the galaxy. However, for you, the love that everyone has for each other is much more spectacular. You decide to emulate this in every aspect of your life! Getting closer to your family, protecting your friends, and helping the stranger. Without a doubt, the visit helped you realize that union is everything.

At the end of the day, you say goodbye to everyone. Time to go home. Planet Earth and its inhabitants already miss you. Fly back to Earth and immerse yourself, as if you were a whale in the water, but in your comfortable room, in your warm bed, which is something you long for from the moment you reached the low temperatures. Take a little moment to analyze how beautiful the trip to Pluto has been and close your eyes. Feel like your body enters a total state of relaxation and finally sleeps peacefully and comfortably.

Attached to Nature

Hello, dear friend, I am glad to have you with me again. On this occasion, you will live a new adventure, full of emotions and smiles. I know that sleep is one of the fundamental pillars to live better, which is why I have come to help you. You just have to relax, breathe calmly and release all those burdens that prevent you from moving forward. Get ready, this is your time of the day!

(Short pause)

There is only one way for you to live this experience to the fullest, and the most important thing is that it is very simple. Find the most comfortable place in your home, such as a king's throne or a bear's den. Just think of a sacred place for you! After choosing it, you must connect with your desire to feel free, inhale, exhale, and lie down with your back straight, in a position where you feel comfortable and free of tension.

(Short pause)

Close your eyes, think about how wonderful nature is, how pure, clean, perfect, and impressive. Leaves falling in autumn, one by one, slowly and the animals playing happily around the trees. Your relaxation is very important. Feel how tranquility and peace take over your body. Your spirit is a flowing waterfall that everyone is shocked when looking at its beauty.

(Short pause)

You are a wonderful person, you have many positive qualities, which make you stand out in your environment. Despite facing difficulties, you know how to fight them without ever giving up. I'm proud of you! A being of light, like you, is not seen every day, so value what you have and never let anyone tell you that you can't pursue and achieve your dreams.

(Middle pause)

Concentrate and feel like you can take small steps through the soft grass of the forest. Birds sing, bees collect nectar and pollen from flowers, trees begin to bear their first fruits, and the sun smiles. Seeing how splendid nature is, you are capable of being part of it, you only have to connect with the feeling of everything that surrounds you, since, believe it or not, and even the earth has its feelings and criteria. Do not worry if at some point you are sleepy. Remember that this is the purpose. You can go to rest and here I will be waiting for you when you need me.

(Long pause)

Your walk through the forest is very relaxing, a straight line, and full of trees, flowers, and little squirrels running from one place to another. A relaxing sound attracts you; you can close your eyes and allow your instincts to guide you to its origin. Fluidity, serenity, there is no doubt, it is a river. You can sit on the little dock and dip your feet in that warm water. The tiredness disappears, little by little. The fish are constantly jumping, just to look at you and come closer and closer, as if your good energy is attracting them.

It's time to get up. Because although it is very peaceful and causes you to stay longer there, you still have to visit some places. Not far away, some songs catch your attention. A priori, they looked like angels from heaven. It is an excellent, harmonious melody, in perfect rhythm and tone of voice. Your curiosity allows you to discover that it is not about angels, but about nature itself, which represents a mirror of everything we dream of.

The birds fly from one tree to another, going through all the nests and singing in perfect harmony. It is impossible not to enjoy something like that. Appreciate how the feeling of tranquility and calm run through all your senses. You lean against a tree, you watch in delight, like when you enjoy a concert. You are witnessing one! But this one is special, only suitable for you. The birds end their song, but clapping is not necessary, your smile is the greatest gratitude they can receive.

From that same tree, where you lay down, an apple falls. Just a few inches from your hands, as if nature wants you to taste it. Such an offer is irrefutable; therefore you test the fruits of mother earth. It's like biting into a piece of sweet heaven! With each bite, the taste improves. Fruits are undoubtedly created by the Gods. While in your hands, you carry a couple of apples, your adventure continues, touring the wonders of the forest.

You can't leave without seeing the variety of plants. Sunflowers, stand out among all, their intense yellow color, which shines as much as the sun, and when you feel its texture, you can only caress it, just as you do with your pet. It is the same feeling of admiration! To your left, are tulips and to your right, orchids, without a doubt, that is paradise! Inhale the sweet aroma of the environment and realize that despite the problems of the day, there is always something beautiful to value. Something that maybe every day you overlook, but when you focus and connect with it, you can have new feelings, which you never imagined before. Nature is the connection with all human beings, so every time you need it, it will never fail you, there you will find answers.

The river did not become perfect overnight, the birds did not always live there, the trees, at some point did not bear fruit and the plants did not find their place to flourish. However, the effort and perseverance of each one, led them to never give up, until they obtained a simply perfect nature.

You should also do it too. Never give up! Follow your dreams and get up from your stumbling blocks. You will be fluid like the river, harmonious like the birds, resistant like the trees, and wonderful like the plants. Your journey was going to end, but only this once, since the forest is always open to you. You lie down on the grass, to watch and count the stars. Slowly, you begin to feel sleepy, your body relaxes, your eyes close, and you fall into a deep sleep.

The Road and the Trails

Welcome friend. It is nice to know that today you have given yourself a little time. You are worthy of well-being and health, so everything you do to achieve it is worth it. This opportunity that you give yourself seeks that you achieve calm, relaxation, and a night of pleasant sleep. Therefore, I invite you to find a quiet place in your home where you can carry out this activity with the required privacy. Lie on your bed, with your back straight, your head resting on a soft pillow, but one that keeps your neck relaxed. It is important to stretch your body and be free from any type of tension or worry, I wish you success.

(Short pause)

Take a deep breath and close your eyes. You inhale, filling your lungs with renewing energy, and then slowly, you exhale. Check your thoughts and your emotions. If you feel like something is bothering you, hand it over to the universe. Feel the new energies that run through your body to bring you peace, tranquility, and stillness.

(Short pause)

It is important to remind yourself that you are a unique being, your experiences and what you have learned from them have determined who you are today. You are capable of achieving everything you set your mind to, valuing each step you take, and understanding that life is not only about achievements, but also efforts, perseverance, and gratitude. You have to be aware of that.

You achieve everything you set your mind to

Your optimistic attitude helps you overcome any obstacle

Within you are the tools to overcome any difficulties

You are a being of light capable of renewing and change what may be affecting you.

(Long pause)

At this time, get ready to start a great adventure with me. If at this time you don't want to continue because you are sleepy, there is no problem if you wish to rest, another day you'll continue. Do not forget that this is the goal of this experience.

(Short pause)

Little by little, you feel like you become light and the wind begins to lift you. You feel a soft and cold breeze. When you open your eyes you find yourself on a long road, you can hardly look at the end. There, on the horizon, you only see the sky. It feels good to be in that place. You notice that the road is full of snow and beautiful flowers have grown on the sides. You see some tall and very green pines on the way and you enjoy the smell of it. All that place is impregnated with that aroma, which relaxes you and makes you experience a feeling of calm and peace.

You notice that on one side of the road there is a narrow path and you decide to explore it a bit. At that moment, snow begins to fall and you look in the distance at a very beautiful and colorful cabin, from which smoke comes out of the chimney. You realize that even though you are protected from the cold, you have started to shiver, so you decide to go there.

As you get closer, you notice that a very graceful lady welcomes you and invites you to come by. Also, she tells you that she was waiting for you. You feel a lot of emotion, she welcomes you with a soft hug that smelled of cinnamon and vanilla. Upon entering you realize that the cabin is very cozy. You love the rocking chairs and cushions that adorn the beautiful place. The lady introduces herself as Aunt Dolly and invites you to sit by the fireplace. She offers you a beautiful rocking chair with very soft cushions. She goes to the kitchen and brings two cups of hot chocolate and cinnamon-vanilla cookies with her.

You lie down and enjoy the comfort of the place where you are sitting. Then you look out the window and realize that there is a big storm. You are grateful that you are there with Aunt Dolly. You taste the chocolate and the crunchy cookies. Aunt Dolly is very kind and begins to tell you about the natural beauties that exist in that place. She tells you that she and her husband live there with their children and grandchildren. Also, she takes out a photo album and shows you her family. Being there you feel protected.

After a while, you watch an older man enter the cabin, and with a hoarse voice, he says hello politely. He introduces you as Uncle Charlie, when he sees his wife, he takes her by the waist and gives her a strong and warm hug. You watch as they laugh happily and he tells his love that he wants to throw a party in her honor to celebrate her birthday. The excited Aunt Dolly gives him a soft hug. At that moment, the couple's children arrive and the father tells them about the celebration. Then everyone happily starts the preparations.

Both Uncle Charlie and his children leave the cabin, and Aunt Dolly invites you to the little share to celebrate her birthday. You stay seated in your nice rocking chair. From there, you watch the wood burn, and that fills you with a lot of energy. You feel in your interior tranquility, peace, harmony, and happiness. At that moment, the youngest grandchildren enter the house and approach their grandmother, who is resting in a beautiful and comfortable rocking chair. They hug her, kiss her and pamper her. In addition, they bring her gifts made by themselves: a necklace of pebbles, a wreath, a bouquet of pretty roses, and some desserts. They also come up to you and bring you cinnamon rolls.

You all sit at the huge table in the center of the cabin. You toast, make jokes, and tell stories. Everyone is happy, the feast starts with a delicious hot soup, then they serve you meat, salad, potatoes, and fruit. And at last, a cake with apple and almond syrup, which makes everyone happy.

One by one, all the attendees go to their rooms and since the storm keeps going, you decide to stay in the cabin with Aunt Dolly. You sit back in the rocking chair and there you begin to reflect on everything you've experienced. You see that sometimes the little shortcuts in life are opportunities that save you from a storm. You understand that the most beautiful thing that exists is to be hospitable, detached, and kind. You value your family today more than yesterday because, in this experience, you have felt the importance of it for human beings. Good night.

The Ruins of a Living City

Greetings friend. I applaud this opportunity that you have given yourself to participate in this relaxation experience, which will help you find calm and pleasant sleep. This decision to dedicate time to yourself and to give yourself a moment to enjoy is necessary to strengthen you and fill you with new energy, to move forward with new expectations and encouragement.

(Short pause)

I invited you to pay attention to the instructions that I am going to give you. You must be in a comfortable and quiet space. Get into your bed and lie down in a comfortable position, make sure your back is straight. Extend your body and relax your neck. Seek to be free of tension. It is necessary that during this activity you do not have interruptions. This will allow you to concentrate better and enjoy the experience.

(Short pause)

Close your eyes, and become aware of your emotions and thoughts. Release those that prevent you from concentrating, those that distract you. Surrender all concerns to the universe and ask for new energies that allow you to flow in harmony. Free from these thoughts, breathe deeply and thank the universe for being in the here and now, open to learning, willing to relax and find the rest you so deserve.

(Short pause)

You need to become aware of how valuable you are. Feel you are worthy of all the good that the universe has for you. Be ready to receive wisdom, health, prosperity, peace, harmony, love, friendship, and well-being. You must always remember that.

You're a wonderful human being able to love others

Able to love yourself

That is why you deserve health, well-being, peace, and a good life

(Long pause)

Now, I invite you to start this journey with me; immerse yourself in the depth of your imagination. If you feel like sleeping, no problem, you can. Remember that this is the end that you can rest and relax. From your heart, you decide to commit yourself to a wonderful adventure where you aspire to feel happy and have experiences that fill you with wisdom.

You allow your imagination to fly and little by little you realize that you are walking with a group of people of different ages. You see children, youth, and adults. Feel a cold but tolerable climate. You are warm and protected. Looking to the front and the sides, you see that you are in an amazing place. To the sides there is a variety of trees, standing out the pines. In addition, nature there is wonderful; the wildflowers adorn the places, making the walk picturesque. Upon reaching a peak on the route, the guide indicates that these are the ruins of a very ancient city. That this place is considered rich in culture and teachings. He invites everyone to be silent and indicates that everyone should enter there barefoot, that this is a tradition and that is required by the person in charge of taking care of that sacred place.

When you arrive at the place you realize the architecture with which that city was built is impressive and enigmatic. It was built on a mountain on large, solid blocks of stone that were perfectly hand-carved and sculpted. This attracts your attention and that of the other tourists. You are surprised that despite the age of these works they are still intact. In some cases, what is observed is that due to the humidity some small plants have grown in the place.

You can observe some monuments. The central figures of these, are animals such as dogs, bulls, lions, rhinos, and elephants. You also catch the presence of some temples, houses, and community meeting places. You separate yourself a bit from the group and enter one of the old houses. There you see that everything is made of stone: the dining room, the furniture even the bases of the beds. Despite the time, the houses maintain a sense of family unity. At that moment you remind yourself that you are barefoot.

Your feet during the tour have not felt discomfort, rather they make you enjoy the place more. The stones on which the city was built are cool and even a little cold. You perceive as if through your feet you receive energy that nourishes your being. Then you go to a beautiful temple, which has no seats. That is the only place which has some elements that indicate that there, people attend some activities. In the background, there is a very beautiful lighted lamp. The center floor is made of wood. You think that place is a beauty. You walk around that floor barefoot and you realize that it is something wonderful.

That place is considered by you as a place of peace. You decide to sit in the middle of the temple and from there observe the architectural perfection of the place. You thank the universe for being there. You feel the freshness and spaciousness of the site. Then you walk to more crowded places and see museums, markets, areas where perhaps they gave training to the younger generations. At that moment, you hear that everyone must prepare to return because it was already getting dark. You realize the vastness of the place because you could barely see a few areas. Some tourists were in tents on the outskirts because they came not only with an interest to know but also as researchers or they also wanted more time to see the whole city.

On the way back, you listened to the experiences of the group. You reflect on everything seen and felt and you think at that moment, that the most beautiful thing this society left to humanity were its teachings, great respect for nature, a solid foundation in its city, a balanced coexistence with nature, the respect for animals, a family organization that is reflected in their homes, beliefs in a supreme being, spiritual practices, museums so that their way or philosophy of life is understood. You noticed that even though the place was known as the ruins, that city remained alive, transmitting values and sensible ways of living. You realize that now you are in your bed, that the dream is flooding you. Good night.

A Pink Dolphin in My Life

Welcome friend. It is nice to know that today you decided to give yourself some time to relax. Through guided meditation and with the start-up of your imagination we will live an adventure that will bring you calm, well-being, peace, and harmony. Important conditions that will help you to have a good rest and to achieve a pleasant sleep.

(Short pause)

I invite you to find a quiet place, where you have comfort and privacy. Lie down on your bed. Try that your head is resting on a soft pillow. Extend your body and keep your back straight. Your neck should be relaxed and you shouldn't feel any tension. Arrange that place with care so that you feel in a special space, where you will live this beautiful adventure which will help you to rest.

(Short pause)

Close your eyes and begin to breathe gently. Inhale and then exhale. Empty your mind of all those thoughts that worry you and do not allow you to concentrate. If you have any feelings that anguish you, release them and give them to the universe so that it can transform it.

(Short pause)

You perceive that your body is light and that the healing energies run through all the veins and cells. In this tune, you enjoy how your soul rises and feels free. Energies flow through your body that brings you peace, tranquility, and harmony.

You are a being of love

You deserve to be cared for and loved by yourself

Your strengths are within you

You must believe in yourself and always act with common sense

You are a being with a healing capacity

(Long pause)

You have reached a very important moment in this adventure. Together we will travel to a wonderful place, where you will have the opportunity to reflect, relax and learn. If when you arrive here, you feel that you are sleepy and do not want to continue, there is no problem, go rest. Remember that the main purpose of this activity is that you achieve rest and pleasant sleep.

(Short pause)

From your imagination, you move to a very beautiful place, close to the shores of a bay. You go up to the top of a cliff and there a huge tree that offers a lot of shade awaits you. You see some boats sailing on the horizon. You appreciate the calm of the sea and the rhythm of each ship, which makes you feel calm. From there, you also catch the variety of birds that soar through the skies. Then you sit under the tree, at its roots, and lean your back on the trunk. You look optimistically at the sky and seeing it so beautiful, you feel that that day will be wonderful.

You get up with courage, carefully descend towards the shore of the bay. You walk through the wet sand. You enjoy how the small waves reach you and wet your feet. You feel the warm water on the soles of your feet. You feel like diving in and enjoying a nice bath and so you do. Little by little you are submerging your body in the sea. You gently sink your head several times. When the water reaches your shoulders, you stay still looking at the horizon, feeling that beautiful energy that the water transmits to you. Think that the tranquility and calm that you feel are indescribable. You start swimming and floating, which makes you feel relaxed, calm, and grateful to the universe, for the gift of life and for so much beauty concentrated in that place.

While there, you observe that a small boat is approaching and you realize it is Teddy, an old friend. He greets you and invites you for a walk. You gladly accept and get on the boat. He tells you it is time to go see the dolphins, that at that time of year they appear in families and cross this place. You with great emotion tell Teddy you are very excited and thank him for inviting you. At that moment, you see that several boats are also sailing towards the same destination. Therefore, you sit in front of the boat to be attentive to the show you will see.

You watch as several boats stop rowing and everything is silent. You can't perceive how many people are in the boats. Each of them, despite being in the same place, is distant from the other. After a while, you begin to hear the typical sound of dolphins. Also, you hear the voices of children who say the dolphins are friendly. At that moment you see that a dolphin appears at the ship where you are and greets you by shaking its head. You realize that it is a pink dolphin. It lets you touch its head and you vibrate with joy. When laughing, the dolphin also laughs with you and its typical sound becomes louder. Teddy gives you some fish to share with the dolphin that chose you.

When you look around, there were hundreds of dolphins. However, yours was different. From the beginning, you felt a special connection with him. He allows you to caress him with your hands and he also looks for your head to bring it closer to his. You have never felt anything like this before. After a while of enjoying his company, he with his fin, says goodbye, but not before touching your face with his face. You hug it and your friend is surprised by what you were experiencing.

At that moment, you come back to reality and you realize that each boat carried several people. Including children, grandparents, and entire families. That show happened once a year. Many children took photos with the dolphins. You felt everyone's joy and you internally felt that you had received and given a lot of love in a very short time. That experience had filled your soul with infinite peace. Your heart is happy and in your mind, there is only a memory of what you saw, felt, and perceived of that dolphin friend who chose you.

At that moment, Teddy interrupts to tell you that all of the boats are applauding you because this year you were chosen by the pink dolphin. Tradition says that this dolphin reaches out to those who need it to give him wisdom, faith, and hope in life. You, surprised and excited, tell him from your heart: "thank you, dolphin friend, this is how my life will be from now on, it will be loaded with what you have left me." You greeted everyone and everyone wished you many congratulations. You watch, as all the boats together return and reach the shore. You hear that everyone tells their experiences from their perspective. You only remember with great gratitude the connection and love between you and the pink dolphin. Good night.

Reflecting on what happened, you realized the respect and kindness that this dolphin showed you. This inspired confidence in you and you also gave yourself to give and receive love. This is the case in relationships, so we must be sincere and respectful. You feel happy about the experience.

Flashes of Peace

Hello, friend, welcome to this wonderful moment of calm that has been created especially for you and that will be full of relaxation so that you can enjoy the peace and tranquility that you deserve. From this moment in which you will allow yourself to enjoy a beautiful trip, you will be able to feel deeply serene and later, you will achieve that pleasant dream that you have longed for so much.

(Short pause)

Before starting, I invite you to find a quiet and peaceful place where you can sit on a comfortable chair or lie on your bed so that you can stretch your body, relax your neck and keep your back straight, managing to release all kinds of physical tension.

(Long pause)

At this moment, it is time to close your eyes and take this opportunity to empty your mind of all those thoughts that may be currently disturbing you. Remove all negative ideas from your head and release all those chains that do not allow you to be free and happy because that way you can be completely prepared for the experience that you will soon live.

(Long pause)

Let me remind you that this is a peaceful and relaxing moment, created so that you can enjoy a pause in which you will have the opportunity to feel calm again, thus healing your spirit and freeing you of all earthly discomforts to be in a place where nothing matters more than being happy and feeling complete with yourself.

(Long pause)

You are in total harmony with the Universe and with the beauty that is within you.

You are someone positive and optimistic about your future.

Wonderful doors open in your life allowing you to continue creating the happiness you long for.

You are grateful for your life and for the ability you have to continue breathing one more day.

You are the well-being and everything constructive that you could wish for.

(Long pause)

Slowly you begin to experience a serenity that makes you feel free and you begin to observe a small light that gets increasingly bigger. I want you to know that there is no problem if you want to sleep before finishing this experience because that is just what we want and you can come back whenever you want. The light becomes so great that it begins to cover you completely until everything you see is so white and pure that you cannot distinguish anything beyond it, and when you feel your body touching the ground, you understand that you have reached your destination.

(Middle pause)

When you arrive at the place that awaited you, a delicious wind welcomes you moving your hair and giving you the exquisite scent of the sea breeze, so you decide to inhale slowly, letting the air enter through your nostrils, passing through your chest swelling with joy and reaching your lungs to fill them completely with that purity that it transmits to you.

(Short pause)

Your breathing is so calm and peaceful that it combines perfectly with the environment that surrounds you. Then you begin to observe everything that is near you to end up taking a fascinating surprise; in front of you there is a huge beach with beautiful waves that go and they come it slowly, bringing great beauty with their water. Above your head, an impressive starry sky gives the deserved prominence to the majestic full moon that gives the landscape the perfect touch to make you believe that you are located in a painting made by the best artist.

(Short pause)

Sheltered by the beautiful light that the sky gives you, you walk a little to wet your hands with the water from the beach and, when you touch it, it feels so warm and exquisite that you start to spray your face with small drops that refresh you and make you laugh.

(Middle pause)

While you delight in the sight you have, a radiant light begins to appear, bathing the beach in front of your eyes in a surprising turquoise blue that with its reflections illuminates the water like the stars in the sky and leaves wonderful traces on the sand luminous that would dazzle anyone.

(Middle pause)

After a while, you begin to see how the flashes of light shine like diamonds on the sand and completely cover the water, making this enchanted scenery appear to be drawn in shades of silver, green and bluish, among which the bright orange stands out of some crabs that walk calmly, enjoying the beach just like you.

(Middle pause)

Happiness fills you completely when you are in a place as unique and pleasant as this where it seems the starry sky has joined the peaceful sea to give you that fascinating experience, and each shine that the water leaves on the sand looks as if it invites you to walk much more through it.

(Short pause)

With each small step you take, the delicious sand refreshes your body and provides you with a great peace that rises from your toes to your head, while your sight becomes more and more beautiful as you increase your reach to observe that the lights effectively surround the entire space, illuminating every place your gaze can reach.

(Long pause)

Slowly, the night begins to darken everything a little more and the only thing you can observe are some of the few sparkles that are still in the sand adorning everything around you that looks as if it were a play made to impress and bring out all the peace that is inside you and that begins to come out to turn you into a totally happy being.

(Middle pause)

After a while, you decide to lie down on the sand to enjoy it. As you do so, you notice that the warmth with which it embraces you is delicious, that the sound of the sea becomes increasingly fainter, and that slowly it becomes a small whisper that you feel traveling directly to your ears, relaxing you completely. That is how you begin to lose yourself in the immensity of the sea, letting yourself fall peacefully into a deep and pleasant sleep.

Let Go

Hello, partner, I want to welcome you to this new meditation session in which we can both live an exciting experience. Today you will have the beautiful opportunity to experience wonderful things that will fill you with the best energies and will cover you with a great feeling of calm and relaxation that will allow you to finally achieve deep and pleasant sleep.

(Short pause)

I want to invite you to find a quiet place where you can feel at peace and enjoy the silence, there you should sit on a couch or lie on your bed. When you get that space, you must stretch your body, relax your neck and keep your back straight so that you release all the physical tensions in your body.

(Long pause)

Now that you are ready to move forward, you should close your eyes to enter your mind and empty it of all thoughts that are within it. Check every corner of your head and free it from all the negative energies that used to be in it before so that you can receive with the doors open to all the positive vibes that will soon reach you.

(Long pause)

I want to remind you that this is a good pause, a moment of relaxation and peace where we seek to find your North and heal your spirit, all this with the help of the universe that has planned this wonderful experience with the idea of making you understand all that you are worth. and what you are capable of achieving. Starting today, my friend, you will be someone who loves yourself and who loves to live life.

(Middle pause)

You are a healthy and happy person.

You are open to receiving all the good that the world has to give you.

You are the creator of your own destiny and knowing that makes you a powerful being.

You are willing to live with the commitment to enjoy every second of your life.

Your world flows around the happiness and abundance you desire.

(Long pause)

From one moment to the next, the darkness that was previously in your mind is replaced by a beautifully warm, and incredibly white light that powerfully draws your attention, so you decide to get closer to its focus. I want you to know that there is no problem if you want to sleep instead of ending the experience because that is the goal we are looking for. Upon reaching the center of that wonderful light, you feel how peace enters you and thus begins your journey.

(Short pause)

After a moment, you see yourself on top of a great mountain, a beautiful place full of grass and flowers with magnificent colors, something almost out of a storybook. The sky above you is as blue as in a painting and the sun is as bright but also as warm as you have never felt before, even the blowing wind feels completely clean as if being so close to the sky you get the purest air that the universe could offer you, which generates in you the greatest feeling of happiness.

(Long pause)

Slowly you start to get out of the charm and when you start to see much more than what you have in front of you, you see a large zip line hanging as if waiting for you. At this point, fear no longer exists in you and the only thing that really is in your heart is a great feeling of joy that leads you to put on the harness to enjoy that new experience.

(Short pause)

By having the harness, you take a small breath of air and let yourself be carried away by the wind that takes you slowly. The breeze brushes your face making you smile for what you are allowing yourself to live and when you finally decide to look down, you see something fascinating; there are large crowns of green trees that have hundreds of branches and can even be seen in them some bird nests that have made them their home.

(Short pause)

As you continue observing, you see a great place where green is replaced by the wonderful and vivid colors of millions of flowers that cover the ground with their impressive beauty and fill the space with their scent that completely intoxicates you and makes you enjoy their exquisite smell of cinnamon and honey.

(Short pause)

The rope that takes you from one side to the other seems to have no end and the truth is that you do not want it to end because the smooth movement of your harness totally relaxes you while it takes you to see lovely landscapes, such as that of a great river that goes down delicately through the mountain carrying beautiful crystalline water with which a group of birds cools off to continue their way through the wonderful sky that you now feel so close to you.

(Middle pause)

The air continues to move your hair and a smile is reflected on your face to reveal the enormous happiness you feel inside you. The leaves of the trees sway with the wind creating an attractive sound, some birds sing in the distance as if they wanted to set your trip and your heartbeat seems to follow their harmony to make this a much more surprising experience. Definitely, the peace that runs through your body is immense and the tranquility that is in you could not be greater. Feeling as light as a feather, you decide to close your eyes for a moment to enjoy how the wind guides you through space.

(Long pause)

When you realize it, you see that you are on the next mountain that welcomes you with the singing of some birds that, close to you, seem to welcome you. Relaxed by their song, you decide to lie on the soft grass to listen to them. As you lie down, the sweet harmony of the birds leads you to close your eyes and this is how slowly you let yourself be carried away by the wind again, this time to fall into the deep and pleasant sleep that now welcomes you.

(Short pause)

Rest, mate.

The Perfect Combination

Welcome, dear friend, to our meditation session, a moment in which we will both embark on a journey full of calm in which you can relax and fill yourself with all the tranquility you deserve. Today you can experience something wonderful that will lead you to discover beautiful things so that you finally find the peace you need to enter a pleasant dream.

(Middle pause)

At this moment I want to invite you to find a quiet place away from all the outside noises so that you can sit on a chair or lie down on your bed and enjoy the silence by stretching your body, keeping your back straight, and relaxing your neck to free yourself from that way, all the physical tensions within you.

(Long pause)

Now I want to ask you to close your eyes quietly; let yourself be guided by the tranquility that begins to slowly enter you so that you can then empty your mind of all the thoughts that are in it and that do not allow you to be someone completely happy. Do this calmly, it is understandable that some ideas struggle to stay but only you have the power over them and that is why, after you invite them to leave, they will do so and you will start to feel better.

(Long pause)

This is a moment of relaxation and peace where serenity will take control of your body and your mind so that you can travel calmly towards the encounter of your inner peace. This will be a pause that will help you find your North and heal your spirit, becoming one with the universe and thus becoming someone complete and totally whole.

(Middle pause)

You are life, happiness, and love.

You are someone strong and capable of achieving anything.

Your thoughts are full of joy and prosperity. That is what will be reflected in your life.

You deserve every one of the things that the universe has granted you so far and those that will soon come to you.

You are an unstoppable light that carries good energies wherever you go.

(Long pause)

Little by little, you feel how tranquility expands through your body, leaving you feeling full and pleased with what you are living. The happiness that comes from knowing that this experience will fill you with peace leads you to fully immerse yourself in that feeling and that is how your journey begins. I want you to know that there is no problem if you decide to sleep before finishing our experience, remember that this is what we are looking for and that you will soon be able to return. Now that you let yourself be carried away by peace, everything around you is covered in a beautiful light that lets you know that you have reached your destination.

(Middle pause)

Looking at everything before you, you can see that two beautiful landscapes have met to make this experience something fascinating: Towards the right side is the path to a beautiful beach as blue as the sky and when looking to the left, the beauty is complete with a wonderful field full of so many flowers that it seems like a dream because although some are large and others small, they are all so brightly colored that they would surprise anyone who saw them. And in front of you, a gorgeous bicycle on a small road that separates the two spaces and that seems to be there for you to cross it. You decide to take that great opportunity and get on it.

(Short pause)

When you start pedaling, a great emotion enters you, the wind blows bringing to your lungs the mixture of the sweet and delicate smell of cinnamon with the freshness of the unmistakable perfume of the sea, two fragrances so powerful

415

on their own and that when combined with this in this way they make an exquisite smell reach your nostrils that completely delights you and makes you feel deeply happy.

(Middle pause)

The thought that the landscape seems to want to hold your attention comes to you when you see that they appear running through the sand, some lovely dogs that entertain themselves by digging large holes to play with each other, filling themselves with happiness and managing to cause the same effect on you. As you continue pedaling, you see how on the other side there are beautiful butterflies that fly over the flowers, allowing you to observe them in detail, almost as if they wanted to delight you with their wonderful colors and the delicacy of their movements.

(Middle pause)

Continuing on your way, you come across some gentle downhills that take you slowly letting you relax with them, and then with their subsequent uphills let you have fun to leave you with great joy.

(Middle pause)

After a few minutes, you see how the palm trees on the beach move almost as if they were dancing to the sweet song that the wind plays to give dynamism to the place, and near them, beautiful seashells with attractive colors stand out among the golden grains of the sand.

(Short pause)

The gentle bike ride makes you feel complete and deeply relaxed, your heartbeat goes at a perfect rhythm that serves to remind you that you are alive and that you should enjoy to the fullest such a wonderful moment. That's why when you see that on your left among the flowers there is a nice swing, you decide to stop to enjoy it. When you do so, you feel wonderful; the coming and going of the game makes you enjoy that feeling of having in your stomach some big butterflies that move their wings causing inside you a funny tingling that makes you laugh out loud while you enjoy something so simple but at the same time so magnificent.

(Long pause)

Slowly, the peace you feel leads you to feel tired and you stop your movement to lie on the grass that welcomes you with a delicious freshness that makes you close your eyes to inhale it gently. Then it is there when feeling so relaxed, you begin to lose yourself between the place and in the wind that blows taking your consciousness as you close your eyes to enter a night of deep and pleasant sleep.

(Middle pause)

Sweet dreams, dear friend.

The Art of Painting in Your Health

Greetings friend. Today is a very special day because you have decided to take time for yourself and experience a guided relaxation that mainly seeks to ensure you get a good rest and that you can sleep pleasantly. I congratulate your great initiative as it is an important step in your growth as a being. To do this, you will perform a breathing and relaxation exercise. In addition, from your imagination, you will travel to a beautiful place where you will have some experiences that will help you feel peace, tranquility and calm.

(Short pause)

I invite you to find a place in your home where you can feel comfortable without interference. In that place, you should have a bed, where you can lie down. Find a comfortable pillow for your head to rest on. Try to keep your neck relaxed, your back straight. I recommend that you move your body to eliminate any tension that prevents you from concentrating.

(Short pause)

Close your eyes. Review the thoughts and emotions that you present at this time. Give to the universe what causes you uneasiness or does not allow you to be in the here and now.

Release everything that does not allow you to be serene and in harmony. Now breathe slowly feeling the positive effects of the breath in your life as a human being. Be grateful how when you inhale, the air enters you and fills you with restorative energies, and also when you exhale, expel everything that you no longer need.

(Short pause)

Relaxed and with your body light, you feel healing energies flowing throughout your being, cleansing and restoring all that prevents you from resting and having a pleasant sleep. Visualize the flow of energy from top to bottom and vice versa. You feel the magic of that energy and your body, your thoughts, and your being feels wellness, peace and health. You understand from your inner self that:

You are a being of love.

Your being requires your love and care.

You can love and take care of yourself.

You are the priority in your life.

You are deserving of well-being.

Therefore, you will do everything in your power to be happy and healthy.

(Long pause)

420

Friend, the time has come to start our journey from your imagination. If you feel that you are sleepy and you don't want to continue, no problem, rest. Don't forget that the purpose of this activity is for you to be able to sleep pleasantly.

(Short pause)

You feel you are being uplifted and a pine scent fills your soul. Slowly you realize that you are walking through a forest full of beautiful pine trees. You see squirrels scurrying everywhere. You feel it is snowing and that alerts you since you have to get closer to the nearest village to protect yourself from the weather. You advance to a road and when you get there you see some vehicles circulating; one of the drivers offers you a ride and you accept. The ride is wonderful, the mountains are impressive and magnificent. Their peaks are covered with snow. The driver tells you that this town is very nice and has many places to visit, he recommends you to go to the site of the arts.

Arriving at the place, you get off near a square. There, you make your way to a coffee shop that is quite busy. You sit down and order a steaming cup of mochaccino and a piece of cheesecake. You enjoy the delicious tastes and smells of the place. You realize that the weather has improved and you can move on and enjoy the place. You remember the driver's recommendation and begin your search for the art site. To do so, you ask some of the people who were also in the cafeteria. Once you have obtained the address, you start your walk.

You walk very carefully architecturally designed narrow streets. In many houses, the flowers adorn their foreheads. When you arrive at the site, you see a fairly large place with a big sign promoting the activities that take quarters there. Upon entering you are greeted by various guides and they explain the philosophy of the community. The place is divided into several arts: music, painting, cooking, dance among others. In each area, the visitor will not only see but also participate in activities where they learn a little about art.

Initially, you choose the art of painting. When you enter the beautiful place you see that it is a sober and very elegant area, the walls, ceiling, and floor are white. They have created in the living room several individual spaces where the visitor sits. You choose a location decorated with lilac flowers. As you sit down, they explain that the small table has some materials to make your painting. You have an easel to paint, brushes, oil paints, thinner oils, cleaning fluids, and some clothes and paper to clean and dry. They give you to choose some landscapes that could inspire you in your creation. They also tell you that if you need any guidance they are there to help you.

Being in front of all the resources offered, you realize that you do not know where to start. Read a message on the wall and it

422

catches your eye. It says, "Relax and give yourself your time. The muse comes when it least expects it." At that moment, they give you a delicious tea and a shortbread cookie. You enjoy and savor this gift, it also relaxes you. You take the brush, and you remember the beautiful mountains that you could see when the driver brought you to the place. Slowly you realize that your canvas is no longer white and that energy is flowing from you that helps you express the beauty that you captured on your trip. Little by little you have painted some lovely mountains and you have also placed pine trees and a road. You decide to place some people walking. You feel like your painting is still a sketch. Therefore, now you start slowly to give it depth and leftovers.

You then decide to place the coffee shop you visited, you try to remember the details and you capture several people. You feel that you go back in time to it and try to remember the colors that prevailed in the place. As you feel the magic of the art of painting you realize that it has an interesting power, as it distracts, relaxes, challenges your imagination and creativity, makes you forget about the world, any worries, and generates happiness and satisfaction. Little by little you wish to be in bed and rest deeply with the memory of the work you have just finished. Good night.

Those Who Do Not Live to Serve, Do Not Serve to Live

Greetings friend. Today we will have an activity where the main purpose is to make you feel relaxed, calm, in harmony and at peace, so that you can achieve the rest and pleasant sleep that you want so much. Today you have taken a break in your daily activities, to use it to feel good and rise above everything that worries you and makes you forget about yourself as a person. For that, I congratulate you since you have dared to take some time for yourself and enjoy an experience that will strengthen you.

(Short pause)

I invite you to find a quiet site in your house, where you can lie down. In this place, you must have privacy and plan so that you do not have interruptions. Lie down, loosen your head on a pleasant pillow. Try that your neck is free of tension, that your back is straight. Stretch your body and move it gently until you find the best position to be comfortable.

(Short pause)

Breath deeply. Inhale and exhale and feel gratitude within you. You become aware of how important breathing is in your life and for your body. In these moments close your eyes and check your thoughts and emotions. Give to the universe what distracts you and does not allow you to be in the here and now, or to be happy. You release everything that causes you annoyance or concern. You inhale and receive healing energies and exhale taking out everything that you no longer need.

(Short pause)

Today you feel that positive and healing energies flow through your body that brings you peace, harmony and serenity. You decide to enjoy this experience that will take well-being to your life. From your inner being you know that:

You are the most important thing to yourself.

You are a capable being.

To achieve what you propose.

You deserve to be loved and cared for by yourself.

That will help you have a happy life.

You are a wonderful being.

(Long pause)

Now, from your imagination, your being will start a wonderful adventure, where I will be your companion. If you feel like sleeping right now, no problem, rest. Remember that this is the main purpose of this activity.

You feel great tranquility and your being feels very peaceful. That feeling takes you to a beautiful garden, where there is a huge variety of flowers, roses, and bushes. It is a dream place, where nature does its part to create a majestic space. You perceive the scent of flowers and that makes you feel uplifted and in a magical area. You are really enjoying being on that site, so you are grateful and bless that space. You realize that this garden is not yours and you decide to leave. When you are walking, you feel a melodious voice calling you. It is a beautiful old lady from the garden house who wants you to come closer.

She tells you how much she enjoyed watching you enjoy her garden and how good it felt to be there. She then invites you to share a cup of coffee and some muffins. Upon entering the cabin, you found it to be very comfortable and nice. The lady invites you to sit in the dining room and there, you talked for a while and shared the offered snack. You feel happy there, the peaceful atmosphere floods the place and that makes you feel calm. The lady told you that she would bake bread that day and invited you to participate if you wanted to learn that art. She said that her neighbors always came to learn how to make the best bread of the place.

You accept with motivation. The lady offers you an apron, a cap and a bowl. They are placed on a large counter and she gradually explains the procedure to you. She stops initially to explain the importance of making the yeast rise to obtain a soft and delicious bread dough. She teaches you how to make sourdough and explains the importance of sugar in these processes. Slowly the lady starts the kneading process and you do the same as she does. You identify yourself with the dough you are kneading, you roll it out with the rolling pin, fold it and knead it again. That relaxes you and makes you feel happy. Then they cover the two doughs with a damp cloth and let the dough rest and rise.

At that moment, you and the lady clean the counter, and everything is tidy and organized again. She tells you that one of her greatest hobbies and joys is baking bread. You perceive in the lady the great illusion with which she expresses herself and you feel her satisfaction for knowing this art. After a while, she brings out the dough. When you see it, you realize that they have almost doubled in size. She invites you back to the counter. There she pours flour and dumps the dough balls. She invites you to knead and to feel the softness of it. She tells you to close your eyes, perceive its scent, its texture and gently knead. So you do it and you realize that the dough is now soft, homogeneous and its smell is delicious. She shows you how to form the rolls and place them on trays. Gradually, you realize that there are quite a few of them on the counter.

Then they let all the rolls rest and you can watch them grow a little more. The lady and you take the rolls to an artisan oven and place them there. Slowly you appreciate the rich smell of the pieces of bread and this makes you close your eyes to enjoy the sensation of having participated in the elaboration of such delicious food. The lady is taking out the trays and you realize that what you see is a great and provocative spectacle. The golden and toasted color of them provokes and gives a lot of satisfaction. You are proud to have been able to contribute to these roles. The lady invites you to take them and you gladly do so. You feel that they are the most delicious pieces of bread you have ever tasted.

Then the lady fills a basket with the rolls, puts some in a bag for you, and she also saves some for her family. She asks you to accompany her to take them to a place. When you realize you are in front of an orphanage. There, the kind lady gives her rolls to some children and then they hug her and give her lots of love. The lady says to you in a low voice, "Those who do not live to serve do not serve to live." Then they come back inside it. You say goodbye and thank everyone for what you have learned. You feel like being at home and before you know it, you are already in your bed, eager to sleep. Good night.

Receive and Give Love

Greetings friend. Congratulations on having decided to take some time to relax and find yourself. Through conscious breathing and guided meditation, you will see that you will achieve the calm, harmony and peace that you want so much. Also, the rest and pleasant sleep that you long for will come to you. So be ready to enjoy this moment, which you deserve for being a great person.

(Short pause)

Now, look in your home for that place where you feel comfortable and where you can rest. Put your head on a comfortable cushion, taking care that your neck is relaxed and your back is straight. Move your body and find the best position. Avoid feeling tensions, so you can concentrate better.

(Short pause)

Close your eyes, take a deep breath. Inhale and exhale. Feel the benefits of breathing in your body. Capture that when you breathe, healing energy enters your body and when you exhale everything that you no longer need leaves you. By breathing, our whole body is continually renewed.

(Short pause)

You check your thoughts and feelings. If you realize that these create any anguish or concern, give them to the universe and release everything that takes away your concentration. You feel how gradually your body relaxes. Discover how the healing energies run through your body and bring you peace, serenity, harmony, well-being and health. You recognize that you have not had the opportunity to find yourself, that you have not been the priority in your own life. Therefore, you cannot rest or sleep well. Today you have understood that:

You have the power of transformation in your being.

You need to be the priority in your own life.

You have faith that everything can change in your favor.

And the strengths of your inner being will resurface in you.

If you are okay, everything will be okay.

Your being possesses the healing power.

(Long pause)

Friend, in these moments our adventure to that place will begin that will allow you to renew your energies, strengthen your soul and your being. If at this moment, you feel that sleep is over you, no problem, rest and sleep. Do not forget that the most important thing is that you achieve a pleasant sleep.

(Short pause)

You feel relaxed and in harmony, you capture the energies that flow through your whole being, filling you with encouragement and hope. You see yourself walking through a very nice place. You realize that it is a park full of dried leaves and flowers, which form golden carpets that give the place majesty. At that moment, a very beautiful dog approaches you to greet you and throws herself at you. You catch that she wants affection, so it provokes you to hug her and touch her head. When you check her necklace you see that her name is Esmeralda. You tell her name and she jumps with happiness. You realize it is lost.

You decide to keep walking and Esmeralda follows you a bit shyly. From time to time you turn to see if it is there and you realize that it follows you. In an opportunity that you flew, she ran towards you and you feel her embrace. You are moved by all the affection that the beautiful animal expresses to you. After that gesture, you decide to walk with your new friend. At that moment, Esmeralda begins to play with you and you follow her. You watch as she throws herself on dry leaves piled high in the breeze and you run after her. Esmeralda is thrown on you and you fall on top of the leaves. You catch that the sensation you feel on top of it is delicious. Besides, Esmeralda comes over and licks your face. You can't believe all the beautiful emotions that Esmeralda has generated in you.

You stay there, but no longer lying down but sitting. You see that the leaves are dry and clean, so you start to throw them in the air and bathe Esmeralda with them. Again you start to play, you chase her and then she chases you. She knocks you down again with excitement and so on for a while. Living that moment brings back memories of your childhood when the simplest thing brought you joy, made you laugh, and amused you. Then you shake yourself off and gently touch Esmeralda and smooth her fur. You sit on a chair in the park and share a sandwich and other treats with Esmeralda. She happily enjoys being with you and as a thank you, she always comes over and hugs you.

Suddenly you hear a soft voice of a woman calling Esmeralda. You answer this way, here she is. Esmeralda sees her owner and runs to meet her, and you observe the happiness of both of them. She turns to you, runs back and hugs you as a sign of gratitude for everything she has experienced, and goes to where her owner is. The lady greets you and says goodbye. At that moment, you feel satisfaction, because you never hesitated to give love and companionship to Esmeralda. You reflect on life and how sometimes we doubt and distrust ourselves and others. That experience taught you the value of animals and their capacity to transmit love. It also reminded you of the importance of giving love to others and showing it with a hug, a gesture, a smile, sharing something, or simply supporting in the moments that are required.

You look around, and everything is different from how you arrived. For you, the place is more beautiful, you feel that what you have experienced has changed something in you and that you will no longer be the same. You are not afraid to be you, to enjoy life, to smile, to run, to let the sun hit your face, or to receive and give love and many hugs. You go again to the hill of dry leaves and throw yourself there, you lie down looking at the sky. You open your arms and thank life, love, nature, happiness, well-being. You wish to rest, your eyes gradually close until you fall into a deep sleep. Good night.

Hypnosis for a Sound Sleep

Hello, welcome. In this opportunity, I am going to guide you through meditation using self-hypnosis. This relaxes both your mind and your body so that you can finally elevate your consciousness to an undisturbed state of peace, and be able to fall into a deep and restful sleep. You just relax, follow my voice and surrender to the experience. Okay, let's begin.

Hypnosis is a deep state of relaxation, which is accompanied by high concentration. It is like being extremely relaxed, but at the same time conscious and focused, nothing more and nothing less.

The person receiving hypnosis is always conscious. In fact, it leads to an increase in consciousness, thanks to the mental focus that we are exercising on ourselves. It can be used to access past memories or to cultivate healthy thoughts. In today's case, we will use it to prepare for deep sleep.

You don't have to worry, you don't need to be an expert on the subject. The following hypnosis is basic and quite simple, perfect to fulfill the objective of going to sleep without any worry.

First of all, we must find a comfortable place to sit, such as a chair or a couch, this will be your place of peace for meditation. Try to make it as comfortable as possible for you, and also totally free from noises or any kind of distractions from the outside world. Once you have found this perfect space, proceed to sit with your back straight, but without creating tension in it. Do not tighten any of your muscles, just sit and let go of all tensions. The most important thing is that you are always comfortable.

Now, close your eyes and begin to breathe calmly and slowly, using your abdomen. Focus your attention on your breathing, begin to notice how all that fresh air enters through your nose, and then exits peacefully through your slightly open mouth. It doesn't matter if your breathing is deep or not, the important thing is that it feels natural to you. Don't force it, just let it be, it's perfect the way it is.

Imagine, that in each of your feet there is a light switch like the ones in your room, they are turned on and connected to the muscles in your feet. Now, using your mind, you turn off the switch on your right foot; and now, you turn off the switch on your left foot. Feel the muscles in your feet relax, and drop under their own weight.

Slowly stretch your arms and legs, move your jaw and regain consciousness in the present moment. Now, with this feeling of relaxation and well-being, you are ready to go to sleep peacefully. Imagine that, at your knees, there is also a pair of switches, both turned on. With your mind, turn off the first one, then the other one, in the order that feels best to you. You're doing great.

Now, visualize that in each hand you have a pair of spheres of restorative light, it is energy capable of relieving all your tensions and calming you instantly, a divine light. Put one hand on your abdomen, and the other on your chest, notice how this light penetrates both areas and relaxes them. It is capable of relieving any tension in both your muscles and internal organs. Once this is done, allow your arms to rest again on your lap.

Finally, think now that you have a switch on your forehead, this is the one that is connected and gives energy to your thoughts, worries, anxiety and your fears. The switch is on and you, with your mind, turn it off at this moment, turn it off. Now you notice, as your mind calms down, freeing itself from any amount of intrusive thoughts, and your facial muscles begin to relax as well. You may even be left with your mouth half open, this is perfectly normal, it is a sign of the relaxation you are feeling at this moment. Well, you're doing fantastic.

Next, imagine yourself walking through a large field full of colorful flowers, and you come to a small garden; this is your garden. In it, there are your favorite flowers and trees, and also, the temperature is at the level you love. There is also a fountain with water in it, and you hear the sound of water falling from it, it is very relaxing.

Take a little walk through this garden of yours, and take the time to appreciate its beauty and the great feelings of abundance that this beautiful landscape generates in you. You can smell the flowers, sit under the shade of a tree, touch the water in the fountain, or just lie on your back on the grass. Whatever makes you feel peace and fulfillment within you.

This garden, which represents your inner peace, is the ideal place to visit before having a restful sleep. Here you feel safe and calm, in fact, in this area, there are no stresses or responsibilities, you are just here to be yourself, with nothing to carry on your shoulders. You don't even have the obligation to fall asleep right away, just to relax and let everything flow at its own pace.

It's all the same to you, now is the time for you to enjoy your state of tranquility, and to realize that this is the only important thing for you at this moment, just to enjoy. It is beautiful to be so present.

Now, visualize that the energy of this garden goes through the physical space that surrounds you, your room, your bed, your chair, your table, all that you have around you. As if all that you imagined was now a real tangible place. Your bed is now part of that garden, and it is waiting for you, for you to lie down on it, and little by little, fall asleep.

Now, when you feel ready to do so, slowly open your eyes, but don't move immediately. Keep breathing with your eyes open, and appreciate the restorative energy, which the garden of your mind has brought into your physical environment. Now everything is as beautiful and relaxing as it is in your imagination.

Slowly stretch your arms and legs, move your jaw and regain consciousness in the present moment. Now, with this feeling of relaxation and well-being, you are ready to go to sleep peacefully.

That's all for this occasion: rest, sweet dreams.

Meditation to Sleep and Relax Deeply

Hello, I want to welcome you to this guided meditation. Today, I bring before you a meditation to help you fall asleep in a deep and restful way. Maybe right now, you are already in bed, ready to fall asleep, but your body simply does not allow you to do so. Don't worry, it happens, that's what these types of meditations are for.

In that same place, lying down as you are right now, I want you to focus your attention completely on your breathing. Feel the sensations that it provokes in you. Feel how your belly expands with each inhalation, and how it also contracts when you take the air out on the exhalation. At no time should this process feel like something forced, no matter if it seems that your breathing is not deep enough, just let it be, it is perfect as it is.

Gradually, your body loosens up, dropping its weight and sinking slowly into the comfort of your bed. Feel how your muscles loosen, and at the same time, feel how you let go of all the worries, all the stress, and all the obligations you have in your body, let it all go. It's time to come home, to come back to yourself.

Visualize how, with each inhalation, you feel a great inner warmth. You breathe in the energy of peace and serenity, you notice how light is getting increasingly bigger inside your chest. This light becomes increasingly stronger with each inhalation you take. Slowly, you connect with a feeling of tenderness and inner warmth, you are getting ready to enter the mysterious and magical world of dreams, where everything is possible.

You are curious about that experience. Maybe, today you are going to have a dream where you live different types of adventures, and interact with different characters as if you were living in a novel, where you are the author and your mind, the producer. As you continue to breathe slowly and deeply, you feel relaxed and at peace.

All of us, we all have a little child inside us, we always carry it with us. Now, I want you to visualize your own inner child, a mini version of you when you were four to seven years old. Visualize it sleeping next to you, I want you to feel its warmth, its tenderness, while you embrace that little inner child, preparing it to go to sleep and have a good night's sleep.

I want you to observe and feel that inner child and embrace it, filling it with love and security before it goes to sleep, as any of us would like to be pampered before resting. You feel infinite tenderness and love for that little being you used to be years ago.

I want you to visualize, how you bring your face close to its ear and tell it with all your heart, "I love you. Everything is going to be fine. Now just rest, you deserve it." Observe how that little child is now in a state of deep relaxation, smiling, feeling very well and very safe, protected around your warm arms. Now it just relaxes and lets go into itself.

You feel that unconditional love for that inner child, and you also feel compassion because you know that this child is doing the best it can, it does not know how to do everything perfectly, and you feel pure compassion for this little one. As you look at its face, you observe how it is already asleep, and you propose to sleep too, next to it.

You feel a sense of curiosity and excitement about what tomorrow will bring. From this place of calm and serenity, you feel gratitude for the infinite possibilities that tomorrow will bring. For the new adventures you will be able to live, and for all that you will one day have at your fingertips.

Your breathing becomes increasingly warm and pleasant. As you focus on it, feelings of gratitude arise, for being able to return once again to your inner home; for having one more night to rest and connect with yourself, with your goodness and your good feelings.

Now, finally, you are ready to dive into that deep and infinite mystery that is the world of dreams. And now that you are about to enter into a deep state of sleep, you are going to say to yourself internally, a few last motivating words, so that when you enter the dream, these thoughts will be the ones that work in your subconscious. Repeat internally, "I am worthy of the life I deeply long for. I am the captain of my life. I choose the direction of my life. I have all the tools to live the life I want. I live my life from my deepest self. Expressing all my talents. I show myself without fear to the world, just as I am— a perfect being in my own way. There are no problems in my life that I can't solve as long as I put my mind to them. I am in control, and I don't let myself be victimized by ridiculous situations. I resolve to have a deep and restful sleep. So that I can wake up tomorrow with energy and enthusiasm."

You are aware of the great feeling of relaxation that you feel right now in your body. And while you are getting ready to go to sleep, you thank life for the last time, for the opportunity to be alive one more day, to hear your voice, for having given you the time to do this meditation. You thank for this life experience that has been given to you, which has its ups and downs, but the important thing is always to know how to enjoy this exciting journey. Enjoy it, be thankful, this life is your gift.

After you have done all this, you finally get ready to fall asleep. Good night, until next time.

Meditation to End Your Day

Hello, I welcome you to this guided meditation. This time, we will focus on a meditation that will aim to end your day with serenity, calm, inner peace, and synchronicity with yourself, so you can enjoy a deep and restful sleep tonight. We will prepare mentally, physically and spiritually, you just relax and follow the sound of my voice. Surrender to the experience, let's begin.

When we become preachers of peace, we permit others to do the same, leading by example. When we incorporate calm into our lives, old and disastrous self-destructive programs begin to be replaced by more beneficial ones.

Bring your attention to the here and now. Sit comfortably, aligning your body with gravity. Keep your back straight at all times, but without generating tension on it, place your feet gently on the floor without pushing it, and let your hands rest on your lap, freeing them from any possible tension.

Tilt your body forward, and then backward, finally resting in the unique and unmistakable center. Similar to what we did above, tilt your body to the left, and then to the right, finally letting it rest in the middle of both, naturally and effortlessly.

Then, close your eyes and focus your attention on your breathing. Observe how the air enters and flows through you, to be released through your slightly open mouth. Drop the weight of your head onto your shoulders, which are now relaxed.

We will begin with three deep breaths. Inhale now, fill your abdomen with air, and then exhale, remembering to take a moment of rest after each breath; inhale again and then exhale, resting in the silence at the end of your breath; for the last time, inhale as deeply as you can, and then exhale, letting go of any tension along with the warm air you release from your mouth. You do this very well.

Allow your body to breathe on its own, and always allow yourself to be comfortable. At no time should your breathing or posture feel unnatural or cause you any pain. Most importantly, always be comfortable. If you feel discomfort, move your body gently and exhale during the movement.

Allow your consciousness to relax, focusing on the here and now; surrender to love and trust blindly, in that which you cannot know with certainty. Breathe in the present moment. Relinquish all that you obsessively try to control in your life, and surrender to the pleasure of focusing your attention on the breath.

If invasive thoughts or emotions appear, simply observe them without judging them, as if they were raindrops in a rearview mirror.

Now, bring your attention to the space your heart occupies while remaining aware of your breath. Allow your oxygen to go in and out of your heart, leaving behind all those difficulties that came to you today. Inhale, fill your abdomen with air, and then exhale.

You should focus on the fact that this moment is unique and unrepeatable, it does not need any change, it is totally perfect as it is. This is the space you have given yourself during your day, to realize that no matter what happened to you today, you gave the best of yourself and you should be proud of that. There is nothing left for you to do today. You don't have to carry unnecessary weight. You can rest easy in the here and now, while you get ready for a good night's sleep.

Without diverting your attention from the space that occupies your heart, let feelings of gratitude emerge from it, for all that you have experienced today. Bring to your consciousness a feeling of gratitude and love for life, the happiness of being alive, the joy of small daily moments. Bring to the present moment all that goodness that inhabits you: feelings of love for your loved ones, pets, nature, your hobbies, your work, etc.

While you continue to breathe slowly, take the time to meditate on today's events. While not everything went as you expected, the truth is, things rarely happen the way we want them to. It happens: it's part of life. You shouldn't blame yourself for things like that. Life is hard; we are not here to say otherwise. But we are here to tell you that in the end, you are alive, and that is more than enough to feel grateful for. Because, if today wasn't good enough, tomorrow you can get up and go for a much better one.

Now that you have finally rid yourself of that burden of negative energy, and have accepted the love and gratitude that dwells deep in your heart, you are ready to rest and have a deep and peaceful sleep. Very well done.

Keep breathing, while invoking feelings of peace, love and gratitude, which will accompany you during your rest. We will take three deep breaths, as deep as possible, and return to the physical form of the real world. Inhale now, fill your abdomen with air, and then exhale, remembering to take a moment of rest after each breath; inhale again and then exhale, resting in the silence at the end of your breath; for the last time, inhale as deeply as you can, and then exhale, letting go of any tension along with the warm air you release from your mouth.

Become aware of your body, feel it now, totally free of tension, and ready to rest in the comfort of your bed. When you are ready, slowly open your eyes, returning to the here and now. Stretch your body, feeling every little movement in the process.

Your body is relaxed, your mind is free of intrusive thoughts and your heart is filled with joy and gratitude for life.

450

Congratulations, you have successfully completed this guided meditation.

That's all for this occasion, sweet dreams. See you next time.

A Unique Tree

Hello friend, get ready and make yourself comfortable, a great adventure awaits us today. You and I make a great team, our mission is to make you enjoy the adventure. You can relax and rest; so you can have a great day tomorrow.

Sharpen your senses and realize that calm can not only be identified by silence. Relaxation also has a smell, like a field of fresh roses or the scent of rain falling in the early morning of a cold night.

Enjoy, relax and immerse yourself in the universe of calm.

(Short pause)

Before you begin, you should be aware that the place you choose to initiate this experience is crucial in determining the effect it will have on you. Therefore, you should go to your couch, room, corner, or favorite place and lie down. When you feel that your comfort is complete, then you are ready.

(Short pause)

As your great friend, I should give you a very important piece of advice. It is to close your eyes. It will allow your imagination to soar and your worries to disappear, for peace is stronger than any feeling of stress. Empty your mind and get ready for adventure.

(Short pause)

Just as in nature, everything is perfectly balanced, you should take that example. As if you were part of it, understand that there are moments where you must endure and others where you enjoy to the fullest.

Focus on your relaxation and how a leaf slowly falls from a tree, to rest on the beautiful grass. This is how you should let go of stress, just as if you were a tree.

(Short pause)

It's easy to single out nature for beauty, but rarely do you see people as pure, kind-hearted and genuine as you. With the sweetness of roses, the resilience of green grass and the magic of a sunset.

Keep captivating everyone and show them that you can make a better world, with attitude, hard work and lots of love.

(Middle pause)

Success is not just around the corner, it takes hard work and effort to achieve it. Imagine the perseverance of a caterpillar to become a beautiful butterfly.

Because it is just as nature works, so does the world in general. Not all trees lose their leaves in autumn, but this change does not make them superior or inferior, since it is understood that each one evolves with the tools it possesses.

Dear friend, before we dive into the adventure, I want to remind you that if you feel tired eyelids and your time to sleep is already evident, you should do it. For that is the mission that you and I shall fulfill, from now on.

When you return, I will be very eager to embark on a new adventure.

(Long pause)

After keeping your eyes closed, for a long time. Now, when you open them, you are a big tree!

You are glued to the ground, yes, but you feel much freer than when you could walk. The soft wind blows through your whole being. You are resilient, strong, imposing, friendly, and able to understand everyone around you.

Your large branches are used for birds to rest and make their nests. Insects come to visit you and tell you that being with you they feel calm and protected. Since you can help them all.

Your leaves are very intense green, so much so that from far away they are more noticeable than any other tree. Although some are already changing color, due to the autumn, you are calm, because those that manage to stay, will be eternal.

In the mornings, you are awakened by the beautiful melodies of the birds, who fly all over your trunk, as if they wanted to spread their song throughout your whole being. In the afternoon, humans come to take refuge from the shade you give them. You touch them. They lie comfortably on your trunk and take a few naps. At night, fireflies light up the whole place and your fruits sprout, feeding the rest of the animals.

Autumn is here. But not all the leaves are falling. Some still cling, tightly, to you. Your feeling is very strange, for you think you have totally lost your magic.

It's another day. The birds, insects and humans, keep coming. Attached to the affection they have for you. None of them abandons you and all of them motivate you, encourage you, they know that the good times will come back.

After a few days, you wake up in the morning and are surprised to find yourself with many more leaves than the previous time.

Everyone around you, trees, plants and birds, are congratulating you. All is excitement! For now, you have not only regained your leaves, but you now have many more and your condition is perfect. You learn that those who are by your side, never abandon you, despite any circumstance.

The solidarity of all drives you to never stop dreaming. Everyone's love shows you that your appearance, shape, or moment does not determine the appreciation they feel for you. True love is capable of overcoming any situation.

Now, with more happiness, the birds share their melodies in your branches. Humans take shelter in your shade and your fruits are sweeter and more delicious every day.

Your tree friends explain to you that a strong tree does not remain resistant despite everything, but one that, although not having a good time, can recover and return to its fullness.

You smile and close your eyes, it's time to go back, you have learned your lesson. Besides, you already have many friends, who are always there for you.

You open your eyes, you are, curled up, in your bed, happy for living that great adventure, where you could have been a tree and kept the strength not to collapse, even when you had many conditions against you.

This will help you in your day-to-day life, to be a strengthened tree, in every situation that comes up in your life. You settle into your sheet and relax to sleep. A yawn and a deep sleep prepare you for the future.

458

Relaxation before Sleep

Hello, welcome. On this occasion, I invite you to be part of this relaxation experience, which brings with it the benefits you need to have a peaceful and deep sleep, through the use of simple exercises and affirmations of peace and confidence. Just follow the steps presented here, and surrender to the experience, let's begin.

First of all, please find a comfortable place where you can start your practice. It can be a chair or a couch, where you can sit comfortably, and preferably without disturbing sounds or any other distractions from outside. Look for a place where you can practice in peace.

Now that you have found your space of peace, let's check your posture. Preferably, you should be seated, with your back always straight, but without generating tension on it. If this posture is too uncomfortable, you can always place a cushion behind your back to be better positioned.

After that your back is well-positioned, let's check the rest of your posture. Your feet touch the floor softly and comfortably without pushing it, and without exerting any pressure on it; your hands rest comfortably on your thighs; your neck and shoulders are free of any tension accumulated on them; and finally, you let the weight of your head fall on your shoulders.

Very well, now that your posture is correct and free of tension, proceed to close your eyes and begin to breathe deeply and slowly, taking all that fresh air to your abdominal area.

Breathe peacefully while focusing your full attention on the inhalation and exhalation your body naturally exerts. Do not try to change your breathing to something it is not, do not force it, just let it flow at your pace, calmly, without haste.

Now, we will concentrate on starting to relax all the muscles of your face. Gradually redirect your attention and feel each of the parts of your face that are indicated.

While you continue to breathe slowly with your abdomen, let us begin by directing our attention to our forehead; then, we redirect our attention to our eyelids; then our nose; then our cheeks; then our lips; our tongue; our chin; our jaw, and so on until we feel our face totally relaxed, free of tension and generating a great relief in that whole area.

Normally and without realizing it, we use a large part of our facial muscles day after day. Whether it is making a strange grimace when someone tells us an impressive anecdote, or simply frowning for no reason when walking down the street. These types of habits are also the ones that prevent us from having a restful sleep since many times we continue frowning or squeezing our eyes tightly even at bedtime. Now that you have freed all this area from tension, everything feels different, calmer, less forced, more peaceful, that is the idea.

As you continue to breathe, take a moment to see how good it feels to have this whole area of your face free of tension. Your jaw no longer clenches and is relaxed; your eyebrows don't have that characteristic frown and feel lighter; your eyes and eyelids are no longer tight, they just drop their weight on themselves, which encourages you to rest peacefully.

Now, let's go a little lower in the body. Now focus your attention on your shoulders, feel this part of the body, try to relax them, and let their weight fall on their own as much as possible. The same thing you will do now with your arms, one by one, feel that area and then let its weight rest on your lap, first with the right arm, then with the left one.

In the same way, start feeling your legs, one by one. Bring all your attention to your right leg, feeling this whole area and making it relax, then repeat the same procedure with the left leg. Feel how the tension in this area is released, and now your muscles become increasingly soft. Many times we do not realize the importance of our legs. They are responsible for carrying us everywhere in our day-to-day; therefore, they are in constant tension. Hence the importance of relaxing them before going to sleep.

Take a moment, and feel how well all these important parts of your body are now, which you did not take the trouble to relax before even thinking about going to sleep. It is as if now your whole being is jelly. There are no more discomforts or tensions that keep you awake. You are finally ready to have a peaceful and deep sleep.

Now, take your attention away from all these areas of the body that are already relaxed, and bring your full attention to your breathing. Inhale peace and calm for a restful sleep, and exhale, letting out all the worries of your day along with all that warm air coming from your lungs. There is nothing to worry about, you are tranquil, relaxed, ready to sleep, and to start the next day in the best of spirits.

Continue breathing, and as you do so, gradually, you can open your eyes. Even if you don't move from your place, keep breathing with your eyes open. Thank yourself for giving yourself this moment, which you needed after all the stress of your day-to-day life.

Now you can stretch your body. Extend your arms, your legs, move your head and feel your jaw, all free of tension and ready to go to rest. Remember that it is always advisable to take some time to do this type of meditation, it is the most efficient way to achieve a night of deep and restful sleep.

Well, that was all for this occasion: rest, sweet dreams.

A Holiday Day

Is someone there? Yes, of course! It's you, my great friend. Welcome! I know you will enjoy our trip today.

It is time for you to breathe calmly, many times until your heart enters a normal rhythm and your body is relaxed.

Remember that when you can enter into your inner peace, you can do anything you set your mind to. It is also much easier for you to rest, your body and your mind.

(Short pause)

You haven't made yourself comfortable yet? Then it's time to do so! Remember that a relaxed body results in a calm mind.

Think a little and determine what your perfect place is. Just as a bird spends hours building its nest with materials it likes, so should you. Go to your nest and lie down. Feel the calm and peace circulating in the atmosphere and enjoy every second.

(Short pause)

Look at your room in detail; concentrate on those areas you have never noticed before. That is your abode, your resting place, where your body and mind can rest in absolute peace.

Breathe tranquility and feel the good energies coming in, clearing all the bad thoughts and making you enter into a state of rest.

(Short pause)

Your time of the day has finally arrived! Releasing negative charges is not easy, but with practice, it will become increasingly easier.

Think about your last vacation, how pleasant it was and how you enjoyed, rested and kept unforgettable memories.

Everything can be improved, even the good times. That's why you should do your chores very well and your reward will be a well-deserved vacation.

(Short pause)

You are a wonderful human being, you are capable of brightening the days of others.

Your smile certainly attracts people.

You can turn a bad day into a good one, just with your great attitude.

Never forget that and never stop smiling at life.

(Middle pause)

What does your perfect vacation look like? I bet you have lots of ideas, beaches, forests, glaciers. It could be anything, no doubt, you'd have a great time. Summer is the perfect time to clear your mind, the heat melts away the negative charges and stress you have and makes you want to cool off. Your body and mind must be synchronized for great enjoyment.

The trip you are taking today is for you to have the vacation you deserve so much. Don't worry if for some reason you feel tired. You are totally free to go to sleep and whenever you feel you need a vacation, then I will accompany you.

(Long pause)

You look at the sky for a few seconds and observe that radiant sun that illuminates you, that looks at all your achievements and makes your days the most special. You go a little closer to the park and watch the children laughing, playing, and enjoying themselves as if there was no tomorrow. Happiness is present in every step you take!

You walk through the park and a dog runs in your direction. You extend your hands and the dog jumps up to meet you, the two of you share a hug. He licks your face and you stroke his fur, with a satisfied smile. The dog decides to join you on your vacation day, so you both go to a nearby beach.

The sound of the waves crashing against the shore makes you feel a great serenity, which you had forgotten to feel. The busy days have prevented you from taking a little time for yourself. You take off your shoes and feel the soles of your feet touch the warm sand of the beach. You run with your partner next to you and both take a big dip on the beach. After so much heat, you need to cool off, so you buy two ice creams and savor them on the shore. You take pleasure in holding the ice cream for your friend to lick wildly. You smile at the prank.

After the ice cream, it's time to enjoy yourself with your doggy friend. The dog digs up a ball and brings it to you in his muzzle. You take it and understand what it's all about. You smile. You throw it hard, and the dog, at full speed, goes out to catch it in mid-air.

The people-watching is impressed and some even applaud, they think they've been practicing for years, but no, it's your first time! And since you've never done it before, you didn't know it was so good.

Following an afternoon full of emotions, you decide to go to the forest to pick some fruits and take them home.

You meet friends who play soccer. They invite you. You're surprised. You haven't tried it before either, but you accept. Even the dog runs onto the field to chase the ball. You and your friends laugh out loud.

Your team achieves victory and you discover that you have many good qualities, that by not trying new things, you didn't know how far you could go.

You realize the importance of rest. You are surprised to feel that a single day of vacation can completely change your week or your month.

You got a new canine companion who is loyal, loving, and willing to accompany you on your adventures, you shared with your friends, you did outdoor activities and most importantly, you took a break.

You return home after picking fruit and welcome your dog to its new home. In honor of the day you had, the dog will be named, "Rest." You smile. You feel at peace, content and happy.

You go to the kitchen, prepare dinner for yourself and "Rest." From now on your faithful friend and his name will remind you of the wonders of thinking of you and taking a break.

There are two hot chocolates, one for you and one for your canine friend. You drink it calmly, relaxed. The warm drink soothes your body.

You sit in your favorite chair and stroke at "Rest." You thank him for being there, cuddled up with you. You feel relaxed, at peace, happy.

Your eyes are closing. You are sleepy. You both fall fast asleep.

One Day at Rose's Cabin

What a pleasure to meet you, my friend, I missed you already. I'm glad you decided to join me in this new adventure! I know that during the day you do a lot of activities that lead you to stress and worries. So, I have good news for you, to start with this adventure, you must not make any effort at all, just relax, breathe and enjoy the wonderful thing that is to be calm!

(Short pause)

Inhale deeply, hold your breath for a few seconds and then release the air. Repeat the process several times and feel how it brings you into balance much faster.

Concentrate and look at all the details of your room, see how beautiful it is and the details you have never seen before. That is your site, there you can be and act as you want, enjoy the place that is designed just for you and your rest.

(Short pause)

Close your eyes and concentrate. The silence makes the place acquire all the necessary calm, your body feels how it is released from all the tension and enters into a state of rest. Your mind prepares to live a great adventure that will help you learn and fall into a deep sleep.

(Short pause)

The arrival of calm is the most important thing because it is what you should enjoy every second.

After an arduous day, finding tranquility is sometimes difficult, however, you must know that only you have the power to do it. It is a challenge and you are ready to face it.

Go out, gather the wood to light the fireplace, and heat your room. This effort will undoubtedly bring you a reward.

(Short pause)

Friend, I can't pass up the opportunity, to tell you how smart, insightful and feisty you are.

No doubt there have been many rocks in your path, but you have never let any of them stop you, that's why you keep moving forward and always get stronger with every obstacle you encounter. Never stop proving to the world that you are made for great challenges.

(Middle pause)

After resting in the place you chose, you wake up in a cozy cabin. Through the window, you can see how the snow is falling unceasingly.

Winter is present in that place, there are snowmen outside the cabin where you are. That's what impresses you the most. No problem if you feel sleepy at some point, the cabin will always be ready whenever you want to come back.

(Long pause)

Although you feel comfortable in the warm bed, with special, hand-woven sheets and a fireplace nearby, you decide to get up, for you should find out where you are and what you are doing there. In the hallway, you come across different paintings. Some of them even appear to be made by amateurs, but without a doubt, each work conveys a different feeling to you.

You understand that things are always different when they are done with love and that is what the artists want to emphasize.

After looking at the paintings for a while, you meet a lady who is in the kitchen, preparing a hot tea. The lady's name is Rose and she is the owner of the cabin.

She tells you, "I will teach you valuable lessons, moreover, I will make you feel very comfortable, relaxed, and very soon you will want to come back."

You nod and smile when Rose gives you a cup of tea. Rose begins to tell you a little about the history of her cabin. She tells you that it is inherited from one generation to the next by the guardians of peace. That is, the owners are experts in balancing the emotions of their visitors.

Rose looks you in the eyes and notices how tired you are. She tells you, "Your daily routine exhausts you too much, plus you always let your mind dominate you; you find it hard to relax and be at peace."

You're surprised by Rose's successes! It seems as if she has been watching you all your life. But she only knew it when she looked at you for a few seconds.

Rose explains to you that the routine can't be modified. Just as the snow falls, nothing can be done to stop it. But you can do something to live better.

With a soft voice, Rose tells you, "It would be very easy for me to just complain when winter comes, not bundle up and suffer from colds. However, I can't change the weather, but I can learn to live with it. By keeping warm, heating my home, and maintaining a temperature that helps me to do all my activities normally. That's how routine is, you have to find little things, that make big changes and help you live and enjoy everything."

Your surprise increases, because you never imagined that such a simple comparison could be so true and touch your heart.

Besides, Rose continues to focus on helping you. She takes your hand and says, "Believe it or not, good work, study, or labors, depends if you can harvest a good dream. In my cabin, you can always sleep; the environment is relaxing and inspires you to rest. I know you are the right person and you are always looking to improve, so my biggest advice is to take a good rest from time to time. Remember, whatever you're doing, it's never going to matter the quantity; it's going to matter the quality and for that, you need to be rested, with maximum energy, as every day comprises a different challenge."

You smile and finish your tea, you have learned your lesson. You know that some things are true, but you needed someone else to confirm them. You give a big hug to Mrs. Rose who, in the cabin, took care of you and treated you as a special guest, you also thank her for the great teachings.

You walk back down the hallway and return to your room, but not before looking out the window again and remembering those important words, "You can't stop snow from falling from the sky, but you can learn to live happily accompanied by it."

You lie down on the warm bed, close your eyes, feel the relaxed atmosphere. You are very sleepy.

A Season of Hibernation

Welcome to a new story, my friend! Today, I reserved for you, the best place, so you can clear your mind and relax, as only you deserve. It has been a tiring day, but it has come to an end. It's time to relax, to empty your mind and get calm; only then will you be able to enjoy today's story to the fullest.

(Short pause)

You should get used to spending the right moments in the right places. That, without a doubt, makes you enjoy an experience, not only good but unforgettable.

Take your time and go to your room, lie down on your bed, put your back straight, stretch your feet and relax your body. Let your mind start the journey and I will guide you to total satisfaction.

(Short pause)

After getting comfortable, it's time for the next step. Close your eyes and breathe deeply, concentrate on enjoying this moment of calm and relaxation. I know that every day, your mind is busy with many things, but you should also take the time to rest, not only physically, but mentally because I want you to be renewed and with lots of energy to face the future.

(Short pause)

Keep in mind that this story will not only serve you to embark on a very exciting mental journey, but I also seek to help you make your days much better than they already are.

Your relaxation is vital for the development of the story because when you close your eyes, you feel like you can walk on a surface, which is not the floor of your house, it is icy. The temperatures are low and obviously, the snow falls without stopping, but you feel warmly wrapped and that helps you to move forward, despite the difficulties.

(Short pause)

Your character has brought you here, you are an incredible person! I admire you a lot and not only for your good qualities, which are many. But because, despite having mistakes, you are capable of realizing them and correcting them, for your own good and the good of your environment.

This ability to improve as a person day by day makes me think that you represent love as it really should. Keep it up and never change, because your essence is what makes others move forward.

(Middle pause)

Right, left, up, down, all directions and you see only big mountains totally frozen. Your eyelashes wring out the snow.

You are at the North Pole. Everything is frozen, but it is strange because you can feel that despite the weather conditions, to which you are not used to, you are not cold.

Surprise! You have claws, which allow you to walk better in all that icy environment; and a big body, which makes it easier for you to travel long distances and enjoy the wonderful views. You're a beautiful polar bear!

Remember, the trip is long, but if you have to take a break, to sleep, I will wait for you and we will see each other next time.

(Long pause)

Fortitude, strength, personality, confidence: Without a doubt, you now possess all the characteristics of a polar bear.

You decide to take a walk on the glaciers and you can feel how the wind ruffles all your fur, but it is not uncomfortable. On the contrary, it is very pleasant; it feels like freedom is flirting with you.

Your friends, of the same species as you, run to walk beside you. They don't need to cross gestures; they feel safe with you and you with them. They all form a big family, protecting each other and at the same time taking care of their cold home.

The cubs, they run around you. You are captivated by how cute they are, so you can't resist. You bow your head and play with them.

The snowstorm thickens. Your friends back off; you want to keep moving forward because you feel so confident; nothing can stop you. Obstacles are small when it's you they have to face!

Good attitude but, remember, nature is very powerful. However, crossing that storm is not the same without your friends, who recommend you to withdraw and hibernate until the big storm passes.

Your impulse tells you it's a good idea to continue, but the logic of your friends makes you see reason and you don't rush into making a decision.

You and your polar bear friends go to a cave to begin hibernation. Being there, it's easier to connect with everyone. You make jokes, share tasty meals, play games, tell stories and laugh non-stop.

It's all great fun and the moment comes where tiredness and relaxation take over everyone and they fall fast asleep. In the cozy cave, you and your friends lie down on the warm floor and snuggle up next to each other. The fur provides you with enough warmth to sleep comfortably and feel as if you are sleeping on top of the clouds.

After a while, you wake up and everyone comes out of the cave. The storm has passed, the weather is spectacular and the whole atmosphere is now much more enjoyable.

At that moment you realize that if you had decided to continue, you would have made a mistake. It was good to listen to your friends, who were in charge of guiding you on the right path and teaching you that to make an important decision, you need to be careful because big decisions carry a lot of responsibility.

On the visit to the polar bears, you not only enjoyed the wonders of the North Pole, but you also saw that it is not good to get carried away by the momentum. Important and momentous decisions have to be reasoned out to ensure success in life. In addition, you learned that after the storm, there is always calm, and times are always better. Sometimes you need to ride out it and then enjoy the peace.

Your journey has come to an end, but you liked it and I know you will be back soon.

You lie down in that comfortable cave again, which is now your warm bed, where you fall soundly asleep from exhaustion and relaxation.

Conclusion

When you have finished reading, you will have acquired new habits and behaviors to help you to fall asleep and enjoy a deep, undisturbed sleep all night long. Through reading the stories, you will unconsciously have achieved a state of relaxation that allows you to forget about all your overwhelming problems by simply visualizing the characters, settings, and stories being told, regardless of the genre.

This book will become a tool for those who want to, who need to disconnect from day-to-day reality, relax, and sleep deeply; a kind of sleep medicine, which you will recommend to anyone who tells you they want restful and quality sleep. All in all, the pages contain differing genres. Some are funny, romantic, adventurous, or fictional. Others aim at the reader's reflection on certain topics to show them the best way to achieve a deep and comforting sleep through healthy changes before sleeping.

Nowadays, most people have some degree of insomnia due to stress. It has become a fashionable "Disease" for a variety of reasons. It is part of our daily lives, and we all experience it to a greater or lesser degree. When it is temporary or passing, it is said that stress is beneficial. However, when stress is maintained for an excessive time, is too frequent or too intense, and damages the organism, negative consequences usually appear.

Most people have trouble falling asleep at night, and when they do, they do not sleep deeply because it is sleep full of interruptions, where their brain does not stop working and thinking about all those things that disturb their peace of mind, which stresses them.

The stories throughout the tales will calm your body and thoughts to help you forget about your day-to-day and concentrate on reading. Without realizing it, you will experience a state of total relaxation that leads to achieving a night of deep and comforting sleep, allowing you to wake up the next day relaxed, rested, and encouraged to undertake a new day.

Reading is one of the most effective methods to fall asleep at night. This is because it puts the reader's imagination to work to visualize the general story, characters, and scenery. When this happens, the person has disconnected from everything around it and has concentrated on reading, which produces a state of relaxation that induces deep sleep, an uninterrupted sleep, a restful sleep.

Reading is very pleasurable when we enjoy what we read, it is educational when it leaves us with some learning, and it is curative when it helps us overcome an ailment or illness that threatens our health.

When we get used to reading daily, we inadvertently train our brains; we are strengthening it. Daily reading promotes mental health, enriches vocabulary, improves memory, increases imagination, improves spelling, quality of sleep, reduces stress, and helps prevent Alzheimer's. Using the words therein as inspiration, readers will feel inspired before going to sleep, wake up the next day with energy, in good spirits, not forget things, and easily fixing any problems that arise.

The book is more than a book of stories; it is a self-help book to achieve a deep conception of sleep through varied stories that transport the reader to other settings through positive affirmations that promote self-confidence, relaxation, meditation, and stress reduction.

The content included has these three qualities, so it is so beneficial to read it because while reading its stories, we experience a feeling of pleasure, joy; a smile on our face without even realizing it. We enjoy what we read. It is educational because it teaches us new methods to follow to help us sleeping pleasantly. It is a book seeking to establish in the stressed adult good habits to follow before going to sleep, to achieve quality sleep that allows you to charge the batteries for the next day. It is curative because it helps us relax to get a good night's sleep that helps us recover energy and calm our thoughts.

This book will become the inseparable friend that will always be by your side when you need it.

Printed in Great Britain
by Amazon

57120190R00274